MW01579171

He Made Me

The Second Booker & Cash Story

Oliver Tidy

Print ISBN: 978-1-912175-29-1

For My Sisters

1

Of all the coffee shops in all the seaside villages in all the UK she had to walk into mine. I was at my usual table. And I mean *my* table. They were *my* chairs too. One of the nice things about owning your own place is the opportunity to designate seating for your exclusive use, if you choose. I chose. Bogart I could never be, but as a big fan of *Casablanca* I understood Ric better for these new feelings of proprietorial snobbery. And there had to be some benefits for being solely responsible for a shot-in-the-dark business venture.

We'd been open a little over a month. The place still had that new smell to it – paint, plastic, coffee and confidence, although the last, as with many things misplaced, had to be sniffed hard for, like the last few scattered grains of cocaine on a glass-topped coffee table.

I'd inherited a small fortune from book-dealing relatives who'd had their lives prematurely and violently ended by a trio of small-time psychotic, paranoid, vintage machinery enthusiasts. The desperate acts of desperate and deluded men that I still struggled in vain to begin to understand – men who thought that torture and the taking of life was a justifiable reaction to a little harmless eavesdropping. In a reactionary fit of sentimentality, I hadn't taken the money – sold my relatives' bookshop, their stock, and liquidated their investment portfolio – so that I could go and lie on a beach drinking cocktails for the rest of my life. Having lived in self-imposed exile abroad for a number of years, and having sworn an oath never to reside there again, I had decided to give living on Romney Marsh – my homeland – another roll of the dice. I'd invested a chunk of my windfall into renovating and converting the downstairs of the property and turned their bookshop in Dymchurch high street into a book-themed coffee shop. Like most CEOs' decisions, it hadn't been an idea that I could take credit for. But, like most CEOs, I was where the buck stopped. It was still feeling like a good idea. Just. I had hopes that given time one day the place might break even.

Normally, I have no objection to tall, green-eyed women with flowing flaxen locks seeking me out but we had *Closed* up on the door and it had been a long day.

Mel, one of my ladies, came out from behind the counter to block the woman's way, handling her mop like a policeman at a G8 summit wields his riot stick.

'We're closed,' she said. 'It's on the door.' She pointed.

The woman stopped in her tracks and without condescending to look down in Mel's direction, said, 'Are you the owner?' Those pools of electric green were turned on me, like they were lit from behind. I had been poring over some invoices, wondering where all the money was going and why not enough of it was coming back.

'Yes.'

'David Booker?'

I nodded.

'I need to talk to you.'

I made a sympathetic face towards Mel and gestured to the empty two-seater leather Chesterfield opposite me. Mel gave me her 'you typical man' look and went back to the floors.

I set my pen down on the bills and reclined in the matching leather wing back. The boss is entitled to nice chairs.

'What can I do for you? Mrs…?'

'Swaine. Rebecca Swaine.'

The name Swaine rang a bell. It wasn't common on Romney Marsh. I wondered if she was related to the Swaines of Aldington. Old money and most of it gone. Or so rumour had it.

'I need to talk to you on a private matter, Mr Booker.' She glanced in Mel's direction.

'Then you'd better keep you voice down, Mrs Swaine,' I said. She didn't look happy. 'I have a matter of a delicate personal nature that I need to discuss with you. Don't you have an office for this sort of thing?'

I realised her mistake. 'You're not looking for me,' I said. 'You're looking for Jo Cash. She has an office upstairs. The coffee shop is mine. The investigator work is hers.'

'Oh. I'm sorry. My mistake. I was told to ask in here.'

'No problem. If it helps, you're not the first. I'll give Jo a call, see if she's in. You want something to drink?'

She smiled tightly, like maybe it hurt her. 'No, thank you.'

I took out my mobile and called Jo. Jo used to be police – a DC working out of Folkestone police station – but she got carried away saving my life and killed two men – one with bullets the other with a monkey wrench. They were both French – which somehow didn't make it so bad – and killers themselves, looking to up their tally at our expense. Despite the obvious self-defence element of her actions, her employers took an unsurprisingly dim view of that sort of thing, especially as she'd gone off the procedural straight and narrow. They also frowned upon officers thinking outside the text book. It could have been her police work rather than her handiwork that pushed them into their decision to let her go. At least she avoided prison.

I said she saved my life – twice actually. I felt the debt. When she lost her job and her source of income it seemed the right thing to offer her help. Suddenly I could afford it and if it hadn't been for her I'd have been dead. With no income and the bailiffs and mortgage lenders waiting in the bushes with their repossession orders, she'd accepted. And we had an arrangement. The place I'd inherited had many rooms above the business premises. She rented a couple for accommodation and one for an office. She'd gone freelance.

We'd started out in our new ventures at similar times and we were experiencing similar stuttering beginnings. It was to be expected. We both had to get known. Fortunately, money was not a problem for me and because money was not a problem for me I wasn't going to let it be a problem for Jo. Like I said, I owed her. That's not to say she milked it. She kept accounts and knew to the penny what she owed me. It didn't matter to her what I owed her.

'David.' She sounded occupied.

'You in?'

'On my way out.'

'Got a client in the shop looking for you. Got time?'

'You know I have. Give me two minutes.'

To Mrs Swaine, I said, 'She's on her way down.'

Mrs Swaine stood and flicked something off her nice overcoat. 'This is new, isn't it?' she said, letting her gaze roam around the interior.

'It is.'

She gave no impression of being enamoured. 'You think you can make something like this work in Dymchurch?'

'Not a chance. I only opened the place because I need to lose some tax money.'

She gave me a sharp look and had her mouth open before she realised I was being funny. We were saved further awkwardness by Jo pushing through the front door. She waved to Mel and crossed the very expensive industrial grade laminate wooden flooring in our direction. She was looking good in a casual dress-down sort of way. She'd lost some weight with her worries and she was working out hard in her spare time. She had a lot of spare time.

I said, 'Mrs Swaine, this is Jo Cash. She's the one you're looking for.' They nodded to each other and I made a note to speak to Jo about her people skills. A smile and a handshake wouldn't kill her. To Jo I said, 'We're shut so you can talk down here if you like.'

To Mrs Swaine, Jo said, 'OK with you? I have an office upstairs if you'd prefer.'

'Over there will be fine, I suppose,' said Mrs Swaine, indicating with an upward jerk of her fine chin a secluded group of furniture behind a low divide and a pot of indoor shrubbery.

'You sure you don't want something to drink?' I said. 'It's on the house.' I got another no thank you from Mrs Swaine and an order for a fresh orange juice from my tenant and saviour.

Mel was all but finished. I told her to go home and I'd lock up. I took the juice over to Jo, came back and poured myself another mug of the black stuff. Another benefit of owning your own coffee shop is that you can help yourself to good coffee any time you feel like it. I sat back down with my bills and tried not to listen to what was being discussed a few tables away.

A few minutes later I heard a chair push back and I turned to see Mrs Swaine getting to her feet. The women shook hands, which I took as an encouraging sign. Mrs Swaine walked over to the long wall of bookcases. She tilted her head this way and that as she examined some of the spines through the safety glass. I let her. It's what they were there for.

When she came back past me she stopped and said, 'I heard you have every one of the Booker Prize titles. Is that true?'

'Every one from every list,' I said.

'We have books and a library too,' she said.

'They certainly furnish a room,' I said. 'Every home should have some.'

'Good luck with your shop. I think you'll need it.' She didn't say it meanly.

I watched her walk away and she must have known I would. She let herself out into the miserable, darkening January afternoon, pulled the door firmly shut and then her collar up. Without a backward glance, she walked off.

Jo came to sit in the two-seater opposite me.

'Job?'

'Maybe.'

'Want to talk about it?'

'Client confidentiality. Sorry.'

I waited. She was going to tell me. I knew it and she knew it. That's how close we'd become. Not lovers. It seemed we would never be lovers. And sometimes I was strangely glad of that. Sex ruins everything, eventually. In my experience, it's the beginning of the end. What Jo and I had was an honest friendship borne out of our shared near-death experience and nurtured in the bosom of our recent companionship. We were equals but not partners. We shared a roof but not a home. And we never shared a bed. Not once. Harry and Sally we were not.

'She wants me to find someone.'

'A missing person?'

'Not exactly. She says someone's blackmailing her husband. She's not supposed to know. She found out by accident.'

'For how much?'

'She didn't say.'

'Blackmailing him over what?'

'She didn't say.'

'For how long?'

'She didn't say.'

'What did she say?'

'She said someone's blackmailing her husband.'

2

I asked Jo where she thought to start with that. She said she was going to go and see the woman the following afternoon. Her husband would be out.

'Aldington?'

'Yes. How did you know?'

'Lucky guess. Swaine's an unusual name on the Marsh. In fact, the only ones I know of live off Giggers Green Road, down a track that runs behind Goldenhurst.'

'What's Goldenhurst?'

'Goldenhurst is that impressive old Tudor manor house on the left as you crest the hill after crossing the Royal Military Canal.' I thought I'd show off a bit. 'It was once owned and lived in by Noel Coward.'

Jo gave me a blank look. 'Who's Noel Coward?'

Sometimes she could disappoint me horribly. 'Only one of the finest playwrights this country has ever known.'

'Oh. The theatre.'

'He acted in films too.'

'Such as?'

'*Our Man in Havana*.' Nothing. '*Paris, When It Sizzles*.' I might as well have been talking to a potato. '*The Italian Job*.'

'With Mark Wahlberg?'

'No. The one from the sixties.'

'I didn't know there was one from the sixties.'

I changed the subject to something less sad for me. 'Where are you going?'

'Mind your own business.'

'What time will you be back?'

7

'Mind your own business.'

'I'm doing a curry tonight. Want some saved?'

She smiled at me for that. 'What time's it ready?'

'Sevenish.'

'I'll be here. Want me to pick anything up? Booze?'

I shook my head. 'I've got it.'

She left. I locked up after her and went back to my bookwork and my coffee.

I soon tired of that. I tidied the piles of invoices, pushed them to one side for paying and filing and took out my new project – something that held far more interest for me.

A couple of months before, I'd done a man a favour. I'd kept him out of something and probably out of jail. His only son had been murdered by the same men who'd killed my aunt and uncle. He had known I was looking for them and had offered me a piece of land that joined the property I'd inherited if I kept him in the loop. He didn't just want to be in at the kill – he wanted to be part of it. I'd kept him ignorant of my progress and he'd ended up more grateful. They got what was coming to them and that's what mattered. There was also the not inconsiderable matter that his son was one of them and had been involved in the deaths of my relatives. He'd given the land to me anyway to show his gratitude and his regret for the actions of his wayward offspring.

It had been about an acre of overgrown builder's yard, littered with the rusting, rotting surplus of his business. It wasn't now. He'd had plans to develop it for residential property one day. My plans were a little different.

Six months before I'd been an unhappily married ex-pat living in Turkey and working as an English teacher. I owned nothing that meant anything to me and nothing of value. My material situation shaped my outlook. Now I had money and property and my outlook had changed. I was no longer feeling transitory – a migrant worker. These days I was feeling the need to root myself somewhere and establish something. I had to hope this wasn't the male biological equivalent of nest building. As far as I was aware, my biological clock either hadn't been wound or was missing its battery. Oh, and my Turkish wife had divorced me for an infidelity that never was.

My plans for the yard were to develop it. I wanted a home for myself – nothing ostentatious or expensive. I nurtured a great interest in a having a small cabin-type home made using sustainable products, employing energy-saving systems and being something entirely remarkable for the village. I had been interested in renewable energy as a concept for a long time. I could only ever dream about being in a position to realise my fantasies. Well, now I was. Solar panels, wind turbine and an ecological footprint about the size of a toddler's slipper. Jo referred to the idea as my eco ego.

I wanted to plant trees and I wanted free-to-roam farmyard animals: a rescue donkey, a few chickens, ducks, maybe a friendly pig. I could have been turning into a hybrid fantasy love child of Johnny Morris and Steve Irwin, without the shorts.

On the patch of land immediately behind where the old concrete panel fence had been, and which had separated the property I had inherited from the yard, I wanted an area of outdoor seating and an all-weather children's playground to go with the business. I also had plans for extending the back of the coffee shop to provide a further enclosed seating area for my potential c-word customers.

From my coffee shop's opening day, children had been an issue. Or rather their parents were. Despite being a teacher of young learners by profession, I don't hate kids. But it has been my sad experience that too often too many parents don't want to play the responsible adult when they take their offspring out to eat and drink. Too many parents made Edward VIII's wayward idea of duty and obligation pardonable.

I wanted my coffee shop to be an oasis of peace and tranquillity in a seaside village that rejoiced in its reputation as 'The Children's Paradise'. I wanted it to be a haven, a sanctuary, a place of refuge for those wishing to escape the omnipresence of the little shrieking blighters and enjoy some time away from them.

As it was, refusing entry to people on the grounds that they had kids with them in the same way that I might refuse entry to someone with a snarling, leashed pit bull made me morally uncomfortable. It made me feel like someone Roald Dahl could have written about. It also could have been actionable in the European Court. I didn't know and I didn't want to find out the hard way. But I'd had too many well-deserved and much-looked-forward-to coffee shop breaks ruined by parents who either could not control the fruit of their loins or couldn't be bothered to try. And when it came down to it, this was my place and, within certain limits, I made the rules.

I wanted to cater to families for the sake of the business and my conscience. I also wanted to give those who didn't want to suffer other people's screaming children tearing around and ruining the ambience of a place somewhere they knew they could get what they were looking for. My plans for out the back signalled my intentions for the long term. I longed for the day I could offer the choice to my customers: children or non-children.

My plans, the land and a healthy bank balance were all I had. But it was a start. That morning my architects had sent over their rough interpretations of my cruder drawings and arm-waving gestures from the site meeting and I had been waiting to shut up shop so that I could study them in peace.

3

I heard Jo thumping up the stairs with all the finesse of a house-trained Shetland a little after seven-fifteen. Light on her feet she wasn't. Not unless work demanded it, of course. She knocked on the door that divided our living spaces and I shouted her in; it was open.

'Smells good.'

'Thank my uncle for that.'

'Did he teach you how to cook?'

'I meant my Uncle Ben,' I said, wishing I'd just said I'd bought a cook-in-sauce and avoided reminding myself of a recently deceased and sorely missed close relative. 'Wine or beer? It's all in the fridge. Help yourself.'

Jo did. She poured a tall glass of white wine from the five-litre box. 'Why do you think they don't sell lager in cardboard boxes?' she said. 'Save on all that recycling.'

'It'd go flat.'

'Someone could invent something for that.'

'Maybe the lager companies have vested interests in the tin and glass recycling industries,' I said. She looked like she was considering it.

Jo said, 'I had a call from Mrs Swaine while I was out.'

I was plating up. Jo clattered our knives and forks onto the tabletop, sat down and helped herself to a poppadom. She crunched it noisily.

I said, 'Changed her mind?'

Jo shook her head. 'Wants you to come along.' She knew that would make me stop what I was doing and look in her direction.

She gave me a satisfied smile and took another slurp of wine and another crunch of the giant crisp.

'Why?'

'It's about how she wants to pay me.'

I set the steaming plates down on the table, got my own drink and said, 'Any chance you can be a bit more explicit?'

'Mrs Swaine can't afford my daily rate in pounds and pence.'

'So what? She wants to pay you by doing things to me? I can't see that I'd have a problem with that if you don't.'

'She's quite a looker, isn't she?'

'Your type too? Maybe we could share her. Maybe that's what she's got in mind.'

Jo didn't rise to my kidding. She raised an eyebrow and gave me her 'grow up and get over it' look. She said, 'You boys must have your little fantasies, I suppose.'

'For some of us that's all we've got.'

'What happened to... what's her name? Donna? She seemed keen.'

'Keen and mental and schizophrenic and possessive and a closet Catholic, would you believe?'

Jo laughed at me. 'Oh dear. Poor you. And there was me thinking that all those evenings behind the locked dividing door you two must have been at it like rabbits.'

It was my turn to laugh. 'Not a chance. She just liked to talk. And watch television. And eat.'

'Sorry.' She looked like she meant it.

I shrugged it off and tucked in.

I believed Jo hoped I would land myself a serious and decent woman sooner rather than later if only to ease her conscience. When we'd first met, Jo had been part of an investigation that, for a time, suspected me of complicity in the deaths of my relatives. She'd sensed my attraction to her and when that horrible episode of our shared existence was concluded she knew I'd be looking to build on our detective/innocent victim relationship. We were not to be. I had felt temporarily stupid and, more irritatingly, let down. But I only had myself to blame for that. She had given me no active encouragement, although she must have known about the growth of my feelings for her.

'So, Mrs Swaine can't afford you?'

'Apparently not. Not in cash or credit, anyway. Actually, I think it's got more to do with keeping her employment of the services of an investigator to herself and she can't do that if she's dipping into the household budget to pay for it.'

I made a face. 'I heard they'd fallen hard but I didn't realise it was as bad as that. They used to own a lot. Where do I fit into her thinking?'

'She wants to pay me in books.'

And the penny dropped. Mrs Swaine associated me with the dead Bookers in more than locational terms. 'She wants to pay you in books,' I repeated.

'That's what she said. She also said that if you know anything about books you'll be able to convince me that a few of her Reader's Digest collected editions are going to be worth a few days of my time.'

'A few yards of Reader's Digest collected editions aren't worth anything other than the time to read them or the warmth you'd get from burning them.'

'OK. I might have made that bit up, but you get the idea.'

I didn't need to think much. 'I'm in. I'd like to see what's in her library. She must think she's got something worth flogging. What time?'

'She said to go up between two and three. What meat is this?'

I smiled. 'You like it?'

'It's delicious. Even the sauce can't hide that.'

'It's veal.'

Jo put down her fork. And stared hard in my direction.

I said, 'What?'

'You know how they farm veal?'

I speared another lump, shovelled it in and shook my head.

'You could have said.'

'You could have asked.'

'I just did.'

'And I just told you.'

We could have been married. She resumed picking at her rice.

'You want to see the rough plans for out the back after?'

She said she wasn't doing anything else.

4

Gluttons aside, people generally don't want cake until elevenses. They might want proper coffee before then. But then they'd probably want something to eat with it that wasn't cake. There were at least two other cafés in the village doing bacon sandwiches from breakfast-time onwards and I had no intention of making Bookers competition for them.

One of the promises I made myself when I opened my coffee shop was that I would not sink to the lowest common denominator of seaside village eateries. There would be no surrender: we would never sell chips. And we wouldn't be doing English fry-ups or bits of griddled pig in bits of cheap white sliced bread. This wasn't about the money for me. It was about living a dream. It was about being different. It was about creating something I could be proud of. I could think of a few 'dragons' who'd roll their eyes at that.

Because people generally don't want cake early we didn't open early. Our winter opening times had quickly evolved to one shift – eleven to four. There was never going to be a great deal of local trade in at least two seasons of the year and so Romney Marsh was not where I was looking for my clientele, though each and every Marshen that came through the door was just as welcome as someone who'd travelled thirty miles or more. I was aiming more for the kind of place people would make part of their day out at the seaside, come rain or shine. And generally speaking people driving to Dymchurch for a trip out in the winter months didn't arrive much before eleven and had all cleared off before four.

My years of living in Dymchurch, and visiting, had taught me that a lot of people, particularly the elderly and retired, will think nothing of driving some miles at least once a month just to walk on the beach – or the sea wall if the tide is in – and to stare wistfully at the sea as the British are often wont to do – it's in our DNA. And after some bracing, fresh, salt air they feel entitled to seek refreshment in the village. I wanted to appeal to that mentality. I wanted the treat, the ambience, the experience of having coffee and cake in Bookers to be something that people would travel for, plan for, look forward to and see as part of their jaunt. I had a great belief that given time, patience and word of mouth Bookers could be that kind of place. It was a 'build it and they will come' philosophy. Maybe Phil Alden Robinson would one day be interested in making a film about me: *Coffee Shop of Dreams.*

I was very pleased with the way my plans had been realised for the interior. The original, solid, locally made oak bookcases and the matching counter had stayed. I'd had another oak bookcase made to line another long wall. It didn't yet have the patina of the original it mimicked but give it thirty years and it would be close. I'd gone with high quality dark wooden flooring and dark leather seats in small groups with matching low tables. Full, we could comfortably seat thirty. We had potted plants, quiet music, sometimes, and the books, of course. The colours leaned towards neutral and the lighting was soft and intimate. We had new windows, a new front door and a very tasteful green-and-white-striped awning that stayed tightly furled through the winter months lest a Channel gale rip down Dymchurch high street and tear it from its fixings.

A lot of books had had to go. I couldn't have fitted coffee tables and chairs in otherwise. But a lot of books had been retained and they filled the shelves of the bookcases with one of the finest, most colourful, dazzling displays of modern first editions one is likely to see anywhere. My word on it. The complete collection of all the Booker Prize lists of winners and losers was the jewel in the crown here as it had been in my uncle and aunt's time when the bookshop had been their life and livelihood.

I'd had lockable close-fitting glass fronts fitted to both protect and secure all the books. It wasn't that I didn't trust people. Actually, it was. I was under no illusions that people might come because of the books. It stood to reason that if people liked the books and the books weren't for sale but just on show one or two of them might view the act of helping themselves to something that caught their eye as something less than a crime. I understood this because I was a book thief myself. Or, as I preferred to refer to it, a book rescuer. If ever I saw a good condition title of a collectable edition in a genre that interested me on a pub bookshelf, for instance, it invariably went home with me under my jacket. I never lost sleep over 'saving' books from ignorant and uncaring owners. And I was equally sure that they were never missed.

One of the great things about my new life was that I no longer had to get up at an ungodly hour. As a teacher for the previous ten years I'd been regularly rising to begin my daily ablutions at a little after six o'clock. Weekends I usually didn't rise before eight – I'm not a great one for lying around in bed all morning unless I have the company to encourage me to do so. I was rarely getting up before eight in my new life and then I either went for my constitutional – a three-mile run along the sands to St Mary's Bay and back – or just took it easy, mentally preparing for my day.

I was usually the first into the shop downstairs and by the time the first of my employees arrived coffee was ready and I was reading a book or the paper or on the Internet on my laptop enjoying the exclusivity of a place that I felt entirely comfortable and at home in. It surprised me how quickly I had adapted to my new life.

That Tuesday, I'd run, showered, breakfasted and spent most of my morning outside in the cold and blustery weather in wellington boots, a woolly hat and a thick coat with a tape measure comparing the plans for development with the space I had to work with. I was tremendously excited with the potential of the place. I was starting to feel that I might really have a future in this unusual corner of Kent.

I made a call to the architect and we discussed details and I went back out to check and re-check. It came as a great surprise to me when Jo pitched up in the shop to tell me she was leaving in an hour. I persuaded her to have a coffee with me and then to come outside and compare something on the plan with what was there. She indulged me as she unwaveringly had since we'd become friends. Jo was good like that. She never begrudged me my new-found wealth and prospects when the bottom had fallen out of her world. She never acted as if I owed her anything at all for saving my life twice. If anything she would sometimes exude a frustrating embarrassment at being behind on the rent agreement that she had insisted on drawing up.

5

We took Jo's car, but only because it was blocking mine in and we weren't going far. She was soon busy turning a pleasant ten-minute potter on narrow winding roads through the flat Romney Marsh landscape into a terrifying rally time trial when I said, 'Will it matter very much if we're late?'

'We're not going to be late. It was just an about time.'

'So why are you driving like this?'

'Like what?'

'Like someone who's late for something.'

She huffed and eased off the accelerator. 'You're turning into an old woman, do you know that?'

'Physiological considerations aside, I'd rather turn into an old woman than a blind corner and a tractor or a dyke. I'm too young to die. Plus, these days I've got things to live for. Find out anything about the Swaines?'

'Quite a bit, actually. There're a few websites that mention them. How old do you think she is?'

'Thirty-eight?'

'Forty-seven.'

'Blimey. See what a life of ease can do for the ageing process?'

'This is her second marriage. He's five years her junior. They tied the knot two summers ago. She kept her family name.'

'How romantic. What's his?'

'Tate.'

'What does he do?'

'As far as I can make out, nothing productive. Another one who lives off the blood, sweat and tears of the proletariat. He share deals.'

'Is that a nice way to be speaking about your employer?'

'He's not my employer. She is. Potentially.'

'What happened to the first husband?'

'Dead. Old age. He was twenty years older than her.'

We rounded a bend made blind by a hedgerow that even in its winter nakedness managed to obscure what lay in wait. The road was full of sheep. Jo braked comfortably to a stop and we sat while the shepherd cajoled and manoeuvred his flock through the open gate of an adjacent field. He touched his cap as the last shot past him. I noticed that he was using bright orange agricultural twine to secure his overcoat around his ample middle. The clichéd anachronism made me smile.

Misinterpreting my enjoyment of the moment, Jo said, 'If you say anything resembling I told you so I'll make you walk the rest of the way.'

'Then you wouldn't have anyone to value the books she wants to trade.'

'OK. You can walk home then. It's going to rain.'

I shut my mouth as we crossed the Royal Military Canal, that impossible undertaking of brute force and, to me, military stupidity. The canal was commissioned and built – or should that be dug? – in response to the threat of invasion by Napoleon. It was over twenty miles in length and ran along the base of the hills that surrounded Romney Marsh, from Seabrook just this side of Folkestone, through and past Rye in East Sussex. It was no more than twenty feet wide for most of it. I'd always had a hard time believing that twenty feet of fairly shallow fresh water was going to keep out a determined invading army under Napoleon that had just crossed over twenty miles of quite deep English Channel. Maybe the military strategists of the time knew something I didn't, although if they were the ancestors of those cretins who ordered tens of thousands of patriotic men to walk blindly into German machine gun fire in the First World War I doubted it.

Immediately we left the Marsh we climbed the steep narrow road hemmed in by bare trees atop high-sided verges that wound its way up towards Aldington. At the top, just as the road levelled out, stood Goldenhurst. I spared a thought for the history of the place as we sped past.

'Slow down,' I said. 'The track's just up here on the left.'

Jo slowed and we turned onto a rutted track only wide enough for one vehicle at a time. We bumped down this for perhaps a hundred metres before it opened out to reveal our destination on the far side of a large gravelled area. Jo had tutted all the way down. I waited.

She said, 'Did you know the track was going to be that bad?'

'No. It's my first time down it. Why?'

'If you'd said we were going off-road we could have brought the tank. Did you hear my car ground on that rock?'

I knew it would be my fault.

Silverhurst was an imposing property. I imagine that it always had been, since the oldest parts of it looked to have been constructed somewhere around the sixteenth century. The side that confronted us looked both ancient and striking – vertical darkened timbers dividing the white front elevation in traditional Tudor style, all under an uneven Kent peg-tiled roof with dormer windows made wonky with age and subsidence. Despite its age it looked in general good order, as did the gardens, considering the time of year and the high winds the area had suffered recently.

The area of gravel was bordered with rampant hardy evergreen shrubbery. Jo brought the car to a halt in front of the garage. As she rummaged for something in her handbag I stared at the building and the opening lines of Daphne du Maurier's *Rebecca* sprang unbidden into my mind. Though there was little I could see to compare to the physical description of Manderley, I experienced a palpable and unsettling feeling of foreboding and unease – a haunting feeling that did something to the hairs on the back of my neck. I had driven past the place countless times but never before visited – never having had either cause or invitation. And yet, I experienced the strangest feeling that I *had* been here and that once inside the house I would know what to expect. Things would be familiar. The spell was broken by a curtain twitching at an upstairs window.

Mrs Swaine opened the front door as we walked towards it. We said our hellos.

'Glad you could come, Mr Booker.'

'Glad to be invited, Mrs Swaine.'

When we were in the warm with the door firmly shut, she supplied us with guest slippers, pointed to where we could hang our coats and then led us through. The house was nice – tastefully, sparingly and appropriately furnished. There was artwork on the walls. Some of it looked original. The place was warm and smelled clean. Somewhere a real fire was burning. I stopped at a strikingly clunky impression of a Paul Nash Dymchurch sea wall painting. Whoever had done this seemed to my amateurish eye to have captured the spirit of Nash's outlook.

'That would be worth something if it were an original,' I said, showing off a bit.

'It *is* an original, Mr Booker. But selling it would be out of the question.'

I was made temporarily speechless. We followed our hostess down the darkened winding passageway to the library. And it too was impressive. The large, light room was at the side of the property that looked out over the Marsh. From our height the uninterrupted views must have been pretty commanding and spectacular on a clear summer's day. But Mrs Swaine hadn't invited me up to look out of the window, admiring the scenery. I turned my attention to the books. I was confronted with a bookcase of discouragement.

Because we had been taken straight to the library I took my cue that Mrs Swaine didn't want to socialise with me, at least, and that I should get on with what I'd been invited along for, like a tradesman. 'Anything you want me to look at in particular?' I said, getting immediately down to the reason I was there, thereby letting Mrs Swaine know that two could play at that game.

She gave me a keen, appraising look, like someone thinking about buying a piece of furniture. 'I take it you do know about books, Mr Booker.' After my painting comment I could forgive her this.

I tried to smile confidently back. 'I know enough, Mrs Swaine. Tell me what you have in mind.'

Her gaze intensified and I felt a little awkward for it. 'Am I able to expect the same level of confidentiality with you that I trust I can with Ms Cash?'

'Absolutely,' I said, just a little too loudly and pompously, like someone accused of something they didn't do.

'Good. I'd like to raise a little capital. Since the idea occurred to me to sell some of these old books, I thought that I might as well take the opportunity to raise a little more. I need ten thousand pounds. And I'd like to do it with as few books as possible. Clearing out whole bookcases will make holes in the collection, which I might be obliged to explain.' She didn't say to whom. 'And I do not wish to. Do I make myself clear?'

I nodded and said, 'Crystal, Mrs Swaine. Ten thousand pounds is a lot of money for books. If you want to raise the capital quickly your best bet is to sell to a dealer and, as I'm sure you appreciate, dealers have to make a living. You won't get open market price or anything like it, assuming, that is, you have books to attract those sorts of offers in the first place.'

'I understand,' she said, although she didn't look happy about it. 'And your fee, of course, Mr Booker?'

I hadn't thought about that. 'Let's see what you've got first, Mrs Swaine, before we decide whether my fee will be something we have to consider. Incidentally, what's the provenance on the library?'

'Why do you want to know?'

'Any dealer who is looking at parting with large sums of money for books will naturally want to know where they came from.'

'My late father liked books. He was a collector all his adult life. Everything here was his. Will that do?'

'It'll have to, Mrs Swaine,' I said, trying to hide the irritation I was feeling for simply asking pertinent questions and getting frosty responses.

'Good. I'll leave you alone while I show Ms Cash what she needs to see. I can't offer you hot refreshment, I'm afraid – the housekeeper only does mornings.' Clearly, Mrs Swaine wasn't able to make tea for herself or her guests. She offered no cold alternative. She gave me one last look up and down. It made me feel she was checking to see if I wore clothing with poacher's pockets. As if I would.

'We'll be just next door,' she said, before leading Jo away.

My first impression of the library was that I would have to make a big hole in it to start getting the kind of returns Rebecca Swaine was looking for. But ask any old Trojan warrior and he'll tell you that first impressions aren't always the most reliable. He might be smiling, too. I'd been looking at the popular fiction section. Around the back of one of the four bookcases that came at ninety degrees off the wall was a set of volumes that made me inhale sharply. And my first thought after *bloody hell* was that maybe Rebecca Swaine wasn't entirely ignorant of what she had and she was testing me. I didn't aim to disappoint her. Just to be sure, I took out my Internet-enabled smartphone and looked them up on the biggest booksellers' website in the virtual world. Even at dealer's prices they would fetch a good part of what she was looking for. I had to remove each of them to ascertain their condition and edition and when I was satisfied that all was as it should be I considered myself privileged to have been in the same room as such important books and allowed to handle them privately.

Encouraged, I looked along the other shelves. I whistled to myself a few more times along the way. I felt like Aladdin moving through his cave. I ran my fingers over beautifully tooled spines. I slid a few out, opened them and inhaled their majesty. Mr Swaine senior had had a good eye, a sensitive nose or deep pockets to indulge his book collecting passion – or maybe he was another book thief – to have accumulated such a splendid and valuable little library. Maybe he'd been a rescuer of books. While his collecting leanings were not in my particular sphere of interest that didn't mean I couldn't appreciate what I was looking at. I did a bit more Internet research and whistled some more.

The door to the library being pushed open hard made me start. It wasn't the door that Jo and Mrs Swaine had left by. A man stood there. He was a bit taller than me but thinner. His thick bright-blond hair was combed harshly back from his brow and held there with some form of goo. His green eyes told me he was mean and intelligent. His expression told me he was suspicious and angry. Then his thin tight mouth opened and asked me what the hell I thought I was doing. It was then I noticed he was carrying what looked like a poker.

6

'Whoa there,' I said. 'I'm a guest of Rebecca Swaine. She's in there.' I jerked my thumb at the door behind me.

'Who gave you permission to touch those?'

'The same Mrs Swaine who invited me in and provided me with slippers. Go and ask her if you don't believe me.'

He looked to be made angrier by my disrespectful response, and I had to consider the possibility that he might go for me yet. He had that sort of look in his eyes.

'Who are you, anyway?' I said, pushing my luck.

'None of your bloody business. Rebecca!' He had a good shout on him. It sounded well practised. I hoped this wasn't the husband returned unexpectedly to surprise us all. That could be embarrassing.

Rebecca Swaine came quickly out of the room next door.

'Sigmund, what are you doing up?' Mrs Swaine's rebuke told a story.

'Who is this?' he said, pointing the poker in my general direction.

'He's a friend of someone who is visiting me. Calm down.'

'Who is visiting you? Why didn't you say something?'

'Sigmund. Go away. I'll come and find you and tell you all about it later. Go and watch some television in your room.'

He shot me a murderous look then he looked down at what was in my hands. 'Put that back,' he said. 'Some of those are valuable.' He turned and left us, slamming the door behind him.

Rebecca Swaine heaved out a big sigh. It was full of melancholy and regret. 'Sorry.' It sounded as if that was an effort she didn't make often. Jo had wandered out to see what all the commotion was about.

She said, 'Was that your husband?'

Mrs Swaine snorted like a spooked horse. 'Lord, no. That was my brother.' I could see on her face that she'd rather we hadn't met each other.

I said, 'I don't think much of his manners.'

She shot me a sharp look and relaxed it quickly. 'No. Have you found anything... appropriate? Saleable?'

'Mrs Swaine, you have some of the finest books it has ever been my pleasure to handle and my uncle was a book dealer all my life.'

'Is that a yes, Mr Booker?'

Fine. It was like that. Couldn't say I didn't try. 'Yes. It's a yes. This set here,' I moved back to the three leather-bound volumes of William Henry Pyne's detailed and comprehensive early nineteenth-century history of royal residences, 'should fetch a healthy four-figure sum for starters. There are some other single volumes that will take the total to the figure you're looking for. Is this library insured?'

The question surprised her, or perhaps it was my impertinence. 'We have contents insurance, of course.'

'If you want my advice, you'll have someone come out and value this lot and then get them properly insured. Incidentally, why not get a dealer out in the first place. Something tells me that you know more about these than you've let on.' With nothing to lose, I was challenging her in her own home and I was enjoying the feeling.

She smiled that thin painful line again. 'I've dealt with dealers before, Mr Booker. I didn't enjoy the experience. You have an honest face. Will you help me sell what I need to or not?'

I wanted Jo to get the job and in order for her to get the job her prospective employer would have to be in funds.

'I'll help you, Mrs Swaine. I still have details of a number of contacts in the trade in my uncle's office.'

She looked at me differently then. 'They died rather unpleasantly, I believe.'

I held her gaze. 'They did.'

'And you… saw that their murderers got their just desserts?' She sounded curious.

'Actually, Mrs Swaine, it was Jo, Ms Cash, who did that. At the time they met their makers, I was temporarily incapacitated.'

She looked between us both and something she found amusing played at the corners of her mouth.

She sighed heavily and said, 'Well, let's hope we don't need anything heavy-handed this time. Take what you think you can sell for what I need, Mr Booker.'

'If you have a pen and paper I'll write them down for you.'

'I prefer to trust you.' She turned to Jo. 'We understand each other, Ms Cash?' Jo nodded. Then to me, Mrs Swaine said, 'As soon as you can sell the books, I can pay your bills.'

She provided me with a small holdall and I carefully placed the three Pynes and five other promising titles into it. There wasn't much of a gap on the shelf.

Apparently, Jo and her client had concluded their business. Mrs Swaine saw us out and closed the door before we reached the car.

As Jo manoeuvred the car around so that we could exit the driveway front first I looked up to see Sigmund Swaine's furious features at one of the dormer windows.

'What a surreal little experience that was,' I said.

'Sigmund? I reckon Freud would have had something to say about that, don't you?' said Jo, as she began easing the car back down the muddy track, heading for home and smiling at her wit.

I said 'boom boom' and it started raining.

7

The drive home started sedately. I attributed this to Jo being full of thought.

As we recrossed the canal, she said, 'She got me up there to show me a document she'd found in her husband's desk. She said it was demanding the return of fifty thousand pounds or he'd be exposed for, quote, what he is.'

'Fifty grand's a lot of money.'

'It is to some of us,' she said, and she might have been having a playful dig.

I waited until she'd passed an approaching Land Rover on the narrow road before saying, 'That was it?'

Jo nodded her head once. 'Yep.'

'Did she give it to you?'

'No. She couldn't even show it to me. She said he must have removed it because now she can't find it.'

'So what are you going to do? I can't see how you can do anything.'

'I told her to talk to her husband.'

'Good move. It's not like you need the work, is it? So why is she still talking about paying you?'

'Because she said no to option A. You're being quite dumb this afternoon.'

'The question still stands: what are you going to do?'

'For a start, assume that it's genuine – that's what she's paying me for. I think she's more concerned about the bit threatening to expose him for what he is than she is about anything else. She's worried about her reputation. That's my guess, anyway. She wants me to find out about any skeletons he's got rattling around in his tallboy.'

'So you're going to investigate him?'

'That's the plan.'

'Can you do it?'

Jo took her eyes off the road and looked in my direction for answer. I gestured for her to look back where she was going before she got us both killed.

I said, 'He works in the City?'

Jo made a noise in her throat and then said. 'Yes. Why?'

'You'll be going up there?'

'What on earth for? What would be the point?'

'I don't know. I thought you might want to see where he works.'

Jo started laughing. She laughed most of the way home. As we pulled up on the gravel out the back of the shop, I said, 'I'm going to have to take these books to London. I was just thinking that if you were going to see where he works we could go up together.'

'That's very sweet, David. I'll let you know.'

I let us in the back door. Jo said she was going to start her new job by looking for information on the Internet. She said it should prove more fruitful than staring at the building he worked in. I had to suffer her laughter as it died away. I went into the shop for some respect.

8

There wasn't anything that needed the owner/manager's attention. Mel and Linda said they could cope with the two geriatrics who were sipping their afternoon tea and behaving themselves. I got myself a drink and sat down with my laptop. While that was powering up I nipped upstairs to my uncle's old office. It was still pretty much as I'd inherited it. It depressed me to go in there, but the thought of throwing everything out was worse. It was easiest just to leave the door shut. It wasn't as if I needed the room. I lifted the contacts books off the shelf and started flicking through it. Then I remembered I'd just left a few thousand pounds' worth of antiquarian books in a very portable bag in the shop and hurried back down to do a bit of Internet research myself.

I was still there two hours later when Jo came looking for me. The shop was shut up and the ladies had gone home. I had the books out of the bag and on a clean table next to me. Jo made herself a drink and sat down. She set her mug on the same table as the books. A little bit of brown liquid slopped over the side. I made a meal of moving all the books to another table. Jo rolled her eyes.

She said, 'Are they really worth ten grand?'

'More, on a good day.'

'Amazing.'

'Aren't they.'

'I mean amazing that people would waste ten grand on a few grubby old books. More money than sense, if you ask me.'

'Don't knock it. And don't knock your drink over it. That's your fee, remember.'

'When are you thinking of going up to town?'

'Day after tomorrow. I've found someone who's interested to take a look at these.' I patted the book on top of the pile, like I might the head of a small boy who was being good. 'Why? Changed your mind?'

'I never said I wasn't interested. Nigel used to work at Hudson's. They're an investment management company. Looks like he might have left under a bit of a cloud. I've found someone who said they'll talk to me about it.'

'Who's Nigel?'

'The husband. Keep up.'

'I didn't know. No one mentioned his name to me. And you didn't say he'd lost his job.' I was aware that I was sounding a bit defensive and whiney.

Jo said, 'I only just found out myself.'

I said, 'Why didn't Mrs Swaine tell you?'

'Maybe she doesn't know.'

'How did you manage to get someone to talk to you?'

'I asked. Sometimes that's all it takes.'

'Great. We can go up together then. I'll buy you lunch.'

'Talking of food – got any of last night's curry left?'

'I thought you didn't like it.'

'Only on principle.'

'I have actually. I'm warming it up later. Want some?'

'No. If you're having that I'll get a Chinese.'

Sometimes I had to honestly wonder if it was me.

9

As neither of us had a significant other in our lives, Jo and I would often gravitate to each other for company of an evening, if company was what we were looking for.

We ate our meals off our laps watching the local news. Then we watched a film. Over the last few weeks I'd been introducing Jo to some of what I considered classic movies of my DVD collection. The whole exercise had been a bit hit and miss. Mostly miss. Recently, she'd lasted ten minutes of *2001 A Space Odyssey*, and fallen asleep halfway through *Silent Running*. For that evening I'd chosen Hitchcock's *Vertigo*. It was a sure sign she wasn't enjoying it when she started yawning.

I said, 'Are you excited?'

'Actually, for a psychological thriller, I think this is a bit boring.'

'Not the film – your investigation. Your job.'

'Of course I am.'

'If nothing else it'll make a change from all that insurance work you've been doing.'

'And the spying on cheating partners and that missing cat.'

I dissolved into a fit of proper laughter at Jo's bitter memory of being called out to investigate a missing moggy.

When I realised Jo wasn't laughing with me, I stopped and said, 'I'll be honest with you: when you said you wanted to start up on your own I didn't think Romney Marsh was going to provide you with an income.'

'It doesn't.'

'You know what I mean – having an office here.'

'The wonders of modern technology and communication systems, David. I might be stuck out in the middle of nowhere but I'm only an email or a phone call from someone who needs me.'

'You're sounding like something out of a Marvel comic.'

The cushion hit me square in the face.

'Besides, I can't afford offices in a big town yet. I need to establish myself as a name to be trusted, someone who gets the job done.'

'Now you sound like the A Team.'

I dodged the next one.

I said, 'You'll leave then? If you get the chance?'

'Of course I will. If I'm still working out of this place in five years' time I'll kill myself.'

I must have looked hurt.

'No offence. But it's just not me. I'm a city girl. Or at least a decent-sized town.'

'I don't blame you. I felt like that up until six months ago. Funny how things change. Who's the guy you're going to see on Thursday?'

'Marion Pardew. *She* works in Economic Crime.'

I furrowed my brow.

'It's a department within the City of London Police.'

'She's a police officer?'

'Well done.'

'I still don't understand how you've got a complete stranger to talk to you.'

Jo just smiled and waggled her eyebrows.

'You think that whatever whoever is threatening to expose him over will be something financial? Some dodgy insider trading, perhaps?'

'I have no idea. But I've got to start somewhere and work's as good a place as any, especially when it involves lots of money and he's recently been let go. This got much longer to go?'

'About an hour.'

'Bloody hell, really? Mind if I call it a night?'

'Of course not.'

She didn't give me a peck on the cheek. She didn't squeeze my shoulder. She just said goodnight and left, carrying her tray with her. And the room was colder and emptier for her leaving. Still, at least I could stretch out and watch Jimmy Stewart getting it on with Kim Novak. I fell asleep before the end and dreamed of dangerous women. As if there's any other kind.

10

Wednesday was always going to be just the day before I went to London to see a man about a bag of books. The sky was overcast and oppressive. It weighed heavily on Romney Marsh, seeming to pressurise the cushion of air between the heavens and terra firma. I blamed it for my headache. The coffee shop did a slow trade. We were getting a few regular callers mixed in with the newbies – distinguishable by the way they edged in, gawping in wonder at the place and looking generally lost regarding how things worked. After lunch the wind blew and the rain fell. I'd managed a run in the morning and that had set me up mentally for the day. I dithered about with the plans for outside again, made a few phone calls, drank too much coffee – which, contrary to what I've always understood from the movies, didn't help my headache – and wasted too much time talking with old man Croker.

John Croker was the last surviving village character from a bygone era – a living relic, a caricature, a legend in his own lunchtime. He still had his fingers in a few shepherds' pies but left the work to others these days. At ninety-three he was entitled to. He looked like he was dressed by the Salvation Army but was worth thrice what I was and change. He was the last of the Dymchurch dynasty of fish and chip shop barons. Behind his back they called him 'The Codfather'. I think he secretly approved. Since I'd opened, he liked to visit – regularly. He'd park his mobility scooter outside, blocking the pavement, shuffle in leaning on his stick, drink free tea – he wouldn't touch coffee (filthy brown muck) – and because he was something of a village celebrity, as well as someone I respected for what he'd achieved through hard work and single-minded grim determination from extremely humble beginnings, I accommodated his demands and tolerated his scathing negativity when he'd tell me how my kind of place would never work in a village like ours. He wasn't mean with it. He might even have been right. Time would tell on that.

By the time dusk was descending and the women were mopping the floors I'd about had enough. It was soon too dark for me to think of going outside for anything other than a smoke but since I'd packed them in I was denied even that distraction. That's another thing about coming into money – it made me more health conscious. I couldn't speak for others, but for me having a small fortune in the bank made me value my health and my prolonged existence that little bit more. I'd given up the smokes but the booze, in moderation, would always be a feature and a pleasure in my life.

I hadn't seen Jo all day. Her car had been missing since I'd come back from my morning run along the beach. We didn't have the kind of relationship in which we felt obliged to keep each other informed of our whereabouts.

I was still in the shop when the lights of her car swept in and briefly illuminated the back yard to the sound of compacting gravel crunching under her tyres, like a distant wave washing up a beach. Her return lifted my spirits. I hoped she'd see lights on in the shop, know I was in there and come in for a chat. And we had to talk about arrangements for the following day.

I was still more comfortable in the shop than I was in my dead relatives' flat. It is no exaggeration to confess that I was somewhat smitten, somewhat in love, with the environment downstairs, especially when we were closed. The decor, the books, the furniture, the smells, the quiet, the space. I'd created an ambience where I felt I belonged. When it was dark outside, the calculated soft yellow lighting of the wall-mounted fittings created an impression of warmth, refinement and intimacy, an effect that daylight meddled with and spoiled. Sometimes I'd put on some low, slow jazz, or some classical piano and just sit and enjoy being there. Sometimes I felt like a character in a novel.

I understood I was still gripped in the first heady throes of proprietorial infatuation, like a teenager moons over a first car. There was also the not inconsiderable influence on my feelings about upstairs – almost nothing had changed from my aunt and uncle's time. I had ploughed all my energy and creativity into the shop. The flat was essentially just for eating, sleeping and washing – the mundane routines of life. I needed to do something about all that. And what I was intending to do was to build a cabin and move out, gut the flats, refurbish and let them.

I had my feet up and was renewing my acquaintance with the most famous detective duo in fiction when Jo rapped on the back window. I unlocked and let her in. She brushed past me into the warm, making a brrr noise for a greeting. I caught her smell. And not for the first time, I felt something akin to desperate longing for her deep in my centre. Not a sexual longing, but an intimate relationship longing where each partner is half of a whole.

I almost asked her where she'd been all day, but Jo didn't like questions like that. Instead I went with, 'How was your day?'

'Interesting. Yours?'

'Not particularly. Want to talk about tomorrow now?'

I locked up after her and followed her into the shop, where she'd plonked herself down on a Chesterfield.

I suggested a timetable: train from Ashford, I go see my bookseller contact in Cecil Court off Charing Cross Road while she sees her appointment, I buy her lunch in Covent Garden, we could have a mooch around and then back before the evening rush.

'I'm meeting my contact for a lunchtime drink.'

'Oh.'

'How long will you be in with the book guy?'

'Depends. He knows what I've got and he's very interested. Perhaps an hour.'

'Why don't you meet me and my appointment for lunch?'

'Won't she mind?'

'If she does you can sit at another table. Have a drink. Read a book or something.'

'Thanks very much.'

'I shouldn't think I'll be very long with her. Then we can eat.'

I agreed. I was more than a little hopeful that Marion Pardew wouldn't mind me sitting in.

11

We got into Charing Cross mid-morning. The weather that was afflicting Romney Marsh obviously wasn't a local phenomenon.

Cecil Court is a shortish walk up Charing Cross Road. We detoured only slightly so that I could appreciate Trafalgar Square, pay my respects to Nelson's Column and feel proud to be British. It didn't happen very often. We ambled up past the National Gallery, the National Portrait Gallery, the Garrick Theatre. So much culture. It felt good just being near it. Life was passing me by.

We turned into Cecil Court. 'Fancy a look in a gallery while we're up here?' I said.

'You can if you like.'

'My treat?'

'David, even I know they're all free admission. I'm just not that into paintings.'

'How about a matinee? There're bound to be some tickets for a show round here.'

'We'll see.' Which I took as code for 'no'.

I stopped and turned to face her. 'Look, I think you'll just be bored in here with me.' I gestured up the narrow alley that was home to several of London's book-dealing community. I really didn't want Jo huffing and tutting about the place, yanking expensive volumes off the shelves and being careless with them when I was trying to conduct business. It was going to be hard enough for me as it was. I had absolutely no experience of what I was about to involve myself in. And I was playing with someone else's money.

'No, I won't. I'll behave. I promise.'

'You'd better.' I flexed my grip on my bag and turned away.

Jo said, 'Would it be all right to take an ice cream in with me?'

She was letting me know she still had a sense of humour.

12

Jo had arranged to meet Marion Pardew in a hostelry called The New Moon on Gracechurch Street. It wasn't a huge trek from Cecil Court and I suggested we hoofed it. Actually, what I did was sing her a line from Ralph McTell's hit from the sixties. She just looked embarrassed for me. I don't think she'd heard of it. She asked if I had toothache, which was her way of saying I couldn't sing.

I'd never been what you might call a regular visitor to the metropolis and so when I did drop by I'd always rather walk the streets of London than take the Underground or a taxi. You never saw anything that way and part of the pleasure of any visit for me was a bit of sightseeing.

We retraced our steps to Charing Cross, headed down the side of the mainline railway station on Villiers Street to Victoria Embankment and turned left to walk alongside the Thames. There weren't many boats about. Not many tourists either. A chilling and challenging breeze was channelled along the ancient waterway. We were walking into it. The sky was heavy and I thought it could snow. I wished I'd brought a warmer coat. Maybe a hat. Maybe some gloves. Maybe some tissue for my nose that was now running. I started to wish we'd taken a taxi or the Tube. Or risked the bus. At London Bridge we turned our backs on the river and in towards the City in search of Gracechurch Street. The wind dropped abruptly.

I liked The New Moon immediately – spacious, comfortable, cared for. Jo took a table. I got our drinks. As I put them down Jo was finishing on the phone. I took a good slurp of my real ale. Lovely.

'She'll be here in a few minutes. You happy with what you got for the books in the end?'

I shrugged and made a face. 'He has to make a profit too. I don't think I could've pushed for more. If he hasn't got a buyer lined up he's now got quite a bit of capital tied up in those. I think I can convince Mrs Swaine that she should be satisfied. At least she can afford you now.'

Jo raised her glass to me and took a sip. 'I'll drink to that. This is nice.'

'The place or the wine?'

'Both. See what I mean about cities and big towns. It's where the life is, David.'

'So what were you doing policing a crummy mid-sized town like Folkestone?'

'Kent Police were my employer. You don't get to choose where you're posted. I planned to transfer somewhere more alive.'

I felt suddenly sad for her. 'Do you miss it?'

'The police?'

I nodded.

'Yes and no. But there's no point in crying over the way things turned out. I don't regret any of my actions. I did the right thing. If I hadn't, well, we wouldn't be here now, would we?'

I thought Jo was putting a brave spin as well as a brave face on things.

'What about you?' she said.

'What about me what?'

'Do you miss teaching?'

I think she was being serious but I couldn't stop the snort of derision exploding out of my nostrils along with most of my last sip of beer. As I cleaned myself up, I said, 'Definitely not. Listen, kids are energy vampires. They suck the life out of you all day every day five days a week and what they take from you energises them so that they become even more demanding. Looking back on it, I think that shutting a single grown-up in a room with thirty young learners for forty minutes at a stretch should be against the Geneva Convention. I was permanently exhausted when I was in a school term. If I lost all my money tomorrow I'd rather work in a petrol station than go back to teaching. I mean it. It was fun while it lasted but my time with chalk dust respiratory problems and classrooms stinking of wee-soaked five-year-olds is over.'

We were spared further talk on that subject by the arrival of her contact. Marion Pardew looked nothing like a police officer and every inch the city slicker – nice clothes, good hair, a tangible confidence that generally only money and/or madness can bring. Jo signalled her and stood to greet her. Either they knew each other or Jo had been primed to look out for a woman carrying a red umbrella.

I stood and we shook hands. And then I was dispatched to the bar to get our source a dry white wine. By the time I returned they were talking easily with each other.

Marion thanked me with a nod and said, 'Are you ex-job too, David?'

'No, he's not,' said Jo. 'But he's trustable.'

Marion nodded and turned her attention back to Jo. 'Nigel Tate worked for Hudson's a little over five years. They parted company a couple of months ago.'

'Not an amicable split?' said Jo.

Marion smiled. 'They let him go. There are strong rumours that he was involved in something the FSA were interested in. Hudson's didn't want the bad press or the attention so they got rid of him.'

'The Food Standards Agency,' I said, showing off. 'What have they got to do with it?'

'Financial Services Authority,' said Jo, with a mixture of embarrassment and disappointment. 'Any idea what it was?'

Marion swallowed a mouthful and said, 'Possible insider trading. Allegedly. The FSA,' she looked at me, 'the Financial Services Authority,' she was still looking at me, 'the body that regulates all providers of financial services in the UK – are still investigating. They won't let it go just because Hudson's let Tate go.'

'How much are we talking about?'

'Impossible for me to say. From a police perspective it's all just gossip and rumour for now, but there's definitely something in it. I know someone over there.'

'Would I be able to talk to your source at Hudson's?'

Marion shook her head briefly. 'As a favour, I'll ask. I can promise you that. But I wouldn't hold my breath. What's it about? What's your interest in him?'

'His wife claims he's being blackmailed. She wants me to find out by whom. This sounds promising. If I could talk to your source I could find out who might be in a position to know about Tate's alleged dodgy dealings.'

Marion chewed her lips for a long moment. 'Tell you what, I'll ask for you. It'll save time and to be honest I've got a better chance of getting that information than you have.'

'Fine with me,' said Jo.

'How much is he being blackmailed for?'

'Fifty k.'

'Are the local police involved?'

'No. The wife isn't even supposed to know. Says she found the letter by accident. And she categorically doesn't want to involve the authorities.'

'Interesting. Give me a day or two. We'll keep in touch over this, won't we? Might be something in it for me.'

Jo smiled nicely and said, 'Of course.'

I said, 'Where did he go to from Hudson's?'

Marion said, 'TJC.'

'Are they another city bank?'

She said, 'No. The Job Centre. I asked around but it seems he wouldn't have been able to secure a position with another financial institution even if he tried. And I'm not surprised if he had the FSA breathing down his neck. No one would touch him with a bargepole while he's in limbo with them. Guilty 'til proven innocent. Financial institutions can't afford to risk giving anyone the benefit of the doubt. They trade on their reputations and customer confidence – and after the banking disasters of the last few years customer confidence is always going to be a very brittle thing in their business.' Marion threw back the last of her drink. 'Right. I should be off. Nice meeting you, Jo.' We all stood. They shook hands like old friends. As an obvious afterthought Marion turned to me and said, 'Bye…'

'David.'

'Right. David. Nice meeting you.' She turned away from us and I watched Jo watch Marion walk away.

'You never told me how you got her to come out and meet us, let alone divulge such sensitive information,' I said.

'Friend of a friend.'

'What does that mean?'

'It means I called up an old friend who's still in the job – she's in the Met now. Fraud. Not her, her line of work. I asked her if she would be able to get me a meeting with anyone who worked for Hudson's who could help us and she came up with Marion.'

'Did you have to pay her for her information?'

'David!'

'What?'

'She's a police officer. Did you see me give her money?'

'No.'

'There's your answer then. But I'll owe someone a favour.'

'I shouldn't think Mrs Swaine would be too pleased to learn you've been breaking confidences with total strangers,' I said.

'Who's going to tell her? You?'

I smiled at Jo. 'What's my silence worth?'

'How would you like the rest of your beer over your head?'

I laughed. 'Hungry?'

'Your treat, you said.'

I nodded.

'In that case, I've never had lobster before.'

Out of habit, I looked at the prices in the menu. Then looked at Jo. I think my mouth was open. She was laughing at me and said she'd have a ploughman's and another drink.

Jo's phone rang and I took the opportunity to go to the bar and order our meals and refills. The pub was warm and the beer was already working its magic. Sometimes when I had a drink in a decent pub I really had the urge to settle in and make a session of it. I was feeling like that when I returned to our table. Jo didn't look happy.

'Bad news?' I said.

'Nigel Tate is dead. Pretty bad news for him, wouldn't you say?'

13

I asked Jo if she wanted to rush back. She eyed me strangely and
said what for? She wasn't related to him. It was a good point.
I asked her if she still wanted to eat and she said yes. She
downed the wine quickly and I went back for another. Behind the
bar they were getting to know me.

I set the glass down in front of her and said, 'Who called
you?'

'Rebecca Swaine.'

'How did she sound?'

'Like a woman who's just lost her husband. How do you
expect her to sound?'

'What I mean is…'

'I know what you mean. She sounded composed, not a
gibbering wreck. She seemed under control.'

'Did she say how he died?'

Jo seemed to have slipped off somewhere. Aware that I'd asked
her something she said, 'What?'

'I said, how did he die?'

Jo was still thinking about something else. But she was
looking hard at me. It was disconcerting. 'Suicide. She said he
killed himself. She didn't say how and I didn't ask.'

Eventually, our food arrived. I was ravenous but I felt
uncomfortable, disrespectful, about diving into my steaming steak
and kidney pudding with the news of sudden death hanging in
the air. The pub was quite busy. There was a good sociable noise.
It helped.

I said, 'Did she give you any instructions?'

'Asked me to go and see her.' And I realised why Jo was looking so down. She'd just lost a decent opportunity, something that might have looked good on her CV.

'Sorry, Jo.'

'What for?'

'You lost a job. A good one.'

Jo frowned. 'No. She wants me to find out who killed him.'

'You said it was suicide.'

'Yes. But someone drove him to it.'

14

The skies had darkened considerably by the time we left the pub. I didn't suggest a gallery or a show or a bit more sightseeing. I hailed a passing black cab and told him Charing Cross. Jo didn't try and talk me out of it.

We were ten minutes early for the train but it was at the platform waiting. I asked Jo if she wanted anything for the journey and she didn't. I fancied a couple of tins but, owing to Jo's lunchtime imbibing, I'd be driving when we got to Ashford so I dared not. I settled for a black coffee and went to look for some.

Jo had found an almost empty carriage. When I returned, I arranged myself opposite her in a pair of seats.

She said, 'You could have said you were getting coffee.'

'I asked you if you wanted anything.'

She made a face. I offered to go and get her one. She told me to stay where I was. Women.

We arrived back at Ashford International a little after three.

When we were back at the car, Jo said, 'How about I give Rebecca Swaine a call? We could pay her a visit on the way back? You've got business to discuss, haven't you?'

'Yes, but I'm not sure she'd be too happy to have me barging in talking about money and books when she's just lost her husband rather unexpectedly.'

'Fair enough. You can wait in the car if you like.'

Before I could protest further Jo had her phone to her ear and was walking away from me in search of privacy. She was back in two minutes.

'Well?'

'Silverhurst, Jeeves.'

A bleary dusk was settling in by the time we were driving through the woodland that crowded the road to the Swaine residence. I needed the headlights on.

There were no vehicles in evidence on the Swaine's parking and turning area. I'm not sure what I'd expected but I had expected something: emergency services, unmarked police cars, undertaker's vehicles, family and friends come to comfort, perhaps. There were lights on in the house. As arranged with Jo, I sat in the car with the heater and the radio on while she went to see what was what. I watched the front door open and Rebecca Swaine was backlit. The women exchanged a few words and Jo hurried back to me, tapped on the window and beckoned me with a crooked finger. I was pleased. I'd rather be in the house than stuck out in the dark. Alone. My Manderley feeling was back and it gave me the willies.

Mrs Swaine greeted me with the air of someone disconnected. I expressed my sympathy for her loss. She didn't cry. She didn't look as though she had been or that she might. After the coat and slippers routine, she showed us through to a different room. It was a fine and spacious living room. There was a low ceiling with exposed old beams. They looked original to me. Some nice artwork, some nice furniture, nice curtains, nice lighting. It was quite nice. This is where the fire burned that I'd smelled on the previous visit. It wasn't burning now and the room was chilly and desolate for it.

Mrs Swaine bade us sit. We obliged. She sat too. We stared at each other for an uncomfortable, long moment.

'He hanged himself in the woods behind the house. He must have done it sometime in the previous night. When we realised he was missing and that he hadn't slept in his bed we went looking for him – Sigmund and I. Nigel's car was still in the garage so he couldn't have gone anywhere. Sigmund found him. It's shaken him up. I shouldn't have let him look with me. He is very sensitive to… violence.'

Mrs Swaine seemed to be bearing up quite well. But probably that was the effect of the stiff upper lip classes she'd taken at finishing school.

'Mrs Swaine, did you tell the police about the blackmail threat?' said Jo.

After the briefest hesitation, Mrs Swaine said, 'No.' She stared into the coldness of the empty fireplace.

Jo looked shocked. 'Why?'

Something in Jo's tone touched Mrs Swaine. She turned those effective eyes on Jo. 'He's dead. He killed himself. Finding out why he did it won't change that unalterable fact. It won't bring him back and it can't change anything. I imagine that will be an end to the matter of blackmail.'

'I have to advise you to tell the police, Mrs Swaine. They could investigate and charges could be brought. A crime has been committed and it's led to a man taking his own life.'

Mrs Swaine raised her chin a notch in preparation for argument and said, 'There is no evidence to back up any assertion of blackmail.' There was something of a rebuke in there for Jo's impertinence. And then Mrs Swaine softened. 'So you see, Miss Cash, there really is nothing for the police to be interested in.'

A bit of an atmosphere descended. The air felt a bit tense. Jo was not happy – I understood that much. Mrs Swaine was resolute. I was ignored. A creak of floorboards indicated someone moving about upstairs. Mrs Swaine glanced at the ceiling.

'Also, I've now changed my mind about asking you to investigate further. When I spoke to you earlier I was... emotional. I wasn't thinking rationally and sensibly. I see now that it would serve no purpose to investigate the matter further. Naturally, I shall pay you for your time and effort and I shall be happy to add something extra for your... understanding.'

After a brief uncomfortable pause, Jo said, 'That won't be necessary, Mrs Swaine. You're my employer. If you want to terminate our association, that's your right. I'll send you a bill for my time and expenses and it will be commensurate with the rates we discussed.'

'As you wish.' Rebecca Swaine turned her whole trunk in my direction, signalling that she'd closed the subject with Jo. 'About those books. I think I'd like them back, Mr Booker, if you don't mind.'

'I'm sorry, Mrs Swaine. I sold them today to a dealer in London.' I reached into my inside pocket and withdrew the cheque made out to her. I passed it across. She studied it and bit her lip.

'That's the full amount. It's not far short of what we discussed. It's a good price,' I said.

She breathed out a little too heavily. 'Well, if they're gone they're gone, I suppose. Thank you. You have both been very efficient. What do I owe you, Mr Booker?'

'Nothing, Mrs Swaine. I had to go to London anyway,' I lied.

After another brief pause Mrs Swaine stood. Jo and I stood. 'I would be grateful if we could all just forget about this whole sorry business,' she said. 'I only want to get on with my life.' Her composure was extraordinary.

Mrs Swaine saw us out. It had started to rain again. It fell in irregular sweeps. A cutting wind was swirling around the hills that overlooked the Marsh, ruffling the evergreen shrubs into gossip and gyrating the taller bare trees around, like drunk-dad dancing at a wedding.

Again, Mrs Swaine didn't wave us off. The door was firmly shut before we had hurried across the gravel to the car. Instinctively, I glanced up at the window I had seen Sigmund Swaine scowling down at us from on our previous visit. It was too murky for detail but I was sure I saw the man's darkened form looking down at us. Something crawled down my spine.

I risked a quick look in Jo's direction as we weaved our way across the Marsh. The dashboard lights gave her features a theatrical ghoulish countenance. 'How do you feel?'

'Bit annoyed. But, like I said to her, she's the boss. She doesn't want me investigating, I'm not going to investigate.' That sounded brave.

'Don't you have a professional curiosity to satisfy?'

'No. Being in the police has cured me of that. I'm not about to start wasting my time on something I'm not going to get paid for.'

'Why do you think she changed her mind about having you follow it up?'

'Like she said, it would serve no purpose. If that's the way she feels, that's the way it is.'

'I must say, I think you're taking it very philosophically.'

'Thank you. I'll take that as a compliment. I still get paid for two days' work and I had a little trip to London and a nice lunch, which she can pay for.'

'I paid for that.'

'OK, I'll give you the money.'

I tutted. 'That's not what I meant and you know it.'

'I'll give Marion a call tomorrow. Let her know. That won't hurt.'

15

I could tell Jo was disappointed with the way things had turned out. I was too. There wasn't much more conversation. When we got home she disappeared upstairs. The ladies had shut up shop and, after checking everything was switched off and they'd locked the front door, I decided to organise a takeaway and watch a film. I shouldn't have been as hungry as I was after the pub lunch. I considered the possibility that I had worms.

The evening weather had degenerated into the sort to make the battening down of hatches and pugging down on the sofa in front of a good film a good option. Even a bad film. Rain was being driven across the English Channel to lash the front windows. I invited Jo down, but she declined without excuse. Not that she needed to provide one to me.

Two hours later I was comfortably stuffed with Indian food and on my second bottle of Whitstable Bay ale when Jo knocked at the dividing door. I called her through and paused the film just as Nick Nolte was fighting for his life in *Cape Fear*. If I hadn't watched the film at least a dozen times I might have been cross.

'You're too late for food. There's a bit of naan bread left somewhere.'

'Tell me you're not drunk?' She looked serious.

I sat up straight. 'What's wrong?'

She perched on the arm of the chair. 'Mrs Swaine just called me. Sigmund's gone missing. He's not in the house and he doesn't drive. She's worried about him.'

'He seemed big enough and ugly enough to take care of himself. Besides, didn't she terminate your employment?'

'Sigmund's missing. She's worried. She's called the police but they aren't interested, obviously. So she's phoned me. Can *we* go up and help her look for him?'

I laughed heartily. 'You are joking? In this?' I pointed at the front window, which was doing a good impression of a shower screen with someone using it on the other side of the glass, as it bore the brunt of a very wet and windy Channel gale.

'She sounded desperate.'

'Tough.' To emphasise my reluctance to be part of such an idiotic venture I took a swig from the bottle.

'If I help her, she might reinstate me to find out who was blackmailing her husband.'

'She agreed to that?'

'No. David, I can't force you and I won't hold it against you if you say no, but I really want this job. I need this job. I don't want to go up there alone. But if I have to I will.'

The words emotional and blackmail sprang to mind. There seemed a lot of it about.

I sighed rather theatrically, picked up the remote and turned everything off. Jo smiled nicely and said thank you.

16

Jo drove the roller skate. The tempest buffeted her little hatchback as we made our way on the otherwise and unsurprisingly deserted Marsh lanes.

The track to Silverhurst was almost completely under water. We bucked and bounced and sloshed down it. I fully expected water to come in somewhere. I waited for Jo to blame me for something but her mind was on other, more important things.

Mrs Swaine opened the front door as soon as we entered the driveway. She was wearing a full-length waxed coat, wellington boots and a wide brimmed hat, which she held in place with a hand. So much for no outdoor footwear in the house. We got out to join her in the overhanging area in front of the garage door. I'd rather hoped that either Sigmund would have returned or that we might be invited in for a warm and a chat first – draw up our plans of action. I was to be disappointed on both counts.

Mrs Swaine had to raise her voice over the noise of the wind and rain in the trees and foliage that encroached everywhere. 'Thank you both very much for coming. I'm sorry, I really had no one else to call.' Away from the house it was pitch dark. I looked for an outside light but saw none. I tested my torch.

'He's not back then?' said Jo, almost shouting.

'No.'

We knew that he'd been 'missing' for over an hour at least.

'Where is there for him to go?' said Jo.

'There's nowhere. That's why I'm so worried. It's only woodland and fields. There are no outbuildings apart from the greenhouse and I've checked that.'

I said, 'Don't take this as anything other than a good question, Mrs Swaine – are you positive he's not in the house somewhere?'

'I'm certain. I've looked everywhere he could possibly be. And I've checked the garage.'

'Has he done this before?'

'Never.'

'And there is no vehicle he could have left in?'

'No. Our only transport is Nigel's car and it's still here. And Sigmund doesn't drive.'

'What about a bicycle?'

'We don't own any.'

'No one who could have collected him?'

'No.'

'Could he have gone to a neighbouring house?'

She shook her head. 'We don't get on. He has to be around here. I can only think that he's hurt somewhere.'

I could only wonder what had possessed the man to go wandering off in such rotten weather. But then on the one occasion I'd met him he hadn't seemed all there. A thought occurred to me. 'Is his coat missing? Footwear? Is he dressed for being out in this?'

'I honestly don't know.' And she obviously wasn't going to waste time going to look.

Jo said, 'There's no point in us all looking. Mrs Swaine, you stay here. He might come home. You have my number. If he shows, call me. David and I will look around the woods. Is there a favourite route or an area we should try first?'

Before she could answer, I said, 'Has he got a mobile phone?'

'No, he hasn't. He can't bear them. The only access into the woods is through the hedge over there.' She gestured at the darkness. 'There is a path.'

Jo and I trudged off across the sodden lawn. My trainers were already letting in water. We agreed not to split up because neither of us knew the area and I had not thought to bring my own phone. I had brought an umbrella, which was not very clever.

Before we had made it to the hedge it had turned inside out. I swore as much at my stupidity as at the wind.

Jo had a good long raincoat with hood attachment and stout footwear. I just got soaked. The rain plastered my hair to my scalp and ran down the neck of my short jacket. It virtually blinded me to the little my torch beam illuminated. Branches like outstretched limbs of desperate people grabbed and clung to us as we pushed our way deeper into the wooded night. We had to progress in single file. We played our torches around us. The mud under our feet was slippery and dotted with puddles. I tried to see if I could make out recent footprints but I couldn't swear to anything. It was no surprise and certainly no teddy bears' picnic.

We hadn't been searching for ten minutes before I took hold of Jo's sleeve. She turned to face me and I told her what a waste of time I thought it all was. We weren't going to see anything that was more than a foot either side of the path.

'We're here now. Let's at least have a good look.' The noise in the thick of the wood was approaching deafening, as if the mouth of hell had opened up and the tormented souls of aeons were howling in their haste to escape. She had to almost shout the words into my face to stop them being whipped away unheard.

Another five minutes or so of fruitless searching and battling the elements and undergrowth and we came to a low wire fence. The wood ended abruptly. The short pasture of a sheep field characterised the other side. In my thin torchlight the grass definitely looked greener.

'What now?' I said. There was an almighty crash behind us as some rotten tree succumbed to the gale and fell into other trees around it. I couldn't see where it had happened but it sounded close. Too close for comfort. I had no intention of meeting my end out there, crushed to death in all that on a fool's errand. I opened my mouth to share this with Jo but she beat me to it.

'What's that place?'

In the almost total darkness I struggled to make out where she was pointing. When I did, I said, 'St Rumwold's. It's a church.'

'Do you think it's normal the lights are on?'
I didn't. And as soon as I'd said so I knew what was coming. There was a stile set in the fence. We clambered over it and set off down the hill towards possible enlightenment. Literally, we were out of the woods. Figuratively speaking, I wasn't so sure.

17

The geography of the area was not unknown to me. I loved St Rumwold's. One of the most picturesque of the local churches, it sat on slightly elevated ground just off the Marsh proper. It was small, well cared for and in the summer a perfect place to dismount during a bike ride, sit in the sun on one of the graveyard benches and stare out over Romney Marsh. I'd never been around it in thick darkness, pouring rain and gale force winds. I preferred my version.

We slipped and slid down the slope from the higher ground. At least I did in my ruined, waterlogged and mud-coated trainers. The water ran downhill too, as water always does. In the absence of light I went in one puddle up to my ankle. I was sorely pissed off by the time we got on level ground. I was also wet through and bloody cold with it. If Sigmund was hiding out in the church I was going to give the dick a piece of my mind.

To get to the church we could either try to jump a normally narrow and vaultable watercourse, which had inconveniently doubled in width when compared with its usual self, or follow the trail alongside the Royal Military Canal, gain the lane and walk up terra firma to the churchyard gate. I couldn't get any wetter but apparently Jo could. We went by way of the road. I looked up at the church to see a dim light wavering at the windows.

As we approached the main door at the northern side of the church through the graveyard I realised that the light inside was not created by electricity but by candles. Great, I thought. As if the whole expedition didn't have enough spooky effects about it already.

Jo was close behind me. I turned the big cold metal ring of a handle and the main outer door, being unlocked, opened into the covered porch. The door banged back on the wall with a resounding thud, making so much noise that anyone inside should have heard our entry. There was no light in the vestibule except that provided by our torches. I exchanged a look with Jo. Her features were hollowed out and made ghostly and were running in water. Our distorted shadows crept along the walls. I realised I was in an isolated rural church in a graveyard on a stormy night with only a torch. My bowels started making themselves known to me.

I turned the magnificent old wrought-iron handle of the inner door and in true Hammer Horror style the ancient entrance creaked its way open on protesting hinges. The sound ricocheted around the interior. There was no sign of life, or death, other than the kind traditionally associated with medieval rural churches. Half a dozen stout candles burned quite brightly in the chancel off to our left. Jo and I edged our way towards them without speaking. Pale impressions of us danced on the whitewashed walls.

A foot behind me, Jo barked out a sudden hello, which almost fast-tracked my curry. I turned to stare at her. 'Let me know next time, eh?'

She rolled her eyes and repeated her call. 'Hello. Sigmund, are you in here? Is anyone in here?'

We were now standing in the middle of the nave facing the chancel and the altar. I used my torch to look for wet footprints on the stone floor but there were none in evidence. However, a small pool was quickly forming where I stood.

After some long seconds waiting for something to happen, I released the breath I'd been holding and said, 'Perhaps they just keep candles burning through the night here. Are we in a period of Christian celebration for anything?'

I played my torch beam around the place, steering it into the darkest recesses. Jo was still close behind me. I took a couple more paces towards the source of light and, like game spooked into flight by a beater, something exploded out of where it had been hiding in the forward pews. I instinctively swung my torch beam around to illuminate the contorted features of Sigmund Swaine bearing down on me, arms raised and clutching something that I instinctively knew would hurt me if he managed to make contact. He was shrieking like a banshee possessed and my fear rooted me to the spot.

Jo barged me out of the way and I fell to the floor. Sigmund slashed air and stumbled. He whirled around and braced himself for more.

'What are you doing?' I shouted at him, scrambling to my feet. 'Your sister sent us to look for you. She's worried about you, you arsehole.'

I had him in my torch beam. His eyes were like those of terrified pony – all whites and rolling irises. It was clear he'd been crying. His chest was heaving with the exertions of his breathing. 'You're lying. I know what you want. I know why you're here.' Some spit hung from his chin. He raised his club again and rushed at me. I brought my arms up to shield my head. I felt my wrist jar painfully as he brought his weapon down hard, hitting my torch. That clattered to the floor and died.

Jo grabbed him from behind and was trying to get some kind of lock on him. But he was strong, scared and demented – a potent combination. He bucked her off and she crashed into a pew. Her torch bounced away and we were back to candlelight. There was nothing romantic about it.

I got myself ready for another assault but Sigmund had other ideas. He bolted towards the west end of the church. There was an arched doorway set in the west wall and he threw himself at it. If he was trying to escape he should have just gone out of the door we came in through.

Jo and I got to our feet. She'd found her torch and it was still working. We moved towards him. I left the talking to Jo.

'Sigmund. We're not here to hurt you. Just listen to me.'

He abandoned his rattling of the door fittings and turned to face us. Jo waved me to stop where I was. She continued edging towards him.

'Your sister is worried about you, Sigmund. Look, I have my mobile phone here. You can talk to her.' Jo took out her phone and held it up for him to see. Rather than having the desired calming effect, the man seemed only to panic further.

'Liar!' he screamed. 'Get that away from me.' He threw his weapon in our direction. It sailed high and wide to clatter noisily on the flagstone floor behind us. Then, with a surprising agility, he jumped up onto the back of a pew, reached up and used a hefty timber bracket angled away from the wall to haul himself up so that after some scrabbling he got himself over the handrail and was standing on the gallery that ran the length of the west wall some fifteen feet above us. There was nothing for him up there. No escape route I could see. But he had put himself out of our reach. I wasn't sorry. My wrist was pounding.

'What are we going to do?' I said.

'Nothing. Let's back up a bit. Give him some room. Let him see we're no threat to him.'

We did that. Sigmund was squatting down on his haunches with his head in his hands. I'd have bet money on him being on medication. And I'd have doubled it that he'd missed his meds recently.

'And now?' I said.

'I'll phone his sister. She can come over here and talk him down.'

Before Jo could make the call Sigmund stood and came to the front guardrail of the rickety-looking gallery. Jo still had her torch pointed in his general direction. He grabbed the handrail with both hands and leant far forward. Even from that distance and in that light the tracks of his tears were clearly visible. 'I know what you want. I know why you're here,' he repeated. Sigmund Swaine hopped up onto the handrail, demonstrating incredible balance for someone clearly unbalanced. It put another three feet on his height. In a hoarse, pitiful voice that was made terrifying for its raw and undisguised emotion, he said, 'You can't blame me. He made me.' And then he pitched off into space. He knew what he was doing. He led with his head. He made no attempt to bring his arms up to lessen the impact. The dull sickening thud of his skull connecting with the medieval stone flooring gave me little hope he'd survive it. His body crumpled over awkwardly. We rushed forwards but it was quickly evident that if he hadn't caved his skull in on impact he'd certainly broken his neck. Jo's torch picked out his open wet eyes and his tear-stained cheeks before I could turn away. And the heartbreaking image was emblazoned on my retina.

18

Jo dialled 999. She walked away from me to attend to the details. I sat in one of the pews at the front and shook from the cold and wet and the shock of it.

Rebecca Swaine called Jo's phone while we were waiting for the emergency services to arrive. Jo let it ring. She'd seen her fair share of dead people, she'd even killed a couple that I knew of, but she took Sigmund's death particularly badly. Maybe it was because he had been her client's kin. People didn't employ investigators to locate their siblings only to have them instrumental in their sudden deaths. It would look bad on Jo's CV, put prospective clients off.

Jo had felt his neck for signs of life and found none. The church was colder than the weather or the season. It was also deathly quiet. The only sounds were our limited movements and my breathing and the high winds creeping in to whine at what we'd done.

As much to make some noise as anything else, I said, 'What will we tell them?'

She looked at me strangely. 'The truth, of course. Never lie to the law.'

I considered myself rebuked but had to ask: 'Even what he said?'

She tested me. 'What did he say?'

'Something about he couldn't be blamed, someone made him. Made him do it, I suppose.'

'That's what I heard. Mean anything to you?'

I shook my head.

'Me neither. The ramblings of a confused mind,' said Jo.

'And what will we tell his sister?'

'I'll deal with that,' she said. She ran her fingers through her hair. 'I'm sorry, David. I've involved you in something that I shouldn't have. I've had training in this sort of thing. I've got experience. I can deal with it. You don't need this in your mind, in your nightmares.'

'Jo?'

'What?'

'Shut up. Right? No way I'd have let you come out in this, looking for him by yourself. You didn't force me into anything. You asked for my help and I gave it willingly. If you ask me the same thing tomorrow, I'll still come.'

She softened a little and smiled at me. 'Thanks. You're a good egg. A good friend.'

Rebecca Swaine called again, shattering the silence with a burst of something wholly inappropriate, and still Jo didn't answer. She was right not to. No one should hear about the sudden death of a loved one over the telephone. And I suppose that Jo didn't want to have to deal with a potentially distraught family member descending on the church to complicate matters.

The police arrived first – uniformed officers, who soon called up for reinforcements of the non-uniformed variety.

19

Naturally, the police had a good many good questions for us. There were two from Ashford CID and both clearly knew of Jo's reasons for doing what she was doing these days. I might have expected some resentment from them for the meddling of the private sector in their world but quite the opposite seemed apparent. They were friendly and surprisingly human, which just goes to show that it's always who you know in life that counts. That said, they were also quite interested in what we knew.

Following her own good advice, Jo told them what had happened in a concise chronological order. No frills. No embroidery. It was another reason the law seemed happy to talk with her. I didn't hear her repeat what Sigmund had said.

My part in the unfolding of events was scrutinised for the rule book's sake but the information that counted was Jo's. And the evidence to back up our assertions was there for all to see. The only bits of the puzzle that were missing were the whys. Why had Sigmund Swaine sought refuge – sanctuary, perhaps – in a remote church on a dark and stormy night? Why had he attacked us without provocation? Why had he looked so hopelessly terrified of us? And the big one: why had he deliberately taken his own life? No one had the answers to any of those.

Because Jo was on first name terms with the detective sergeant in charge, we got a lift back to Silverhurst when the police were done with us. I think the additional fact that Jo offered to be the bearer of bad news influenced her decision.

No one spoke on the ten-minute drive. I was freshly conscious of my soaking, freezing clothing. I hadn't stopped shivering since Sigmund had expired.

As soon as the tyres crawled noisily over the gravel, Rebecca Swaine was at the front door. She'd lost the outdoor look. Her blonde hair was pulled back harshly into a ponytail. The little light that filtered out was enough to illuminate her body language, which emphasised her anguish. She watched the four of us get out of the police car. I left the four of them to it.

The rain had eased but the wind was still a force to be reckoned with. I remembered I had an old jumper in Jo's car – a relic of a picnic in better weather. While the police and Jo spoke to Mrs Swaine I stripped off my top layers and pulled something dry on. I was still bloody cold. I sat in the car and put the heater on. No one seemed to mind my absence.

In five minutes Jo was letting herself in. She sat behind the wheel and just stared at the closed garage door. I had questions: how did she take it? Did she blame us? What happens now? Could she say what was wrong with him? But I kept them to myself.

The police disappeared inside the house and the door was shut. Jo started the car and we left.

We were almost home before either of us spoke. I said, 'What happens now?'

'We go into Ashford police station and give our formal statements. Other than that I have no idea. I can hardly hope to be reinstated to investigate her husband's suicide when I've just been instrumental in her brother's, can I?'

I agreed with her without saying so.

It was well past midnight when we got back home. The storm had all but blown itself out. Normal service had been resumed. I let us in. We said goodnight. I took a long hot shower and guessed Jo would be doing the same. Then I put on a clean T-shirt and tracky bottoms, made myself a hot water bottle and went to bed. I was just drifting off when I heard a gentle tapping downstairs.

'Jo?'

'Can I come up?'

'Of course.'

I put the bedside light on and sat up a bit. She pushed open the door to my bedroom and leaned against the door jamb. She was dressed in loose-fitting sweats. Her hair was wet.

'What's up?'

'If I ask to get in with you, will you get the wrong idea?'

I already had and was struggling to suppress my body's natural reaction to it. I didn't trust myself to speak and not say something quite stupid. I shifted over and threw back the duvet. Without another word passing between us she moved in, turned off the light, gave me her back and reversed in. I stayed wide awake well past the time it took her breathing to find an even, deep regularity. Her smell, her warmth, her presence comforted me and diverted my thoughts from replaying on a loop Sigmund Swaine's swan dive to oblivion.

20

From the strength of the light in the room, I could tell it was later than usual for me to wake up. Jo was gone. I wondered whether I'd dreamt her visit. Then I found a hair on the pillow that wasn't mine. It could only have been Jo's.

I lay back, comfortable. I didn't want to get up. I had things to think about, things to remember and I always found staring at the ceiling from my warm pit short on distractions and therefore good for thought.

In a couple of minutes my phone rang – Jo. We enquired after each other's health and didn't mention sharing a bed.

She said, 'You around this morning?'

'No plans. Architect's coming to see me after lunch.'

'Ashford CID want to pay us a visit.'

'I thought we were going there?'

'They've changed their mind. It's a copper's prerogative.'

'I thought it was a woman's.'

'She is a woman. A DI I don't know is in charge. She's in a hurry.'

'To do what?'

'Talk to us, among other things.'

'Suits me. I'd rather not traipse into Ashford. Parking can be a bitch. What time is she coming?'

'An hour OK with you?'

I said it was, got up and got dressed.

An hour meant we'd be open downstairs. I hoped they wouldn't mind conducting their business in the shop. With hot fresh coffee on hand, I doubted it.

21

I might have sworn an oath not to stoop to serving up the mainstays of British breakfasts in my premises but that didn't mean I had stopped eating them. I had no personal, ethical or business conflicts regarding buying bacon rolls from the baker's next door and eating them in my coffee shop. I just didn't like customers doing it.

I was burping dead pig, brown sauce and black coffee when Jo showed. She'd declined my offer to join me for breakfast. She helped herself to a hot drink and came and sat opposite me.

She looked tired and gloomy but still good, as usual. Under different circumstances, to bask in the knowledge that we'd shared a bed the previous night would have buoyed me. Actually, it still felt special.

'What are you smiling at?'

'I'm not smiling. It's wind.'

'Nothing happened.'

'Maybe not for you, but for me...' An image of Sigmund Swaine lying crumpled and bloody on the cold stone floor returned to remind me of something more serious. 'How are you this morning?'

'Not great. I keep wondering if I could have handled that better. If I had he might still be alive. My sloppiness has cost a life, David.'

'Don't be so hard on yourself, Jo. You weren't sloppy. He was off his head. He was terrified of something. He was crazy. What happened last night is nothing for either of us to reproach ourselves over.'

Jo took a sip of her drink. 'My friend from Ashford – the DS from last night – gave me a call this morning. Her DI is new and keen. She's also, naturally, professionally curious about two suicides so close to each other in the same household.'

'I get the picture. So you don't know this one?'

Jo shook her head and didn't look happy about that.

We didn't have long to wait. I recognised one of the women from the previous evening. She and Jo greeted each other less warmly than they had less than twelve hours previously but that was probably because the DS had a senior officer with her who looked like she'd swallowed a bumble bee on the way in. Or it could have been that the DS was feeling as tired as she looked. I felt a bit sorry for her when I thought of the night she'd had and now she was back on duty.

Jo's friend nodded to me. The new one, the detective inspector, introduced herself and didn't offer to shake hands. There was something standoffish about her. Maybe she didn't like private enterprise in her field. Maybe she didn't like the look of us. Maybe she didn't like the fact that Jo was disgraced ex-job and a killer of civilians. I could wonder all day about what she didn't like. It wouldn't get us anywhere.

I offered them coffee and they accepted without fuss.

DI Francis took a turn around the shop. 'This place yours, Mr Booker?'

I said it was without sounding smart about it. No point in getting her back up.

'Nice. It's like Waterstones meets Wetherspoons without the booze.'

'Maybe I should have called it Waterspoons,' I said for fun.

'Weatherstones might have been better,' came back DI Francis.

'Trouble is neither of those is my name,' I said.

'If it's that important to you, you could have changed it by deed poll. How's business?'

'Slow, but it's early days.'

'You don't seem too worried about it.'

'Money is not an issue, yet.'

'So I heard.'

She came and made herself comfortable. She regarded Jo with what I took as an acute professional interest. She had to have known about Jo's history. As someone who'd taken on and slain one nasty piece of psychotic work and one giant albino idiot with anger management issues, and then escaped jail, Jo had a reputation among her ex-peers – generally, in a good way. In gunning down the bad guys, she'd lived out some of their fantasies.

DI Francis got down to her reason for being there. 'Two suicides within twenty-four hours in the same family. You can understand why the police are interested, I'm sure.'

We both nodded.

'What exactly is the nature of your involvement with the family?' She looked between Jo and me and waited.

'I was retained by Rebecca Swaine to look into a personal matter. A private matter,' said Jo.

'What private matter?'

'You'll have to ask her about that. I can't discuss it. It would be unethical.' She'd changed her tune, I noticed.

DI Francis had to accept this. 'What about you, Mr Booker?'

'Same meat, different gravy, Inspector. It just so happened that Mrs Swaine needed my services too. I don't think I'm breaking any confidentiality clauses when I say it was about books.'

'What about them?'

'Sorry. I'd rather you asked her. I said I could keep a secret.'

'Where were you both when the husband took his own life?'

'We don't know when he took it,' said Jo.

I knew she did, so I knew she was lying to the police. Tut tut.

'When we heard about it we were both in London. Together,' I said.

'He died between the hours of midnight and dawn.'

'I was in bed asleep,' I said.

'So was I,' said Jo.

'I suppose you can corroborate each others' stories?'

'No,' said Jo, unhelpfully. 'And why do we need to?'

'Just an expression. You know how it is.'

'I know that's how it is if you suspect someone of wrongdoing.'

It suddenly felt a bit tense.

'Calm down, Miss Cash,' said DI Francis. She set her mouth in her idea of a patronising smile. She pulled off broken twig.

'I am calm. But I'm not sure I like your thinking, Inspector.'

'Just exploring avenues of enquiry. You've got to admit it's all a little strange. And like it or not, you two are involved.'

'Involved in what?' said Jo.

'Events. Broadly speaking.'

We said nothing.

'Tell me about last night.'

Jo said, 'Mrs Swaine called me late evening. Told me her brother was missing and she was worried about him. She asked me to look for him.'

'Why?'

'You'll have to ask her, but the police weren't interested, apparently, and she didn't have anyone else to turn to.'

'Did she ask that both of you go?'

'No. I asked David to accompany me. When we got to Silverhurst, Mrs Swaine pointed us in the direction of the woods. We followed the trail and came to a fence by a field. I saw lights on in the church and we decided to investigate.'

DI Francis was frowning. 'Why? Why investigate?'

'It seemed odd that there were lights on in the church at that time on such a night.'

DI Francis was still frowning. It looked like it pained her.

'We were right,' said Jo.

'And what happened when you forced your way in?'

'We didn't force our way in. The door wasn't locked. We just turned the handle and there we were. Sigmund Swaine attacked us.'

'Why?'

'He didn't offer an explanation.'

'Had you met him before? Would he have recognised you?'

'I had,' I said. 'I met him when I visited the house earlier this week.'

'So he would have recognised you?'

'It would make sense, unless he was not in his right mind.'

'What makes you say that?' and there was a professional barb attached.

'He acted very oddly in the church.'

'Go on.'

I wanted to look at Jo to see whether she would want me to *go on* but that might have seemed suspicious. DI Francis seemed suspicious enough. I had a clever thought.

I smiled falsely at Jo and said, 'Why don't you tell them? You've got more experience at this sort of thing than I have.'

They both looked at her and she looked at me. I recognised her deadpan expression and thought she'd have some unfriendly words for me when we were alone.

'He was clearly agitated about something. He was ranting and violent.'

'What did he say?'

I waited for Jo to show me what a good cooperative citizen she was these days by telling them what he'd said.

'He was shouting incomprehensibly. I didn't understand any of it. Did you?'

I realised she'd sent the ball back over my side of the net. I shook my head slowly and made an exaggerated downward curl of my bottom lip. It felt so fake, I nearly blushed. I couldn't hold DI Francis's stare.

DI Francis huffed. There didn't seem anything personal in it.

'If anything should occur to either of you, I'd appreciate you giving me a call.' She laid two of her cards on the table. Face up. Insanely, it crossed my mind to shout, 'Snap!'

The DS took our statements while DI Francis made some phone calls, had another coffee and a slice of cake on the house. It might not have been time for elevenses but she was police. There are exceptions to every rule.

22

When they'd gone, I said to Jo, 'What happened to all that guff from last night about always tell the truth? Never lie to the law.'

'Do as I say, not as I do.'

'Very funny. I'm serious: why?'

'Because Mrs Swaine is going to want answers and if I tell the police everything I might not be the one to find them for her.'

'So you kept something back so you could be ahead of the police?'

'Listen, they're going to lose interest pretty quickly anyway. They don't have the time, the manpower or the motivation to investigate the reasons why people take their own lives, and they can't bring charges against dead people for committing that particular crime so they move on, quickly, to something that isn't a waste of their valuable resources. I've just given them less to bother their consciences over when the time comes to signing it off.'

'What do you think he meant?'

'Who?'

'Sigmund. When he said, "he made me"?'

Jo breathed in deeply and then out heavily through her nose. I recognised it as a sign of deep thought, as if she needed more oxygen for it. It was a mannerism, one of the few I'd come to recognise in her.

'Can we recap what happened after we entered the church? What do you remember?'

'You want the truth, the whole truth and nothing but the truth or the police version?'

'You do know that sometimes you're not funny, don't you?'

'Yes. But your reaction is always worth it. He attacked us.'

'No. He attacked you, not me.'

'OK. He went for me.'

'Why do you think that was?'

'Because he recognised me? Because I was a man and therefore more of a threat?'

Jo raised a mocking eyebrow.

'Maybe it was just because I was closest to him. He was screaming, so it's fair to say he was furious.'

'Or terrified.'

'OK. Or terrified. He slashed at me with whatever it was. Thanks, by the way. Shoving me aside maybe saved me a headache this morning. I told him we were there looking for him because his sister was worried about him. I called him an arsehole.'

'I meant to talk to you about that. You need to work on your people-management vocabulary.'

'I was brought up to call a spade a spade.'

'You can't say that these days. It's racist.'

'That's not what I meant, and you know it.'

She was half smiling at me. 'Yes. But your reaction is always worth it.'

'I meant what I said to those two: he didn't seem in his right mind, if he had one that is. When I met him in the library he seemed... highly strung. And in the church, well, he seemed crazy. Wouldn't you say?'

Jo nodded and made an mmm noise. 'Mad. What did he say before he lunged the second time?'

'Didn't you hear? He was shouting loud enough.'

'I want to know what *you* heard.' She took out her little pocket notebook and a pencil.

I said, 'You can take the woman out of the police...'

'Blah, blah, blah.'

'He said, "You're lying. I know what you want. I know why you're here."'

Jo looked impressed. 'Very good. That's what I got. He was frightened.'

'At least.'

'What did you hear just before he jumped?'

"It's not my fault. He made me."

Jo consulted her notes. She said, 'How about, "You can't blame me. He made me."'

'Same thing.'

'No, it's not. I thought you were an English teacher.'

'It's not my fault and you can't blame me amount to the same thing.'

'Sometimes.'

'The important bit is *he made me*. What could he have meant by that?'

'Another male made Sigmund do something that, presumably, he was either ashamed of, embarrassed about or was against the law.'

'Maybe. In that case, I'd say against the law would be favourite, wouldn't you? He did kill himself.'

'But you said he might not have been in his right mind. And people do die of embarrassment. And shame.'

Even I cringed at that. '*He made me* could also have meant that another male made Sigmund the person he was in some way.'

'He made me the man I am today?'

'Something like that. And there's something else we shouldn't discount, especially given the location.'

'Go on.'

'*He* could have referred to God. We were in *His* house after all.'

23

Jo gave the police time to get back to Ashford before ringing her DS friend. She wanted a private word without DI Francis within earshot. I was coming to appreciate that it's not just the old boys who have networks. She asked whether her friend could let her know the details of the post-mortem of Nigel Tate and while she was about it could she also her let her know the same for Sigmund.

Then she called Marion Pardew and gave her the news. They spent a few minutes chatting.

Jo's phone rang the moment she hung up on Marion. It was Rebecca Swaine. I knew this because Jo clicked her fingers at me and mouthed 'Rebecca Swaine'.

It was a brief conversation. When it was over Jo was smiling. 'What did I tell you?'

'She wants you back?'

'Just like Michael.' In response to my thick-face, she added, 'Jackson, dummy.'

I let my eyes roll up into my skull. 'For how long? An hour? Two? Before she casts you aside like a Dymchurch day-tripping baby's soiled nappy on the Parish Council car park gravel after a Bank Holiday Monday.'

(There were eight bins in the car park and yet at the end of every Bank Holiday Monday the ground was dotted with soiled nappies where the lazy-bastard parents couldn't be bothered to Keep Britain Tidy. These were the kinds of people I was spending a fortune on encouraging into my business. I must've been mad.)

Jo made a face. 'I'm going to insist that she sees it through this time or I'm not getting involved.'

'How can you do that?'

'Watch and learn.'

'I'm coming?'

'I want you to. Of course, if you're too busy...'

'The architect is coming at one.'

'Don't worry. You'll be back home by then, in your wellies and hard hat, clutching your tape measure. I promise.'

24

Romney Marsh was enjoying a bit of unseasonal sunshine. The calm after the storm in this case. You couldn't live on the Marsh without sooner or later realising that the place enjoyed its own micro-climate and mostly it was the exact opposite of what the rest of Kent was either basking in or drowning in. I'm not saying it snowed in July but as a native of the place I was used to standing on the beach at Dymchurch in a T-shirt, shorts and flip-flops while dark and petulant storm clouds, thunder and lightning prowled around the hills at Lympne, like some mythical beast scared of crossing an invisible line. The magic of Romney Marsh.

Jo had asked if we could take my car. I'd said we could. She'd asked if she could drive. I'd said she could, but only if I could start sitting in the back and she wore a cap and got the door for me. She'd asked if I wanted a punch in the mouth. I threw her the keys to my four-wheel-drive indulgence and tried to make her promise to drive carefully.

All my life I'd made do with battered second-hand cars; I'd never even owned a new bicycle. Until now. The money I'd come into after the deaths of my relatives encouraged me to break that cycle of making do. And I broke it in style, like a thundering volley from outside the box in the eighty-ninth minute of an FA cup final.

I didn't buy a new pushbike; I treated myself to a brand new Range Rover HSE Sport in black. And I loved it and how it made me feel. Like a king. The convenient tipping point in my umming and ahhing over whether to really spend that much money on a lump of metal, plastic, rubber and glass was my very-near-death experience at the hands of the French loonies. You only live once and you can't take it with you. And in my case there was no one to leave it to. My mind was made up.

Of course, Jo saw through my shallow male vanity for the purchase before I had the handbrake on in the back yard for the first time. She poured her own particular brand of good-natured scorn on the fire of my enthusiasm by saying that in profile it put her in mind of a giant surgical shoe. She might have been right, but it still said Range Rover on the bonnet and boot in big shiny metal letters. And that's what mattered most. It's worth mentioning that her reservations regarding the aesthetic appeal of the car didn't stop her asking to borrow it or drive it when we went out together. She said it impressed clients and gave her respectability when she went calling on them. I wasn't having any of it; she was as shallow and vain as me at times.

She drove at a sedate pace for a change. I looked out of the window. We had Adele rolling in the deep on the CD player and the windows down. I could smell winter off the fields and the dykes on the crisp air that was being channelled in and it was nice. I saw an owl on a fence post and a heron standing sentinel with his beady eye on something in the water. He did not bat a feather as we growled past.

We pitched up at Silverhurst a little before late morning. There were two vehicles on the gravel. Neither suggested Mrs Swaine had company of a social nature, unless she'd really fallen a long way off that particular ladder. One was a dented little hatchback that had been improved by at least three models that I knew of since it had rolled off the production line. The other was a pick-up truck full of garden maintenance equipment.

As we stepped out of the car I caught the straining note of a chain saw and the smell of hot tree resin on the air. I thought that Mrs Swaine hadn't let the deaths of her husband and her brother who weren't even in the ground yet interfere with her gardening responsibilities. On the other hand, a garden the size of hers would need regular maintenance and the Swaines didn't strike me as the type to be out in all weathers keeping on top of things. Maybe he was just a regular and this was his day.

25

Awoman who wasn't Rebecca Swaine opened the door to us. I took her for the lady that did for the Swaines. Domestically speaking. She was short and plump and I knew her face from the village. She wore an apron and a sour expression. She had the face and eyes of a gossip and that was something to store away for later.

She knew who we were and after another performance of the coat and slipper show she ushered us through to the room with the fire we'd been in already. The room, not the fire. We were heading for that but first we had to spend some time in the frying pan.

Rebecca Swaine was sitting in a floral-patterned armchair in a floral-patterned dress. It made me notice the William Morris floral-patterned wallpaper. Considering there wasn't a houseplant in sight, it was a very botanical scene. But everything was from different gardens so it wasn't as amusing or confusing as it might have been. Not that any of us was there for a laugh. I reminded myself that she'd lost a husband and a brother within twenty-four hours of each other. Put like that, she sounded careless. Or dangerous to know.

She pointed to a leather sofa of the old style and asked us if we'd like something to drink. Our backsides renewed their acquaintances with the furniture while our manners and our mouths agreed tea would be nice. I looked forward to seeing what crockery it'd be served in. And the standard of the biscuits. You can tell a lot about a person from the biscuits they offer their visitors.

When Joan, she of the domestic help, had withdrawn to organise victuals, I tried the third of the grieving person's Holy

Trinity: sympathy. I said, 'How are you bearing up, Mrs Swaine?' It was a difficult but necessary question, I felt. One couldn't ignore that herd of elephants trampling about the room.

She still didn't look like she'd been crying and she still didn't look like she was about to start, but she did look tired, drawn, pasty and troubled.

'As I'm sure you can imagine, Mr Booker, it is a very painful time for me. Sigmund and Nigel were the only two real people in my life.'

I wondered what that made Joan. Android?

'To have lost them both so suddenly and so horribly... well, I'm still in shock. And there is no reason, no explanation that I can cling to. Something to make sense of the tragic wastes of life.'

'There must be a reason, Mrs Swaine,' said Jo, a little insensitively, I thought. 'An explanation. Two people in the same household don't take their own lives so close together without there being a reason, very good or otherwise.'

'Of course, you're right. I understand that. What I mean is: the reason is beyond me.'

'That's why we're here, Mrs Swaine. To find the reason.'

Jo became almost aggressive. I suppose it was the backlash of her recent brush with the Pinocchio Syndrome – being jerked around by the puppet master – and she needed to get some of that out of her system. Assert herself.

'If you really want me to help you, Mrs Swaine, you're going to have to be completely candid and honest. I won't be able to help you if you're not. It's as simple as that. If it helps, anything you tell me and anything I find out in the course of my investigation is protected by client confidentiality.' Mrs Swaine couldn't help her gaze shifting across to me. Jo noticed and said, 'That goes for him, too. You have to trust us if you really want to find out why your husband and your brother killed themselves.'

I felt like one half of a good cop, bad cop pairing. I wondered how everyone else felt.

Mrs Swaine had a bit of an inner struggle and then she said, 'I understand.'

'And if you decide to employ us then we see it through to the end.'

Mrs Swaine nodded. I thought about that *us*.

Jo went for what she saw as the throat of the matter, and to remind our hostess, her client, that she was still smarting from her jerking, she said, 'When you phoned me to let me know your husband was dead you said you wanted me to find out who drove him to it. By the time I called on you a couple of hours later, you'd changed your mind. What happened in between the phone call and my arrival?'

It was a big, fair question and just as Rebecca Swaine opened her mouth to answer there was a loud crash, which made us all start. Joan had put one of her ample hips to good use and barged the door open. We sat in uncomfortable silence as she bustled over to set the tray down on the low table between us. The china looked good. It looked like Suzy Cooper – all cream and crocuses. And it all matched. I made a mental note to sneak a look at the stamp under the saucer first chance I got – it could've been a cheap imitation. The biscuits were a disappointment. They were still in the packet and the packet advertised a cheap own brand. And they were plain. How the mighty fall.

'Will there be anything else, Mrs Swaine?' said Joan. She made 'Swaine' sound closer to 'swine'.

Rebecca Swaine smiled thinly, and I was struck with the notion that she'd heard 'swine' too and didn't like it.

'No, thank you, Joan.'

There was definitely something missing in the mistress/servant relationship. If I had to guess, I'd say its name was 'respect'.

When Joan had bustled back out to the sound of nyloned-thigh friction, Mrs Swaine bent forward to play mother. 'I told Sigmund I was going to have Nigel's death investigated. He became distinctly agitated. He was very upset over Nigel's death. He begged me to change my mind.'

'Why?'

'He didn't say. If he had, I wouldn't need you.'

'Why do you say that?'

'Because it seems obvious to me that whatever worried him so over Nigel's suicide and my intention to have it investigated was something he knew about and was something he must have been involved in. Can't you see that?' Mrs Swaine looked like she was thinking she'd made a mistake with Jo.

'I see that's how it looks, Mrs Swaine. But things aren't always how they first appear.'

Mrs Swaine's features relaxed a little. We sipped our tea. It wasn't very nice or hot. No one had taken a biscuit.

'Your husband didn't leave a suicide note?' said Jo.

'None was found.'

'He hanged himself in the middle of the night?'

'Yes, as I told you before.'

'I'm just recapping important information. What time did you notice he was missing?'

'In the morning. About eight o'clock. He should have left for work well before that. His briefcase was still in the hallway. I looked for his car in the garage just to make sure he hadn't simply forgotten his case. I searched the house and when there was no sign of him Sigmund and I searched the grounds and then the woods. I think I already told you Sigmund found him.'

'Why did you search the woods?'

'After the house and the garden there was nowhere else he could have been. He might have had an accident while out walking.'

'Was he in the habit of walking in the woods in the middle of the night in winter?'

'He liked to walk in the woods.'

'In the middle of the night?'

A pregnant pause. 'He never mentioned it.'

'And you didn't notice it? Mrs Swaine, I'm just trying to build a picture of how things were.'

He got in from work about seven.

'No. I didn't notice it.'

'How had he been? What I mean is, had he been acting strangely at all? After he'd hanged himself did you think back to how he had been in the last few days and see something that could have contributed to his state of mind?'

Mrs Swaine gently shook her head. 'There was nothing. It was such an incredible shock. It was so out of character.'

I had to agree with her even though I'd never met the man. Habits made character. And one couldn't generally make a habit of suicide. For most who were serious about it, it was a one-off experience.

'How had your husband been the previous evening?'

'Just like any other evening.'

'And how was that?'

'He got in from work about seven. Had something to eat, spent some time with Sigmund and went to his rooms.'

I didn't think much of his normal evening. Wedded bliss it didn't sound like.

'You didn't share a bed with your husband?'

I don't think either of them saw me wince at that.

'We did not share a bed. Or a room. Of late we had been husband and wife in name only.'

'You were married about eighteen months ago, weren't you?'

There was an ugly moment, like bad breath on a first date.

'How do you know that?'

'I'm a detective, Mrs Swaine. Did you know he'd had trouble with work?'

'No. What sort of trouble?'

'Hudson's let your husband go.'

Mrs Swaine fought valiantly to hide the shock of the news. She said, 'Nigel didn't like to discuss work at home.'

'I'd like to see his mobile telephone and his computer, if he had one here.'

'Why?'

'Something tipped him over the edge. It must have been news to him and most news comes through technology these days.'

Mrs Swaine sat a little more erect and said, 'I'd like a guarantee from you before we go down that route.'

'What guarantee?' said Jo.

'A guarantee that anything you discover in the course of your investigation, no matter what the nature of it, remains confidential between us, unless I give express permission for the sharing of it with any outside agency.'

When Jo didn't immediately answer, Mrs Swaine said, 'I have no idea what, if any, secrets you might uncover if you start going through their things. But I do need your assurance that my word will be final on whether they remain secret or not.'

I could understand why Mrs Swaine would ask such a thing and if Jo didn't agree for both of us then I could also understand we'd soon be leaving.

'Like I said, Mrs Swaine, customer confidentiality. It's as solid as doctor/patient, lawyer/client and priest/confessor. If I were to get a reputation for breaking that understanding I'd be finished. You would be my employer in this. The final word for everything comes from you.'

Mrs Swaine seemed placated. She took us through to Nigel Tate's rooms. He had enjoyed the privacy of a small lounge, a small bedroom and a small bathroom. It looked lived in. Jo didn't ask exactly how long they'd been living apart under the same roof and I was glad.

His phone was on his desk next to his laptop. The laptop was off and the phone had run out of battery. We plugged the phone into the charger and were asked for a password. We turned to Mrs Swaine. She shrugged that she didn't know it. We fired up the computer and were asked for a password. We turned to Mrs Swaine. She shrugged that she didn't know it. Someone skilled in these things might have worked some magic but for normal people like Jo and me that avenue of enquiry had just turned into a cul-de-sac. The last time I'd held my breath for a laptop to see if it was password protected I'd got lucky. I was reminded that you can't win 'em all.

Jo asked if Mrs Swaine would mind her having a look around. She said she didn't but she wouldn't stay. She'd be in the lounge when we'd finished. I don't think she liked being in her husband's rooms.

I stood by and watched as Jo rummaged in all the obvious places for something that might take her interest. She found nothing and looked disappointed. She checked out the bedroom and the little bathroom. Nothing.

Just as she was preparing to leave, I said, 'Where's the briefcase?' That got me a brownie point. We looked for it. Everywhere a briefcase could fit. We couldn't find it.

We made our way back to the lounge. Mrs Swaine was sitting quietly. Doing nothing. Just waiting.

Jo and I took our seats.

'What happened to your husband's briefcase, Mrs Swaine?' said Jo.

'Isn't it in his rooms?'

'No.'

'I have no idea then.' She looked genuinely puzzled. 'I can ask Joan. Perhaps she put it somewhere.'

'The police didn't take it?' I said.

Jo snubbed that thought with a quick shake of the head. 'Why would they? Can we talk about Sigmund now?'

The change of topic and the subject of it seemed to startle Mrs Swaine, as if she'd completely forgotten her brother had just died. For a fleeting moment her shields were down and there was something vulnerable and very sad about her. She gathered herself and rallied her features into something more stoical. I think that the empire must have been built on bones like hers.

'How did you know Sigmund had left the house last night?'

'I heard the front door bang.'

'Where were you?'

'In here.'

'Alone?'

'Yes.'

'Where had Sigmund spent his evening?'

'In his rooms. He works, worked, better in the evenings.'

'Worked? What did he do?'

'He was an artist.'

I interrupted. 'What sort?'

'The painting sort, Mr Booker.'

'I mean what sort of paintings did he produce? Still lifes, portraits, landscapes, seascapes? Oil, watercolours, pen and ink?'

Mrs Swaine regarded me with some interest. 'Are you a painter, Mr Booker?'

I shook my head. 'I don't know much about art, but I know what I like.'

'And what do you like?'

'I'm very fond of Miro, his later stuff, Kandinsky, Paul Klee, that sort of thing.'

Mrs Swaine looked disappointed. She said, 'Shapes.' Then she said, 'Sigmund worked predominantly as a watercolour landscape artist. He also liked to paint the sea and the sea wall at Dymchurch.'

'Like Nash,' I said. 'I'd love to see some of his work.'

'Another time, if you don't mind.' And there was something of a rebuke in her tone. I considered myself reminded of why we were there.

Jo said, 'Did he paint for a living or a hobby?'

'He was good enough to exhibit but his confidence in his work was not high. He was far too self-critical.'

'Do you have any idea what happened to make him leave, to go into that stormy night, run across the fields, seek refuge in a church and then when we arrived deliberately jump to his death?'

Momentarily, Mrs Swaine looked like she'd been hurt physically. She said, 'I have no idea.'

'How had he been during the day?'

'I hadn't seen a great deal of him. As I said, he had been very upset by Nigel's death.' I was suddenly glad that someone in the family had been. 'I'd learned to leave Sigmund alone when he was in one of his moods. Besides, I had my own grief to deal with.' I made a note to ask Jo what she thought of that statement later.

'Did Sigmund know your husband was being blackmailed?'

'Not from me.'

'How did they get on, both living under the same roof?'

'They were very good friends. It was Sigmund who introduced me to Nigel. They'd known each other from college.'

'So it was possible that your husband had told your brother about the money demand?'

'It's possible.'

I butted in again. 'Please don't take this the wrong way, Mrs Swaine, but was Sigmund all right in the head?'

She stared at me for a long uncomfortable moment before saying, 'He had some personal problems – his demons.'

'Was he on medication? Was he receiving professional help?'

'No to both. Why do you ask?'

'In the church he acted very strangely, like someone needing their meds. There was something manic about him. I just wondered if that could have contributed to him taking his own life the way he did.'

'What did happen?' said Mrs Swaine. 'I'd like to know. I have the right to know, I think.'

I turned my head to look at Jo, thereby shifting responsibility for that joy onto her. It was her case, after all. And I owed her one from her own employment of the tactic when we'd had the police round.

She said, 'When we entered the church, Sigmund attacked us. He had a weapon. It seemed defensive, like he felt threatened by us. He seemed terrified of us, or something. He was very upset. Hysterical, I'd say. He climbed up into the gallery, then onto the railings and threw himself off. It was quite deliberate and he made no attempt to minimise his potential injuries. He knew what he was doing, Mrs Swaine.'

'Did he say anything?'

'Nothing I could understand.'

Because Sigmund had hated mobile phones, computers, technology in general, had had no friends other than Nigel Tate, didn't watch television or listen to the radio, Jo's avenues for investigation were about as abundant as Easter eggs at Christmas.

26

We crossed back onto the Marsh and the security of the familiar flat landscape rolled out before us, like something Wim Wenders might have given a second look. I said, 'I didn't know you were legally bound by that client confidentiality crap.'

'I'm not.'

'But you said...'

'What she needed to hear. If I hadn't put her mind at rest over that, she would have shown us the door.'

I said, 'Isn't that unethical? Immoral? Dishonest? What about all that "if I don't keep my gob shut I'm finished" guff?'

'I had my fingers crossed.'

'I'm serious.'

'Listen, David, if I find out that some serious crimes have been committed it's my civic responsibility to report it.'

'Who decides if they're serious?'

'I do. What if we uncover a paedophile ring they were both involved in? Would you expect me to keep that to myself?'

'No, of course not, but...'

'No buts. Besides, in my new line of work I'm going to need friends in the local law and if they know I can help them out from time to time with something then my life will be made easier.'

'You'd shop your clients to the police?'

'No, dummy. That wouldn't be very smart, would it? There are ways and means.'

'I'm a bit disappointed.'

'Tough.'

We motored on past the falling down ragstone barn and the kennels.

'Do you think it's a possibility?'

'What?'

'A paedophile ring?'

'Didn't you see photos of naked children in his room?'

I sat up straighter. 'No.'

'Me neither. No, I don't think they were involved in a paedophile ring. It was an extreme example.'

We rounded the bends at Rushfield and Jo had to throw out all the anchors for a tractor.

'Why didn't you tell her what he said?'

'Because I didn't tell the police, and if she talks to them again and mentions that I did have a recollection of him saying something comprehensible that night then it would make me look bad.'

'But she might have had an explanation or a suggestion for what he meant by "he made me."'

'She may have.'

I waited.

Jo didn't elaborate.

I said, 'You gave her a bit of a grilling. Did you forget she's just lost the only two "real" people in her life in tragic circumstances?' I felt my funny thought was worth sharing. 'Hey, what do you think that makes Joan? An android?'

Jo didn't even blink. 'Which reminds me: in future maybe you should leave the questions to me.' Jo mimicked my voice: '"Please don't take this the wrong way, Mrs Swaine, but was Sigmund all right in the head?" What kind of a question was that for a grieving woman?'

'Did you meet a grieving woman? Who was that then?'

'Good point.'

'It was a legitimate question. You saw him. All pony-eyed. The bloke was nearly frothing at the mouth.'

'Yes, I know, but if you want a client to confide, to open up to you, you have to be more... subtle and sensitive.'

'Sensitive? Are you winding me up?' It was my turn to mimic her: '"You didn't share a bed with your husband?"' I nearly died of embarrassment.'

'Sometimes you have to just be straight with them.'

'That's what I was doing.'

'No, you were insulting her dead brother and pissing in the family gene pool.'

I huffed. There were some arguments I could never hope to win with Jo. They were usually the ones where my opinion differed from hers.

Jo said, 'I wouldn't underestimate our Mrs Swaine. Underneath that rather neutral, haughty exterior I reckon there's one tough-hearted, hard-headed woman. She looked like she could take it and I had things to find out. Cases don't solve themselves.'

I said, 'That could be your strapline.' And then, with a heavy Hollywood accent, 'Jo Cash, P.I. Because cases don't solve themselves.'

To shut me up, Jo floored the accelerator. The car leapt forward.

'OK, OK. Calm down.'

She eased off.

I said, 'So what did we learn?'

'You tell me.'

'You mean you didn't learn anything?'

'No, I mean let's hear what you think you learned.'

'Joan doesn't like her boss and her boss knows it.'

Jo gave me a sidelong glance. 'So we're not doing this in order of importance. Or maybe we are, but the order is reversed.' I think they call it dry wit. 'Go on.'

'Didn't you catch it in that exchange over the tea things? And look at the way she presented the biscuits to us. She served up crappy own brand plain ones still in their packet. She was trying to embarrass Rebecca.'

'Since when has it been Rebecca?'

'It's her name, isn't it?'

'Not for us. Not if we want to remain thinking objectively. As soon as you start getting personal or emotionally involved you're finished as an investigating officer.'

That was too close to home, the bone and the truth, and I think it was accidental.

I said, 'Moving swiftly on, what do you think of my surmising?'

'About the biscuits?'

I grunted.

'You read too much Sherlock Holmes. They were just biscuits.'

'My point exactly. But if I'm right, and Joan doesn't like her mistress, maybe she'd be worth speaking to privately.'

'Maybe. What else?'

'The husband didn't tell her he'd lost his job.'

'And what does that tell us?'

'That he didn't want her to know he'd lost his job.'

Without taking her eyes from the road, Jo said, 'Are you sure you've never done this before?' I think she was being sarcastic. 'What else?'

'She thinks he was working. We know that's not true.'

'Which part?'

'Both. She thinks he was working because she said he was coming and going from work. And we know he didn't have a job because your maid Marion said he hadn't been taken on anywhere else.'

'Did you say *maid*?'

'I meant mate.'

'No, we don't. And she didn't. My *contact* Marion said he hadn't been able to find a position with another financial institution. That's not the same as not working.'

'OK. So maybe he had a job flipping burgers at the Golden Arches and maybe he didn't.'

'They don't strike me as having been a close couple.'

'Well, if he didn't have a job, but did have a shit marriage, and money was a problem and he was fearing investigation from the authorities for financial irregularities then that would make a good motive for suicide, wouldn't it?'

'Sometimes.'

'But?'

'But, how does Siggy fit into that theory?'

'Maybe the men were lovers and 'Siggy' just couldn't go on without Nigel.'

'If there weren't other factors to consider, like the demand note, Sigmund's odd behaviour and that *he made me*, which is really bugging me, I could buy that idea. If you ask me, there's something quite odd about that family.'

After she'd negotiated a blind bend a little too fast for my liking, I said, 'Obviously, Sigmund had an idea why the husband topped himself. He wouldn't have asked her to call off the dogs otherwise.'

'Thanks very much.'

'You know what I mean. And so it would be reasonable to assume that if Sigmund didn't want Nigel's death investigated there must be something to hide and that something must involve him in some way and that something is probably not very legal.'

'No such thing as *not very legal*. Either it is or it isn't.'

'Hair splitter.'

'No. It's called the law. Look it up on that fount of all knowledge you're always referring to and relying on.'

'There's nothing wrong with Wikipedia.'

'Apart from the fact that any Tom, Dick or Harry can post anything they like on it and call it fact. Maybe that's where you got your idea things can be *not very legal*.'

I didn't want the 'Wiki' argument again, so I said, 'What do you think of my reasoning?'

'Generally, over Wikipedia, or with the case?'

'The case, of course.'

'I think you might be on to something.'

'Really?' That was good to hear from the professional.

'Yes,' she said, 'Joan might be an android.'

27

There was a car parked up on my pea gravel when we got back. The architect had arrived and my interest in Rebecca Swaine and her lost loved ones shrivelled up, like a singed nose hair.

I asked Jo if she'd like to join us, see what was what with the plans. She said (a) some people had to work for a living and (b) she was sure she'd hear all about it lots of times soon. With an attitude like that I wasn't particularly sorry or hurt when she pushed off to get on with something 'more pressing'.

The concrete panel fence that had once divided the old builder's yard from my relatives' property had been one of the first things to go when I got on with things. A JCB and a few empty ten tonners had made pretty quick work of the detritus of Flashman Builders' occupancy after the vultures had been in and picked it clean.

I'd had a pretty clever idea to get rid of a lot of the stuff that I had no use for and didn't want to pay to cart away and dump. After Flashman had let me know there was nothing left in the yard he wanted I put word around that I was going to have a giveaway. For one weekend I'd throw open the rusting metal gates to the yard and anyone who felt the desire to come and help themselves to whatever they wanted was welcome – no charge.

Other than Harrods on New Year's Day, I've never seen anything like it. They were queuing up around the block in their lorries, vans and family cars before daylight. There were even a couple of hopeful old men waiting on the grid with wheelbarrows. All because of the magic word – free.

The local PCSO had got me out of bed and asked if I wouldn't mind opening up earlier than I'd advertised because the highway was becoming congested and dangerous to navigate. I'd obliged. As soon as I had the chain off the gates I had to stand back to avoid being trampled to death in the stampede of steel toe-capped work boots.

Having seen the numbers of those in front of them, a couple of vans at the back had dispatched their passengers to get into pole position on foot with the idea that they'd get into the yard quickly and stake claim to what they were after before someone else got their calloused and grubby mitts on it.

This did not go down well with those who had been out of bed a bit earlier to ensure their places at the front of the grid. There was some name calling. Some pushing and shoving. A punch was thrown. Then a few more. The PSCO called for reinforcements. The cavalry arrived and calmed things down. And all the while men – young, middle-aged and old – crawled over the yard like ants: ferreting, inspecting, grabbing and claiming. It was like a little gold rush – like the January sales in hobnails.

I didn't need to keep the gates open for the second day. The yard had been picked clean of anything anyone could possibly have had a use for or sell or scrap for profit by lunchtime on day one. Job done.

Now the land had been properly cleared. Only the trees around the boundary had stayed. The old ship's containers had been removed – they'd all been leased. The ramshackle collection of temporary structures had been demolished. All the scrub had been torn up. It was now a flattened, bare patch of brown and it looked twice the size it had when it had been overgrown and cluttered.

Some grotesque memories had gone, too. The worst kind. And I had to let them go or one day I'd have gone crazy out there.

I spent most of what remained of the daylight with the architect. He seemed in no great hurry with his measuring and sketching, his questions and suggestions, and with what he was charging an hour I wouldn't have been either.

We knocked some little stakes into the ground and strung some pretty red and white tape between them so we could form an idea of how things were going to look space-wise. It felt like progress.

28

I was back upstairs stirring a wok of meat and vegetables, sipping boxed promotional wine and listening to Radio Four when I next saw Jo. I was in a fairly good mood. I put this down to the chilly winter afternoon's groundwork outside and the chilled evening's booze inside.

'Smells good,' she said from the doorway.

I pointed at the fridge and she helped herself to a glass of Chateau Blanc de Blanc. Blankety-Blank as she liked to call it.

'How did it go with Archie?' she said.

'Who's Archie?'

'Archie Tect.'

I groaned. 'Does your sudden interest in my project mean you want some dinner?'

'Am I that transparent? Now you mention it, there looks a lot there for one. What's the meat?'

'I found a litter of young hedgehogs in the yard. They didn't take much drowning and skinning.'

'That's disgusting.'

'You think so? You know what goes to make up that elephant's leg in the kebab shop you're so fond of?'

'No and I don't want to.'

'Lips and arseholes from whatever they happen to be slaughtering at the abattoir that week.'

'I hate you sometimes.'

I laughed. 'Find out anything new and interesting on the "Swines"?'

'Post-mortems of both have not made the police suspicious regarding foul play: no evidence of third party involvement, substance abuse or aliens.'

'So they were both in their right minds?'

'I wouldn't go that far. If all you needed to commit suicide was a right mind there'd be people queuing up for the lampposts all the way up the A259. Well, maybe not on Romney Marsh,' she said, dodging the daggered look I threw her way.

I said, 'I've been thinking.'

'Is that wise? I mean thinking and cooking at the same time? You are a man.'

'Don't worry: I wasn't holding anything sharp or hot. You should have a word with Joan.'

'The android?'

'Yes. I got the feeling she doesn't have undying loyalty for her employer. She looked like she enjoys a good gossip.'

'Really? And what do those people look like, Watson?' I noted that Jo had already assumed the leading role of Holmes.

'Er… Joan. I'm pretty sure she lives in the village.'

'Where?'

'Don't know, but I know a woman who might.'

'One of your local condiments?'

Jo found it amusing to refer to 'sources' as condiments, even after I pointed out that's not how you spelled it.

'Yes. We can go see her after dinner if you like?'

'Joan?'

I shook my head. 'The condiment. I'll stand you a pint.'

'Pam over the road?'

I nodded, tried the food off the spatula and said, 'This seems ready.'

29

Pam was the landlady of The Ocean, my closest local hostelry. It was so adjacent; I could read the specials board on the opposite pavement from my lounge window without binoculars. But not at night, of course.

Cold and damp January weekday nights did not generally attract a great many punters out for expensive beer. Like most businesses in the village, the pubs made their money in the summer when the hordes of grockles descended on the Marsh and the caravan parks, the amusement park and the beach for the seasonal wind and rain.

In my old life, Pam had always been a landlady to exchange pleasantries with, but since I'd lost my aunt and uncle – both regular and valued customers as well as friends of hers – and become a local business owner we had more in common and greater empathy for each other. I liked her. I think she liked me. Jo and she got on well enough.

While Jo took a table near the fire, I got us a couple of drinks. After enquiries about how we were each doing, I said, 'If I ask you about someone can you not ask me why I'm asking?'

Pam laughed at me and said, 'Who?'

'Do you know a woman called Joan who works up a Silverhurst? Domestic help, I think.'

'She doesn't come in here often. But she's a regular up at the Legion. Likes her bingo.'

'What night is bingo night?'

'Friday.'

I thanked her and shared my intelligence with Jo.

'Today is Friday,' I said.

Jo said, 'I know.'

'Fancy a game of bingo?'

'Not while I can still choose when I go to the toilet. I'd rather tattoo my face with a quill and Quink.'

'Look,' I said, with mock seriousness, 'if you want to fit in around here, sooner or later you're going to have to get involved in the local community. You know: mingle, socialise.'

'How about I just don't, and see what happens?'

'Don't you want to talk to her?'

'She might be worth a whirl. I'll think about it. In any case, I wouldn't go barging into God's waiting room…' Jo's name for the British Legion '… asking awkward questions of a confidential nature with someone who you have pegged for a gossip and who would probably be tipsy on cherry brandy or whatever's flavour of the month up there. Things likely wouldn't stay confidential for long, would they?'

'Fair point,' I said, and drank some more beer. 'What are you going to do next?'

'I might take my coat off. It's hot in here.'

'You're not always funny.'

'Nigel Tate lost his job weeks ago. He's been going out of the house every morning and coming back late at night pretending he's been working.'

'Or working.'

'True. Or working.'

'I think I should find out where he's been spending his time.'

'How do you propose to do that?'

'Legwork.'

'Why look further afield when probably the answer is at Silverhurst?'

'Because I already looked there and found nothing and the only person at Silverhurst who could have helped us is dead.'

'Maybe Joan can. She's not dead. And then there's the gardener.'

'Maybe, but my copper's intuition says this has got something to do with what Nige was doing out of the house all day.'

'Want some company?'

'I thought you had an empire to build.'

'They're not built in days, don't you know. Anyway, nothing's going to happen for a while yet. Archie needs to formalise the plans, clear them with me, then submit them to the Parish and Shepway councils for planning permission and building regulations.'

'How long will all that take?'

'Weeks. Possibly months. Depends if there's opposition.'

'Is that likely?'

'Only God knows.'

'Blimey. Bummer.'

'So I'm at a bit of a loose end at the moment. The shop's not busy and the ladies can run it without me breathing down their necks.'

'OK. Why not? But it could get pretty boring.'

'If I complain you can say I told you so.'

'If you complain I'll say more than that.'

30

Jo rang Mrs Swaine and asked if she could have a picture of Nigel Tate that was a good and recent likeness. We picked it up from Silverhurst on our way through the next morning. While we were there, Jo asked if she could have a quick look at Nigel's car. Mrs Swaine let her into the garage and she was back out in seconds.

'Not the most rigorous search I've ever seen,' I said, as we were bowling along the road through the woods towards Aldington.

'Got what I needed.'

'Which was?'

'Confirmation that Nigel Tate used the parking facility at the train station. There's a parking permit attached to the windscreen.'

I wished I'd thought of that.

Jo said we'd ask at the station to see if anyone recognised Nigel. I suggested it might have been a more rewarding exercise, information wise, if we'd done it on a weekday and during his normal travelling time frame, meaning before nine o'clock when the commuters were about.

'We won't be talking to them,' said Jo.

'Who then?'

'The railway people.' The way she said it made them sound like the Borrowers. 'They always remember faces better. They work here. They can't help themselves. And Saturday won't be such a busy day for them.'

So we walked into the station and enquired in the ticket hall with our wedding photograph of Nigel Tate. Jo had folded it over so that Rebecca Swaine was not visible and I could understand why. No red-blooded male was going to pay too much attention to Nigel's not unattractive features when there was a beautiful woman, revealing rather a lot of shoulder and cleavage in a summer wedding frock, to gawp at.

The man at the ticket office recognised Nigel as a season ticket holder. Jo asked to where. He said Nigel went all the way. And he didn't smirk when he said it. St Pancras, he added. On the fast train.

I thought that was that then. Job done. Jo had other ideas. I didn't share her belief that we'd have a chance of finding anything more out; London, I reminded her, was a big place. She was not to be deterred. I asked when we should go then. She said, no time like the present. And we were already halfway there.

So we bought a couple of day returns and went through to our platform. She said it was only going to be forty minutes each way and that it took longer to get from Dymchurch to the platform than it did to get from Ashford to central London. She was almost right.

She asked a couple of guards who were loitering around the staffroom door if they recognised Nigel. They both did. A regular early bird, they agreed.

The high-speed rail link left Ashford every half an hour so we didn't have a lengthy wait. We got on and settled in. It wasn't long before the call of 'Tickets, please' came echoing up the aisle. Jo showed the train manager the photograph.

'Yes, madam,' said the friendly man. 'I recognise him. A frequent traveller. He usually catches an earlier train than this one, though. The seven forty-five, unless I'm much mistaken.'

'Do you know where he gets off?' she said. There were two other stations that the high-speed train stopped at en route to the metropolis and I suddenly appreciated why Jo was asking. Jo couldn't simply assume that Nigel Tate went 'all the way'. It needed checking.

'He goes all the way every day, madam,' the man replied. It was obviously an in-joke on the railways. 'St Pancras. Very dapper gentleman. Always polite. Haven't seen him for a couple of days, mind.'

Jo didn't tell him he'd never see him again. We thanked him and he went about his business.

When he came back he stopped next to us. He'd obviously been thinking about things. 'Mind me asking why you're asking about the gentleman?' he said.

'He's gone missing,' said Jo.

The friendly railwayman raised his eyebrows at that. 'I'm sorry to hear that, madam.' As an apparent afterthought, he said, 'You police?'

'Private. Working for the wife.'

'Ah.'

'Seven forty-five you said?' Jo asked.

'Yes, madam.'

'Weekends, too?'

'Saturdays.'

Jo thanked him and he went away.

31

We got out at St Pancras half an hour later. I'd never set foot in that station before. And it fairly took my breath away. As I was marvelling at the space, the structure, the architecture of the place, Jo had taken off in the direction of a gaggle of railway employees hanging around the ticket barrier. I left her to it, figuring she'd have more success on her own. Assuming there was any success to be had, which I thought highly unlikely.

She was back soon, wearing a puzzled look.

'What did you really expect?' I said.

'What are you talking about?'

'They must see thousands of passengers every day. Did you honestly think they'd be able to help you?'

'One of them recognised Nigel Tate.'

'Seriously?'

'He knows where he works.'

'You're kidding?'

Jo shook her head. 'He said he's got a picture gallery near here. Says he walks past it on his way home.'

'A picture gallery? He must be confusing him with someone else.'

'He said it's called Tate's Modern.'

That shut me up.

We exited the station onto Midland Road, followed it south, crossed Euston Road and ended up in Judd Street. That was where we needed to be. According to the railwayman, Tate's Modern would be somewhere down on our left. It was. And it was closed. No matter. It was progress. I had to admire Jo's copper's nose.

Judd Street was very smart up to a point about a couple of hundred metres down where a high-rise loomed over everything, spoiling the view and the skyline. The conservative in me was glad we didn't have to go down that far. The street was a mixture of residential and commercial: a terrace of houses, a front of businesses with flats above and so on. There was a coffee shop, a specialist bookshop, a chartered accountant's, a bespoke travel agent's, a pub and what looked like the headquarters of the RNIB. Nothing tacky. Nothing essential for daily life, unless you were a visually impaired alcoholic looking to buy something to read while you waited at the accountant's to see whether you could afford that holiday of a lifetime you'd been planning.

The gallery was not large. It occupied the ground floor of a three-storey property that could have been Regency or Edwardian influenced – that era of construction remains a bit of a grey area for me. We rattled the door handle even though there were steel grilles over the windows and they were padlocked. We cupped our hands to see better. It didn't help much.

It was definitely an art gallery. There were pictures on the walls and not much else. It looked flashy and modern and pricey.

A man clutching a couple of straining black bin bags came struggling up the stairs from the basement flat. He spared us a cursory glance as he tossed his load into a wheelie bin.

Jo hailed him. 'Excuse me.'

He turned without much enthusiasm for it. 'It's nothing to do with me,' he said. He had half an inch of roll-up stuck in the corner of his mouth. He needed a shave and a haircut.

'What isn't?' said Jo, and she'd closed the gap between them so he couldn't really just scuttle back down to his burrow.

'The gallery. I just live here. Look after the building. Watch them come and go.'

'Who?'

'Tenants, of course. Who d'you think I mean?'

'Right. This hasn't been here long, has it?'

'Few months. Looks like they've thrown in the towel on it.'

'Why do you say that?'

'Neither of them been in for a couple of days. It's always a sign.'

'But the place is still full of paintings.'

He shrugged.

'Who's responsible if the alarm goes off?'

'Not me.'

'You haven't got numbers for the tenants of the shop then?'

'Nothing to do with me.'

Jo said, 'Do you know who deals with the letting of the premises?'

For answer he pointed a nicotine-stained digit down the street on the opposite side. We followed his gesture to see a small estate agent's. When we turned back to him, he was already making his way back to his lair.

Jo called out her thanks. It sounded a bit sarcastic. He didn't acknowledge her.

I said, 'He said *them*. Neither of *them*.'

Jo said, 'I heard.'

We traipsed down the pavement and looked in the estate agent's window. A couple were sitting across from a pretty young girl who looked about twelve and they were all staring at a computer monitor, like friends sharing something on Facebook. Jo led us past a couple more properties to stare in the window of an art and craft shop.

'What now?' I said.

'We wait.'

'For what?'

'For that,' she said, raising her nice chin in a direction over my shoulder.

The couple were coming out of the estate agent's shop.

'Come on,' said Jo. 'And don't speak unless spoken to.'

I said, 'Who are you, my mum?'

'Just follow my lead.'

We went in and were greeted by the pretty young girl showing us nearly all her very white teeth. They were big, too. They were almost comical, like something I'd once made out of reversed orange peel. She was on the phone and it was quickly clear it was a personal call. She terminated it without ceremony and offered us a warm welcome.

'How can I help?' she said in her sing-song voice. She had to work her jaw a lot just to get the sound out of her mouth.

Jo became friendly and helped herself to a seat. I remained standing. 'We hope you can. We've driven a long way and they're shut.'

The girl's plastic smile melted a little in her puzzlement. Her eyes gave away her confusion.

'Sorry,' said Jo, 'I should explain. We've come to the art gallery, Tate's Modern, to pick up a painting. And they're shut. They shouldn't be because we arranged to come today, didn't we dear?' Jo turned and looked up at me and I nodded a bit slowly. A bit stupidly.

Jo said, 'The building's caretaker told us you might be able to help seeing as you were the letting agents. I've been trying Mr Tate's mobile all morning but he must have a problem with it. If you could just give me the phone number for his associate, if you've got it, I'm sure he'd be really grateful, as would we.'

The girl hesitated for about a second before saying, 'Sure. If we've got it. No problem.'

She punched a couple of keys on her computer and said, 'You said you've being trying Mr Tate?'

'Yes, we've got *his* number. It's his associate I spoke to last. The one who arranged to meet us here. My husband's left his phone at home and I haven't got the number.'

'Sorry,' said the pretty young girl. 'It's only Mr Tate's name and number on the leaseholders database.' She still sounded as if she was trying to fit her words to music.

I said, 'What about if the alarm goes off? Is there a different number?'

She studied the screen again. 'I've got two numbers for that. We have to have two numbers. One is the same as on the lease agreement database, so that must be Mr Tate's.' She was being smart and letting us know it.

'What does the other one start with?' said Jo.

The girl read out a couple of numbers.

Jo pounced, 'That's it.' She repeated what the girl had said as she typed it into her phone and then waited for the rest of it. The girl obliged. It turned out that there wasn't a name to go with it. We offered our sincere thanks and left.

When we got onto the pavement, Jo said, 'Well done. That was good thinking. Let me buy you a coffee.'

We retraced our steps until we came to the street's nice little independent coffee shop. We went in. Being in the independent coffee shop trade I took a keen professional interest in the place. I was looking for ideas to steal.

Jo had offered to buy *me* a coffee but it was me standing at the counter ordering with my wallet in my hand while Jo settled herself at a table. About half of the tables were occupied and the place had a good ambience going on – casual, relaxed, easy-going. But this, I soon understood, was created by the clientele. Local professional people dressed down and chilling out on their day off with broadsheets and weekend supplements littering the table tops. There wasn't a child in sight. These weren't representative of my customer demographic. Romney Marsh just didn't have the same sort of job market as central London.

I put the tray down and said, 'Are you going to ring it?'

'When I've thought of what to say. I need to bait it properly or we'll lose them in the time it takes them to press end call.'

'We don't even know if it's a man or woman, do we?'

'True, but I can think of a way to find out.'

Jo caught the eye of a young man who was clearing a table and wearing the apron of the establishment. He came over looking as though he was expecting a complaint. His name badge said Paul.

Jo said, 'Hello, Paul. Do the people from the gallery ever come in here?'

His face relaxed a little. 'Every day, when they're open.'

Jo took out her photograph of Nigel Tate and showed it to him.

'He's the boss,' said the young man.

'We're looking for the other person who works there.'

'Natalie?' Something happened to his face then. If his look had been captured on canvas, I'd have called it *Penny Dropping*. He became guarded but remained interested.

Jo sensed a change in his attitude and went for the heart of the matter: 'Do you know her?'

'Only from coming in here. Are you police?'

'No. Why do you ask that?'

'We had people asking questions about them a couple of days ago.'

'Police?'

'They acted like it.'

'Did they speak to you?'

'No. Harry. He told me about it.'

'And they were definitely police?'

'I don't know.'

'Is Harry here now?'

'No. Day off.'

Jo's questioning had been quick fire and the youth had been answering almost reflexively. With the short pause, he recovered some of his wits.

'Who are you, anyway?'

Jo ignored it. 'When was the last time you saw Natalie?'

'A few days ago. Is she in trouble?'

'Have you got her phone number?'

'No. Why?'

'I need to talk to her. I've got a phone number and it might be for Natalie. If you had her number, you might have been able to confirm it.'

Paul said, 'Why don't you just ring it?'

Jo smiled at him. 'Because she doesn't know me. She might not want to talk to me.'

'You want me to talk to her?'

I sensed that Paul had an ulterior motive for this suggestion.

'Would you?'

'Sure. What do you want me to say?'

'I'll tell you what, if she doesn't want to talk to me, how about I pass her over to you and you can explain who we are and what we want to talk to her about?'

'You haven't told me.'

Jo showed him her Security Industry Authority identification and said, 'The boss is dead. He committed suicide recently. I'm working for the family trying to find out why. I want to talk to Natalie but, like I say, she doesn't know me. All I've got is this phone number that might be hers. If I call she might just hang up and then I've lost her. You understand?'

He nodded and he was frowning.

Jo didn't give him time for further questions. She dialled and the three of us waited. Eventually, Jo made a face and hung up. She said, 'It went through to a personalised answerphone message. If I ring it again can you listen and just tell me if it's Natalie?'

Paul nodded. Jo pressed redial and handed the phone across. He listened until the message had ended.

'That's Natalie's voice.'

Jo thanked him for his help and gave him her business card on the off chance Natalie showed up in the near future.

We had a look in the gallery window again on our way back to the station. Nothing had changed. On an impulse, Jo went down the steps to the basement flat and banged on the door that the unfriendly man with the bin liners had disappeared back into.

He was still being unfriendly when he opened it. 'What you want now?'

Jo dispensed with any pleasantries. 'Have you had other people asking about the gallery recently?'

'Might have. What's it to you?'

Like a magician, Jo pulled out a twenty-pound note and held it up for him to get a good look at.

'Tell me about them.'

He actually licked his lips. 'Man and a woman. Man was a bit bigger than him,' he said, nodding in my direction, 'and older. She was about as tall as you. She was older, too.'

'Were they police?'

'Doubt it.'

'Did they say what they were after?'

'Looking for him. Bloke what runs the place.'

'How were they dressed?'

'Smart.'

'If you had to guess, what would you say they were?'

'Trouble. I told them nothing. She was in charge.'

'Anything distinctive about either of them?'

He thought for a moment. 'He had a tattoo of a small bird on his neck and one of them stupid little ponytails. Fat ponce.'

Jo handed over the money and her business card and said, 'If either of them comes back, or anyone you think isn't after a picture comes looking for the owner, give me a call, eh?'

He withdrew, mumbling something.

As we walked back towards the station, I said, 'I thought they only did that in the movies.'

'What?'

'Pay for information with folded notes.'

'Where have you been living, David? Money opens doors and mouths. Always has, always will. Most people like him will fall over themselves to tell you what they think you want to hear for the price of a good bottle. The thing is, knowing who and what to believe.'

'Did you believe him?'

'Yes. But I might give coffee shop Paul a ring to ask his mate, Harry, for descriptions of them. That tat sounds distinctive.'

'I've never seen police with tattoos and ponytails,' I said.

'No. Me neither. But some of those undercover boys need to blend in with some very nasty people.'

'And they'd get a tattoo on their neck for it?'

'Think about it, David. It would certainly be a touch of authenticity at a time when the police find it harder and harder to break into criminal gangs.'

'Yeah, but still. A tattoo. Would the police pay to have it lasered off?'

Jo said she had no idea and she didn't sound very interested in continuing the conversation.

We were back in St Pancras waiting for the train when Jo's phone rang. She had a brief conversation and finished with a 'Thank you very much for your help.'

She said, 'That was Paul.'

'Coffee shop Paul?'

'The same. He has a common social-network friend with Natalie. He's had a chat with her.'

'Natalie?'

'The friend. The friend hasn't seen Natalie for a couple of days and that's unusual.'

I had one of those bad feelings in my stomach. It must have shown on my face.

'Let's hope not,' said Jo, reading my expression.

'So what's happening?' I said.

'Paul's friend is going to call me.'

'Now?'

Jo's phone rang. She had another short conversation, during which she asked where Natalie lived. Then she asked where the friend lived. Jo suggested they should check on Natalie together. It seemed that the friend agreed.

Jo ended the call and said, 'She'll meet us outside the station in twenty minutes.'

32

Natalie's friend was also a young woman. Early twenties. A little overweight. A lot of peroxide. She'd brought an escort. That was sensible. Natalie's friend introduced herself as Irene. She sounded foreign. If pressed I'd have said Eastern European. Irene's escort was not introduced, as if he'd tagged along uninvited, but it was obvious he was there as Irene's protector. He was all hair, ink and piercings. He was dressed all in black. Even his hair was jet black and I think it was dyed. It certainly didn't look natural. He was fatter than Irene and looked like he was trying to convince everyone he could look after himself if it came to a fight. I smiled at him, trying to let him know I didn't want to fight him. He didn't smile back.

Irene asked to see Jo's identification. Jo obliged. She gave her one of her business cards as well, which seemed to ease some of the uncertainties Irene appeared to be harbouring. Jo summarised the parts of the story she wanted Irene to know. Irene visibly relaxed further with us but became concerned for her friend.

'When was the last time you saw Natalie?' said Jo.

'Tuesday. We are not that close. But I have not heard from her and I have tried. I tried again today.'

'So did we,' said Jo.

'You think she could be in trouble?' said Irene.

'I have no idea, but if you know where she lives it might be a good idea to check on her.'

'I know where she lives but I can't go now. I have work soon.'

'Will you tell me her address?'

Irene made a decision. 'I am worried about her. If you see her, will you tell her to call me? Let me know she is all right?'

'I'll call you myself if you like?'

They exchanged numbers and in doing so Jo acquired a path to Irene if she needed one in the future.

Irene gave Natalie's address. It was out near Finsbury Park. She advised us to get the Tube to Manor House and hoof it from there. We went in search of subterranean mechanical serpents. The day was becoming interestinger and interestinger.

Yale Road was all one might expect from a residential street in that part of London: too compact, too congested, too crammed full of little homes and big cars. A keen bitter draught was being funnelled down the narrow highway, driving litter and debris before it in little playful swirls. The leaves played games with each other. Their irregular dashing and twisting and rushing and leaping put me in mind of energetic little children.

The address we'd been given for Natalie was a two-storey terraced property. Like a good number of the houses down there, the one we were looking for was split into two flats. Irene had not given us a flat reference. As I was staring at the buzzers, working out which we should press, Jo leaned in and pressed both.

In seconds a curtain twitched to our right at the downstairs lounge bay window. An old woman's face loomed out. She looked a bit lost, like someone who'd just gone blind.

Jo gave her a little wave. The old woman took over a minute to crack one of the windows so that she could speak with us. At least she could see.

'What do you want?' she said. She wasn't particularly friendly. It was London, twenty-first century Britain – I couldn't begrudge her her suspicions or her frostiness.

Jo said, 'We're looking for Natalie. Do you know if she's in?'

'No.'

'No you don't, or no she's not?'

'No she's not.'

'But she does live here?'

'Yes.'

'How do you know she's not in?'

'If she was in I'd hear her moving about, wouldn't I?'

Jo said, 'Good point. When were you last aware of her being home?'

'Who are you, anyway?'

Jo took out and held up her identification and said, 'We just want to make sure she's all right. She hasn't shown up at work for a few days and she's not answering her phone.'

'She in trouble?'

'I hope not, Mrs…?'

'Pope. I haven't seen or heard her for days.'

'And you haven't seen her leave with luggage or anything that looked like she might be going away somewhere?'

'No.'

'Have you had any other visitors like us? People looking for her?'

The woman shook her head.

'Thanks for your help, Mrs Pope. You might get a visit from the police now.'

That changed the woman's attitude. 'Why? I've done nothing wrong.'

'They'll just need to check that she isn't in the flat and had an accident or something like that. Maybe she had an epileptic fit. Did you know she suffers with those? People are worried about her.'

'What if I let you in to have a look?'

'If she's not lying on the floor unconscious or worse then you won't get a visit from the police.'

'Wait there,' she said and shut the window with a bang.

'You played on that poor woman's fears,' I said, as we waited. 'And you lied to her. You don't know Natalie's got epilepsy.'

Jo said, 'We don't know she hasn't.'

There was a rattling of a key in a lock and the door was opened. There was no chain in place. We waited to be invited in.

'Hurry up then,' said Mrs Pope. 'You're letting all the heat out.'

We went in. Mrs Pope shut the door behind us and then pulled a heavy curtain across. We were in what was the old hallway of the original house. The passageway that would have led through the house, probably to the original kitchen at the back, had been blocked off – cheap panelling with a cheap door in it. The only way forward was up the stairs. It was tidy and bare. Just a small table for post and a little bunch of artificial flowers in a cheap vase. An ugly energy-saving light bulb protruded from beneath the small central lampshade. A faint smell of cooking hung in the air.

My guess was this was Mrs Pope's home and she lived downstairs and let upstairs to supplement her pension.

'How long has Natalie been your tenant?' said Jo, obviously thinking similar thoughts to mine.

'Six months.'

'No problems?'

'No. She's good as gold. Always pays on time, polite, quiet, keeps herself to herself.' It sounded like a reference.

'Visitors?'

'I don't spy on her,' said Mrs Pope and I didn't believe her. 'And I do ask my female tenants not to bring men back. I'm not running a knocking shop.'

'You've got a key, then?' said Jo.

Mrs Pope showed us the key and said, 'We'll just make sure she's not in and hurt herself. I won't let you poke about.'

'We're only concerned for her welfare, Mrs Pope. We can wait down here if you like?'

'I don't want to go in on my own,' she said, sounding a bit afraid.

We trailed the old woman up the stairs and I thought I could have climbed Everest quicker. There was a little landing at the top in front of a door with a Yale lock that wasn't an original fixture. Mrs Pope fumbled with the bunch of keys and her breathing was heavy. Up close I got a whiff of onions from her. I exchanged a quick look with Jo and I felt like laughing for it.

Mrs Pope got the door open. I saw Jo sniff at the air and I realised why I didn't feel like laughing any more. I inhaled gingerly but only got trapped homely smells for my trouble.

Mrs Pope called out for Natalie. And got no answer.

'Shall we have a quick look, then?' said Jo.

Mrs Pope seemed like she had changed her mind about us all being there, ready to invade her tenant's privacy.

Jo said, 'You stay here, David. Mrs Pope and I can just check Natalie isn't hurt in here.'

They went in and I heard them moving about the rooms. In under two minutes they were back out and Mrs Pope seemed mightily relieved that the seeds of the fear Jo had planted had not rooted and grown into something ugly.

The door was locked and we all piled downstairs again feeling a lot better about things.

When we were standing in the little shared area at the foot of the stairs, Jo said, 'Thank you, Mrs Pope. I'm sorry if I worried you. But it's best to be sure.'

Mrs Pope looked pleased with the way things had turned out. Or maybe she was pleased that she wasn't going to be visited by the police now.

Jo said, 'I used to be a police officer, Mrs Pope. You shouldn't let anyone into your home without first checking their credentials. Always ask to see identification – they can pass it through the letter box – and then you ring whichever organisation they claim to represent. I've seen too many trusting little old ladies taken advantage of by unpleasant individuals. Do you understand me?'

Mrs Pope looked a bit crestfallen.

'Promise me, now,' said Jo.

Mrs Pope nodded.

'Good. Here is my business card. Please, when Natalie comes back, get her to call me, would you? Or you can.'

We heard the chain put on the door and the noise of the curtain going back across as we stood back on Mrs Pope's doorstep.

'A wasted journey,' I said, as we walked back towards the Tube.

'I wouldn't say that,' said Jo. 'Natalie wasn't hurt and she's cleared off somewhere. That might tell us something.'

'You don't know she's not hurt, just because she isn't in there. She could be lying dead in a ditch somewhere.'

'Bit dramatic but you have a point.'

'She could be hiding somewhere, or held against her will.'

'Calm down, David. She might simply be visiting her mum. Let's not get carried away. It's the details – the parts of the puzzle – that we have to collect and then put together. And now we know what Natalie looks like.'

I said, 'I know you have superhuman detecting powers but how on earth can you work out what she looks like without seeing her?'

Jo held up a strip of passport sized photographs. A rather attractive and detached-looking young woman stared back blankly.

We spent the time walking back to Manor House station having a good-natured discussion regarding issues of ethics and principles associated with abusing the trust of vulnerable old women and stealing from the homes of absent tenants. I took the high road of morality and Jo took the low road of expediency and neither of us arrived at the Underground ahead of the other.

The Tube was busy and didn't encourage conversation of a sensitive nature, or any nature for that matter. We were both forced to stand and apart from each other all the way back to St Pancras. I spent most of the journey only inches away from – and fully focused on avoiding closer proximity to – the naked, hairy armpit of a tall straphanger who obviously didn't see the weather as something to influence his dress code, or toiletries as something to waste his money on. Maybe he was just used to smelling that way getting him some personal space on the Tube. It was working. His dirty smell was getting him some dirty looks, too. Other than thinking him a selfish bastard, I had to marvel at his nerve and the obvious lack of figs that he gave for the opinions of others.

With all our London leads knotted there was nothing else to do but grab a baguette and a drink for the journey and head home.

33

We got four seats to ourselves. As we refuelled, I tackled Jo over what was next.

'All right with you if we call in on Mrs Swaine on the way back through?'

'You're going to tell her about the gallery?'

'Naturally. Why wouldn't I? I've found something out during the course of an investigation that she's paying me to conduct. She's my client. She's not employing me to keep secrets from her.'

'And what about Natalie?'

'What about Natalie?'

'Are you going to tell your client about her?'

'Haven't decided.'

'Isn't that keeping secrets from your employee?'

Jo gave me the look and changed topic. 'I'm a bit concerned about her.'

'Me too. Missing since Tuesday is a coincidence that makes me uncomfortable. She might be in danger or hurt or worse.'

'Leaving aside that we don't know exactly when she disappeared, why do you think that?'

'Because coffee shop Paul and the caretaker from the charm school said there were people asking after Nigel. Maybe they caught up with Natalie.'

'How?'

'Perhaps she turned up at the shop and they were around, waiting.'

'Say they found her, it doesn't mean that that they would have hurt her. Paul said they were like police. They could have been any authority: tax officers, bailiffs, local council, selling advertising. They could have been customers.'

'True, so where is she then? Why hasn't she been home for days or in contact with her friends? With those kinds of considerations and two people dead I'm always going to fear the worst for anyone else who's involved and missing.'

'Even though they were both clear-cut suicides, I'll say fair point. Interesting change of career path for Nigel, don't you think?'

'Mmm. Sigmund liked to paint.'

'I remember.'

'And he's dead.'

'I remember that, too.'

'Connections?'

'Possibly.'

'I'd say likely.'

'Maybe. I think I'll give Marion a call, let her know what I've found out and tell her there's a missing person.'

Jo placed the photos of Natalie on the little table between us and spent a minute composing and taking an image with her phone, which she then forwarded to Marion Pardew as an attachment to a text message. Before we reached Ashford, Marion replied thanking Jo for sharing and to let her know she'd find out whether it was local police who were sniffing around for Nigel, and that she'd pass on the concern over Natalie's disappearance.

Rebecca Swaine said she'd be happy for us to call on her. So we did. I couldn't help looking up for the ghost of Sigmund at the window as we pulled up noisily on the drive. We knocked on the door, waited and knocked harder. We got no reply.

Jo suggested we looked in at some windows. Mrs Swaine might just be asleep. I hoped so.

Guided by the sounds of classical piano music drifting on the breeze, we surprised her in her greenhouse exercising her green fingers. She was wearing clothes that suggested she'd been outside for a while. Over the shock of our sudden appearance, she apologised for not being ready for us, saying she hadn't expected us quite so soon.

The greenhouse was very impressive. Not aesthetically – it was all about functionality – but in its size. The only other time I'd been round the back of the property was in pitch darkness so it was no surprise I'd missed it. It was not particularly old. It was well equipped with sprinklers and heating. The temperature reminded me of a butterfly house I'd been in once. There were rows of neat and sturdy staging on top of which dozens of empty shallow green plastic trays lined up for attention. There were a number of black bin liners bulging with the efforts of Rebecca Swaine's labours and the contents from the trays. People dealt with their grief differently. Keeping mind and body busy was traditionally regarded as good therapy by many. Mrs Swaine caught me sizing the place up and it seemed to concern her.

She said, 'Shall we go back to the house?'

'This is fine,' said Jo. 'Your husband's briefcase hasn't turned up, I suppose, has it?'

'Sorry, no.'

'We've found something out this morning. It looks like your husband had recently started up an art gallery in London. Did you know anything about that?'

One thing you could say for Jo, she liked to get directly to the meat of the matter.

Mrs Swaine reacted like she'd been slapped. 'What? An art gallery? You must be mistaken. Nigel wouldn't have known anything about running a gallery. He'd have said something. I'd have known. He couldn't have kept something like that a secret from me.' But it increasingly looked like he had and the elephant trampling about the greenhouse trumpeted 'why?'

Jo said, 'It's up near St Pancras railway station. It's called Tate's Modern. I showed the picture of your husband around up there. He was recognised as the proprietor.'

Mrs Swaine swung her appalled gaze between us looking for something we couldn't give her. I looked around for a seat in case her legs went and as I did I was struck by the idea that she seemed more disturbed by the notion of her husband keeping a harmless secret from her than either of the suicides.

'There's something else,' said Jo, with all the finesse of a boxer with his opponent on the ropes. 'I told you before that your husband was let go by Hudson's. Actually, he was dismissed over suspicions of financial irregularities he was involved in. The Financial Services Authority is, or was investigating his part in things. He couldn't have got another job in the finance industry with those sorts of clouds hanging over him.'

Rebecca Swaine gave an impression of someone inwardly exploring a damage limitation exercise against the clock. It was in her eyes.

'I'm sorry,' she said, after a long pause. 'This is such a shock. Could it explain why he took his own life? I mean if he'd lost his job with no hope of getting another in the industry.'

'If he hadn't opened a gallery, I'd say it could. But he'd opened a gallery. He hadn't given up. He was trying something else.'

'And the demand: it could have been about the trouble with Hudson's?'

'It's possible. But none of that suggests why your brother was also moved to take his own life.'

Mrs Swaine's involuntary bodily reaction to that reminder seemed genuine and painful.

Jo said, 'You said your brother painted. It's not a connection we can ignore, Mrs Swaine. If you want me to continue my investigations, I think it's time I had a look in your brother's studio.' Mrs Swaine jolted a little, as if she'd touched something hot.

Within a few minutes we were trudging back across the moist, spongy lawn in single file, like complete strangers.

Sigmund Swaine's studio was light and spacious. It occupied a good deal of the available attic space of Silverhurst. Unlike the usual depiction of the working space of the committed painter, it was not a terrible mess. Canvases of varying sizes and in various stages of completion hung from walls and the heavy beams that spanned the space and supported the roof. Others leaned up neatly against each other in purpose-made racks, like the kind you could wade through in HMV looking for a cool poster. I didn't see a lot that was finished.

There were three easels, all with half-finished paintings on them. Palettes, brushes, pencils, paint and other equipment and resources necessary to the practice of producing a work of art were tidily organised. It had a touch of the obsessive-compulsive about it – a place for everything and everything in its place.

Mrs Swaine looked around the area as though she hadn't been in there for a long time. Perhaps for her own reasons she hadn't. While Jo poked about in all the obvious and not so obvious places I admired Sigmund's efforts with brush, colour and canvas.

I thought he was good. I thought he was very good. I'd have liked to see a finished one. He had a distinctive style. I didn't know enough about art to say whether it was his style or whether he was imitating someone else's. There was something there that put me in mind of someone else. An influence. All artists have their influences.

I mooched about enjoying the novelty and privilege of being in a working studio, stimulating my senses with the uniqueness of the place. And it occurred to me that it wasn't a working studio any longer. It was the creative centre of a dead man. And with his death the artistic spirit of the place had been extinguished. That was a pretty sad thought to contemplate. A waste.

I stole a look at Mrs Swaine to fathom something of what she was thinking. Would she have to organise the clearing out of everything? Have strangers traipsing through her home destroying the memory of her brother? Eradicating his life? I suspected she'd pull the door shut on it instead and leave it as some sort of, if not shrine, physical memory of his existence. Maybe I was just being a bit sentimental and she couldn't wait to get stuck in with the bin bags.

For something to say, I said, 'I can't see anything that's finished?'

She looked like I'd startled her out of something. And then she looked around, as if she'd forgotten where she was.

'Of course he finished things,' she said. 'They must be here somewhere.' She began poking through the collection. It started as a controlled, careful searching and then it became something more urgent, like someone suddenly desperate to salvage things from a home with a bushfire on the wind. She went from place to place flicking through the canvases.

Before it became something frantic and disturbing to witness, I said, 'Perhaps they are in your husband's gallery. You said yourself Sigmund was good enough to exhibit. Maybe they'd gone into business together.' I think I thought I was making a positive comment. Something comforting for Mrs Swaine to cling on to. But I hadn't thought it through.

She treated me to a very strange look for that. And I realised why. If they had been collaborating behind her back it would be a painful betrayal. Her brother and her husband. Her closest kin. The only 'real' people in her life. And they would not only have not included her, they'd have pointedly and secretively excluded her.

Jo came out from where she'd been poking about looking none the wiser. I don't think she'd heard the conversation we'd been having.

'Nothing here to interest me professionally,' she said.

'I'd like to see the gallery,' said Mrs Swaine.

Jo and I exchanged a quick look.

'We don't have a key for it,' said Jo. 'You could only look in the window.'

'Maybe the letting agents have a key,' I said, which earned me a *shut up* look from Jo.

'Can you ask? Please. Even if they haven't, I'd like to see it. Will you drive me, please? I don't think I could face the train, and I can't drive in London.' She was looking at me. 'Of course, I can pay for your trouble.'

Under the circumstances I would have felt incredibly mean to have refused. So I nodded my head and said I'd do it, even though I really didn't want to. I hoped that she'd quickly forget about the idea.

'Tomorrow?' said Mrs Swaine.

Tomorrow was Sunday – a potentially busy day for us in the coffee shop. They might need me. Sometimes they needed Jo *and* me. But there was something in Mrs Swaine's imploring stare that made me say yes. I avoided looking in Jo's direction.

Rebecca Swaine thanked me and then saw us out.

When we were back on the Marsh proper, I said, 'Well?'

'Well what?'

'Aren't you cross with me? Aren't you going to tell me off?'

'No.'

'Really?'

'Sure. It's a free country, just about. If you want to waste half a day driving her up to London in all that traffic just to look through a window good luck to you.'

'Won't you be coming?' I was aware that a pleading tone had affected my voice.

'No.' She sounded pleased with herself. Like someone who'd just laid two queens in a game of Pontoon.

After a long thought, I tried to sound like someone with an ace and a king. 'Good. The ladies might get busy in the shop, as it's Sunday. And as I won't be there, I'll tell them that if they need help you'll be around.'

34

As we ate dinner off our laps in front of the television that evening, Jo said, 'Maybe I should come up with you tomorrow.'

'You can't. I've already told the ladies you'll be around.'

'Tell them I've changed my mind. Can't Linda's boy come in and help if they need it? He's done it before.'

'Did you see the mess he made of everything last time? And he's such a sullen so and so. I'm trying to build a clientele, not drive them away.' I huffed out noodle and wine fumes. 'Why have you changed your mind, anyway?'

'There might be something to learn. On the off chance you can get access to the shop there's a good chance there'll be something there to help make sense of things. I should really come.'

'Fine. I'll ring Linda. To be honest, I wasn't looking forward to spending several hours cooped up with Rebecca Swaine feeling all she must be feeling at the moment.'

'What is she feeling, do you think?'

I didn't know if Jo was being sarcastic. I said, 'Grief, loss, hurt, anger, frustration, betrayal. Actually, the more I think about it the more potent the cocktail sounds.'

'She seems to hide her feelings pretty well if you ask me. Two deaths and not one tear that I've seen. Why would her husband and her brother have conspired together and kept her out of it? It's only an art gallery.'

'Maybe it's not.'

'Go on.'

'Maybe they were involved in something illegal. Nigel Tate broke the law.'

'Allegedly. Innocent 'til proved otherwise, and all that. What sort of illegal?'

'What about something to do with art?'

'Fraud? Art fraud?'

'I don't know. It's possible. I'm just making use of all we know to make an educated guess.'

'If that's an educated guess, I'd have to *guess* you didn't finish primary school.'

I put my tray to one side, sucked my fingers, wiped them on the old T-shirt I was wearing and picked up my tablet computer. In seconds I had found what I was looking for on the Internet.

Jo was bored with the reality TV show and said, 'What you looking at?'

I turned the screen so that she could see.

'What's that?'

'A famous painting. By a famous painter.'

'Come on, spit it out. I know you want to show off, so let's have it.' She stifled a yawn.

Because she was right, it didn't hurt so much. 'This is a painting by a man called Paul Nash. He is best known for being a war artist in the Second World War. His stuff is worth a lot of money. It says here that this one fetched fifty thousand dollars. Nash has a very distinctive style. Today, in Sigmund's studio, I saw something that reminded me of that style.'

Jo seemed more interested. She popped a bit of chicken in her mouth, chewed twice and said something that sounded like, 'What are you getting at?'

'You said art fraud. What if they were at it? Forging Paul Nashes. Or anyone collectable come to that. You ever heard of Tom Keating?'

'Any relation to Ronan Keating?'

'I very much doubt it, but come to think of it they did both turn out to be a couple of frauds.'

'I used to be in love with him.'

'Ronan?'

'Yes.'

'Do you mind me saying that's really sad?'

'No. I think so too now. Who's this Tom Keating?'

'Only one of the modern world's most prolific art forgers.'

'What's he got to do with Nigel Tate and Sigmund Swaine?'

'Nothing directly. I just wanted to use him as a famous example of how, even today, people can still pull the wool over the eyes of the art world establishment. He was a bit of a hero of mine.'

'I think being in love with Ronan is less sad than idolising a common criminal.'

'Believe me, there was nothing common about Mr Keating. The man was flipping extraordinary.'

'If you say so.'

'I do and I'm not the only one. You remember when we first visited Silverhurst, I commented on a painting? Rebecca Swaine said it was an original. It was a Paul Nash.'

Jo continued to chew and think. She was a woman. They can do two things at once. Allegedly. Normally, I can't abide watching or listening to other people eating. But with Jo it didn't bother me at all. She wasn't noisy; she didn't ruminate like a farm animal. She masticated her food with a subtle, dignified and slow movement that was almost hypnotic, almost sexual. That's what I thought, anyway.

Jo wiped at her chin and said, 'What? Have I got food somewhere?'

I shook my head and said, 'What do you think?'

'It could fit.'

'Really? You think so?'

'I said *could*.'

35

As with many January mornings on Romney Marsh, the early sky had been clear and the low, tepid, torpid, winter sun something to rejoice in and turn one's face to. I'd slept fitfully and was up and about before the paper children. I'd taken a Thermos mug of coffee over to the sea wall with me where I sat and stared at the Channel. I decided I wanted a boat. It wasn't warm enough to stay out dreaming for longer than it took to polish off the hot drink, but sometimes just having made the effort was worth twice the experience to my day.

As the morning ticked by, large heavy clouds began to gather along the sea's horizon and the wind was beginning to stir the trees in the yard at the back. I was back home by then, showered, dressed and getting ready for the trip to London.

I asked Jo if she wanted to drive and she declined without explanation. She installed herself up front as shotgun.

We were due to collect Rebecca Swaine late morning. The thought occurred to me as we were heading once again across the Marsh to Silverhurst that we'd spend at least four hours together on our pointless caper.

'I reckon this'll take at least four hours,' I said.

When Jo didn't answer, I said, 'It's coming to eleven now. Eleven plus four is three.'

Jo found her voice. 'Where did you say you went to school?'

'Three o'clock,' I said. 'That means we'll be together through lunchtime. What should we do?'

Jo said, 'I had a big breakfast.'

'Well I didn't. And maybe your client will want something to eat at lunchtime.'

'David, I'm not her dietician. I'm her investigator. If she wants food, she'll have to say so and get something. You can always stop at a Golden Arches drive-thru.' Jo started laughing, presumably at the thought of Mrs Swaine trying to order and then make her way through a burger and fries.

'Don't suggest it,' I said. 'No one's eating in my car. Ever. Got it?'

'Then you'll have to stop if she's hungry.'

'What, and leave you sitting in the car on your own while we have a pub lunch?'

'No. If you're buying lunch I'll have some.'

'You said…'

'I said I'd had a big breakfast. I didn't say I'm not eating lunch if you're paying.'

Like a Panzer IV, the Range Rover made easy work of the track. Rebecca Swaine had her front door open before I'd had a chance to kill the engine. She wore close-fitting denim jeans and knee-length leather boots. Her jacket was over her arm. She had on an elegant top. She carried a good brand of handbag and an umbrella. There was something determined, stubborn even, in her stride as she approached the car.

'Hadn't you better hop out and open the door for her?' said Jo, as her client came towards us.

I growled at Jo, jumped out and got the rear door on Jo's side of the car just as Rebecca Swaine got there. Up close Mrs Swaine smelled good – understated, but expensive. She'd made an effort with her make-up and wore some coordinating and probably quite costly jewellery. I caught a flash of a wristwatch set with stones that were probably diamonds. If I'd been picking her up for a date, I wouldn't have been disappointed, especially as she was no longer wearing her wedding ring.

We exchanged hellos. She offered her thanks for my attention and I shut the door after her. Walking back around to my side I wondered whether Jo had changed her mind about coming along because she didn't trust my intentions regarding the rather gorgeous grieving widow. Given half the chance, maybe she'd have been right.

As we headed up Giggers Green Road under the arching bare tree limbs, Mrs Swaine said, 'Thank you for this. Both of you. I really appreciate your care and time on what is almost certainly going to be a fool's errand. Thank you for indulging me.'

Jo said, 'You're my client, Mrs Swaine. No problem. All part of the service.'

I really wanted to say something to Jo for that. Something like, you brazen lying cow. Instead, I let my silence speak for me.

No one spoke again until we were comfortably bowling along the M20. Then Mrs Swaine said, 'I've been thinking about what you've suggested regarding the notion that my brother and my husband may have started up a picture gallery without my knowledge.'

I glanced at her in the rear-view mirror to see how she was taking the notion. She seemed composed as she stared out of her window. In that letter-box of reflective material, Mrs Swaine seemed more than a little vulnerably beautiful. And the car was now properly filled with her perfume. That always contributes.

'Why would they do such a thing, do you think?' she said.

Jo said, 'Firstly, we don't know that they did, Mrs Swaine. We don't know that your brother was anything to do with it.'

Almost as though she hadn't heard Jo, she said, 'Sigmund and Nigel were very close. They were better friends than Nigel and I were.'

I hoped she wasn't going to suggest they were also lovers. I'd only been joking about that.

'They'd known each other a long time. They were at college together.'

'What sort of college?' said Jo.

'Art college, actually. Nigel could paint but he gave up. He just stopped one day. I don't think his parents approved. He dropped out of college and went into business.'

I thought that was interesting. The art college bit.

'But their friendship endured,' said Jo.

'Yes. It was Sigmund who introduced me to Nigel.' She might have gone on to say more but I had to brake rather hard to avoid a triple pack of fibreglass insulation that was rolling around the middle lane of the motorway trying to cause an accident. By the time we were past it, she'd stopped reminiscing.

I said, 'If they had been in it together, why wouldn't they have included you, do you think?'

It seemed a reasonable and pertinent question to me. I thought it might encourage Mrs Swaine to reveal something that she might not otherwise. I caught Jo twitch her head in my direction. I gave her a very little smile.

'It's what I was thinking,' said Mrs Swaine, as if her train of thought was back on track. 'Why would they? The only thing I can think is that it was something they would know I wouldn't approve of – something I wouldn't tolerate, that they'd know I couldn't be a party to.'

'And what fits that bill?' I said.

'Something illegal.'

Encouraged, I said, 'Yesterday, when I was looking through Sigmund's work, I was struck by something familiar in his style.'

Mrs Swaine turned her head to meet my gaze in the mirror. That part of her face that held her emerald gaze was perfectly framed in the little rectangle. 'And?'

'I'm no great appreciator of art, but I was struck by a resemblance to the style of Paul Nash. You have a Nash, I remember.'

'I have a couple.' She wasn't bragging; she was just saying. 'Daddy didn't just collect books. Sigmund had something of an unhealthy obsession with Nash's work. With Nash the man, too. He lived in Dymchurch for a while, you know?'

'I know. He rented a cottage in the high street in the twenties.' In response to her raised eyebrows, I smiled, I hoped a little enigmatically.

'Nash and my grandfather were great friends. The Nashes often visited my grandparents' home while they lived in the village.'

'Is that how your family came by the paintings?'

'No. That was all to do with my father's obsession.'

The Swaine males were coming across as a bit obsessive. There was something she wanted to add. I could sense it. I said, 'What was behind his obsession?'

'My father believed that he was the love child of Paul Nash and my grandmother.'

This was news. 'And he convinced Sigmund that he was Paul Nash's grandson?'

'Perhaps he was,' said Mrs Swaine, and she was back to staring out of the window.

I felt that another piece of the puzzle had fallen into place.

36

We turned into Judd Street from Euston Road. It was empty of cars, apart from ours. I couldn't see any pedestrians either. It had a feel of a place deserted – a scene from a zombie movie before all hell breaks loose. We prowled in low gear towards the gallery.

'It's just up here on the right,' I said, to prepare our passenger.

As we rolled to a stop alongside the gallery my heart sank. Police tape fluttered in the light breeze channelled up between the tall buildings. Where the front door had been, a rectangle of thick and sturdy plywood with an emergency glazier's advertisement stencilled on it was now fixed. I glanced up at the alarm. There were no little red lights glowing to show it was working.

'What's happened?' said Mrs Swaine. 'Was it like this when you came before?'

'No, it wasn't,' said Jo, and there was something in her tone to suggest she was cross.

We were parked on a single yellow line. I turned the engine off. It was Sunday. I thought we would be safe from wardens and penalties. We all got out and went for a closer look. The inside of the car had been warm. The breeze was cold. In just a shirt, I felt it keenly.

We did our best to see inside but, like before, the fixed security grilles made that difficult.

In our confusion, Jo said, 'I'm going to talk to misery guts.'

She left Mrs Swaine and me and disappeared below ground level in search of answers. We heard her banging on the door.

I said, 'Shall we wait in the car? It's cold out here.'

Jo reappeared in a couple of minutes. She got back in the car with a brrrr.

'He's not in or not answering,' she said.

I said, 'What now?'

'I called Marion.' To Mrs Swaine, Jo said, 'She's a police officer I know up here. This isn't her patch but she's going to try to put us in contact with someone whose it is.'

Jo's phone rang before further questions could be asked. She got out of the car to have her conversation in private, which I didn't think was very nice of her. She spent a couple of minutes walking up and down the pavement outside the gallery with the phone clamped to her ear.

When she returned, she said, 'That was the detective whose desk this landed on. He wants us to stay put. He's going to come and speak to us.'

'Is that normal?' I said.

'He's keen. I got the impression he was short of leads and couldn't believe his luck when I explained who and where we are.'

'How long is he going to be?' I said.

'He said he'd be over as soon as he could.'

I suggested we waited in the café Jo and I had visited the day before. It seemed a popular idea.

I got our drinks and joined the ladies at a table by a window that overlooked the street. The only thing that seemed to have changed was the date of the newspapers. I recognised some of the customers from the previous day. I recognised the same acoustic guitar strains on the stereo, too. It seemed I wasn't the only one who thought classical guitar and coffee shops went together like things that go together.

Jo asked whether coffee shop Paul was about. He wasn't; it was his day off, but his mate Harry was in. Jo questioned him about the people who'd been looking for Nigel and he confirmed that they were a man and a woman and that the man had a tattoo of a small bird on his neck. He confirmed the ponytail too. He couldn't tell us much more; he'd been busy, he said.

We were on our second round, again got by me, when a nondescript saloon car pulled up behind the Range Rover. A man got out.

'That's him,' said Jo. I didn't ask how she knew.

She rapped on the window for his attention and beckoned him over, which I thought was a bit cheeky. He was the police, after all.

Jo made the introductions. Jo and the detective shook hands and there seemed some genuine friendliness there. I had to wonder how far the jungle drums and Jo's reputation had spread. The policeman bestowed business nods in the direction of Mrs Swaine and me.

A chair was organised. He took off his overcoat. Jo asked what he wanted to drink and when he gave his order she looked at me and smiled nicely and her meaning was clear.

By the time I returned with his drink, the three of them were chatting quite comfortably.

'Cheers,' he said and turned back to the women.

'So you had no idea your husband had opened a gallery?' he said.

'No. It's been quite a shock,' said Mrs Swaine.

Because I'd spent a good five minutes queuing for his flipping coffee behind a dippy woman in a massively oversized cardigan who couldn't make her flipping mind up which flipping muffin to have with her flipping espresso, I didn't know how much they'd told each other.

'What can you tell us about what's happened?' said Jo.

'No secrets here. Nothing much to go on either, if I'm honest. Late last night report of a break-in across the road. The old boy who manages the flats got a dink on the head for his trouble. He's still in the hospital. I haven't spoken to him yet, but I don't hold out much hope he'll have much to contribute. You know how it is?' Jo nodded.

'Did they steal many of the paintings?' said Mrs Swaine.

'Until we can find someone who knows what was in there, I can't say.'

I opened my mouth to mention Natalie but shut it again quickly when I saw Jo's look.

'Can we have a look inside?' said Jo.

This was the sixty-four-thousand-dollar question.

'As you're next of kin,' he said to Mrs Swaine, 'and SOCO have been and gone, I don't see why not. Maybe you'll be able to help with our enquiries.'

We finished our drinks, shrugged our coats back on and made our way across the street.

'Nice motor,' he said, looking at the Range Rover. 'The private sector must be paying well.'

'That belongs to my chauffeur,' said Jo. 'I couldn't afford the petrol for that thing with what I'm making.'

He tore the police tape, unlocked the padlock and grunted with the effort of opening the temporary and ill-fitting front door. He went in first and we all crunched over broken glass after him.

It was one long open space through to a door set in the partition wall at the back of it. Only a big, naked desk and an executive chair halfway down broke things up. The flooring was laminated boards. The walls were plain white. The ceiling had some sympathetic track lighting. There were paintings on the walls. And there didn't appear to be any missing; there were no bare nails sticking out of the plaster.

My eyes were drawn to the artwork. I can look at a painting that's considered important, valuable even, and not be particularly enamoured with it. And I could look at others and be immediately intrigued and involved in them: Hilder's snow scenes, Vermeer's interiors, Nash's war artistry, for examples. Paintings with qualities that grabbed my eyeballs, stirred an emotion, touched on a memory, a nerve or a sense. The images on the walls of the gallery had a similar effect on me. They were mostly landscapes but there was something quite out of the ordinary about them. It was something elusive, mysterious and, for me, a layman in such things, indefinable, like Mona Lisa's smirk.

To Mrs Swaine, Jo said, 'Do you recognise any of the pictures?'

From the moment we'd crossed the threshold, my attention had flitted between her and the paintings. Her expression hadn't given much away but the way her eyes roamed over the works of art we passed led me to believe that she was not unfamiliar with them, or at least their style.

Mrs Swaine gave a small nod and said, 'These are Sigmund's.'

No one felt the need to challenge her.

'There don't appear to be any missing,' I said.

The policeman looked at me and I said, 'You can see from the spotlights in the ceiling that all the parts of the wall where the lights are pointing are occupied.'

He moved across to a bank of switches and turned them all on to prove me right.

'So what would whoever broke in have been after?' said Mrs Swaine.

'No idea,' said the policeman. 'Maybe they were looking for something. Maybe they found it.'

'What's in the room at the back?' said Jo.

Jo and I followed him through. I looked around for Rebecca Swaine but she was lost in one of her brother's imaginings. She looked very sad and forlorn, like a painting herself, standing unhappily in front of something she'd been kept out of. I felt for her.

The room at the back was nothing more than a place for making tea, washing up a cup, keeping wrapping and packing materials. There was a toilet in a small space.

Mrs Swaine was staring despondently at another picture when we filed back out. She was interested only in the artwork and what it all meant to her and for her. The bigger picture.

'When might I be able to have these back?' she said.

'I'm afraid you'll have to go through the proper channels for that,' said the policeman. 'More than my job's worth to let you remove stuff.'

Rebecca Swaine nodded her understanding.

'How badly was the old boy hurt?' said Jo.

'Few stitches. Shaken up as much as anything. He'll be home today, probably.'

We parted with the police on the pavement and on good terms. He'd got something out of it. Information, names and contact details for his forms. But none of us was any the wiser over why someone should go to the trouble of breaking into Tate's Modern and steal nothing and, other than the door, do no damage.

Jo wrote a note for the caretaker and slipped it through his letterbox.

I asked if anyone was hungry or wanted another drink before we pushed off, but neither of them did. I was starving and my stomach was grumbling before we were even back on the motorway.

I waited as long as I could stand it for one of my passengers to share their thoughts over events. In the end I had to say something. 'At least we know that your husband was selling your brother's work.'

'It doesn't explain why they would have kept it from me or why they both committed suicide,' she said. 'And there is no evidence to suggest that any of the paintings were sold. Will you be able to get me my answers, Miss Cash?'

'I still have some leads of my own to pursue, Mrs Swaine. If you want me to.'

'I want you to. I want to know what they were doing. I want to know everything about it. I want to know why they died.' She sounded filled with a barely suppressed cold anger and it encouraged me to just shut up and drive. Hell hath no fury like a woman lied to by the only 'real' people in her life.

37

Rebecca Swaine thanked us politely when we dropped her off. She didn't invite us in for refreshment. I felt that she wanted to be very alone. I felt that she had some emotions to deal with and her kind didn't do that sort of thing in public.

Jo promised to keep in touch.

As we drove home along Eastbridge Road, I said, 'Did you tell him about Natalie?'

'Yeah. He said he'd look into it.'

'Did he know about the two suicides?'

'We talked about it in the café. Weren't you listening?'

'Maybe that's when I was waiting tables.'

Jo smiled at me and patted my leg. 'Thanks for that. And thanks for today.'

Like a puppy that gets its head patted, I felt better. 'What about the two who've been looking for Nigel?'

'I told him about them, too. He said if he had any luck he'd let me know.'

'What do you think about it?'

Jo shook her head and looked out of the window. 'I think she's right. They must have been up to something illegal. Something they couldn't share with her. Maybe they were just using Sigmund's paintings as a front for an illegitimate business. What about this bloke Nash?'

'What about him?'

'Could he have anything to do with it?'

'I doubt it – he's been dead over fifty years.'

'I don't mean literally.'

'If they were up to something, there'd have to be something incriminating, wouldn't there? We've found nothing physical to suggest it.'

'His briefcase,' said Jo. 'If we could find his briefcase... what are you doing, you idiot?'

I'd stamped on the brakes and ended up in the verge as the tyres had slewed across the narrow damp surface.

'His briefcase. The police didn't take it. Rebecca Swaine hasn't seen it. The last place it was seen was at home. If Sigmund thought there was something incriminating in it, or important to him, when he learned that Nigel had done away with himself he might have taken it.'

'It wasn't in his studio,' said Jo. 'You're blocking the road.'

'There's no traffic. Where was the last place Sigmund was seen alive?'

The penny dropped. She said, 'Well, come on then. Turn this tank around and let's go and see.'

I drove on to the next suitable turning area – an opening to a field. As I manoeuvred the 'tank' in a five-point turn in the country lane, Jo said, 'It would certainly explain what Sigmund was doing hiding out at St Whats-it's.'

'St Rumwold's,' I corrected her. 'Maybe he wasn't running away or hiding out. Maybe he knew exactly what he was doing and what he was doing was hiding something in a good place. I'd bet there are nooks and crannies in that place that don't even see a duster during a Lent clean. And we burst in on him and frightened the life out of him and he lost his head.'

I headed back to the Lower Wall crossroads and took a left. The ribbon of raised tarmac was not wide enough for two vehicles. The swollen dyke on our left was a constant reminder of the dangers of driving fast out there. I could tell Jo wanted me to put my foot down, but I'd heard stories of motorists losing control of their vehicles and ending upside down in one of the Marsh sewers in a seat belt that they were suspended from and couldn't undo. A rotten way to go.

A couple of hundred metres on, I took our first right. We navigated bends, blind corners and bridges as we rapidly closed the gap between ourselves and the remote house of God.

Just as I sensed Jo was going to ask how much further it was, I caught a glimpse of the church's distinctive cupola and said so. We recrossed the Royal Military Canal via one of the smaller bridges and I parked up on the verge.

'Why are you stopping here?' said Jo.

'Because we can't park by the church without blocking the road.'

Dusk was fast approaching and with it another gloomy Marsh winter evening.

'It's going to be open, isn't it?' said Jo, as we hurried on foot towards the wonky wooden gate of the little churchyard's cemetery.

'It's always open,' I said, with more confidence than I suddenly felt. I soothed my worries with the knowledge that it was Sunday. Surely, if there was one day of the week the church wouldn't lock people out it would be Sunday. And then I was struck by the idea that there might be people worshipping inside. That could make taking the place apart awkward.

It was unlocked and empty. I'm a practising atheist but the insides of the Marsh churches, any churches, usually brought me a palpable multi-sensory pleasure, a feeling of inner peace. I was just letting this claim me when Jo trampled all over it with a, 'Come on. Hurry up. The light's going.'

I smiled an apology to Jesus as he bled for us on a crucifix nailed to the wall, and turned my mind to thinking about where Sigmund could have hidden a briefcase. As I stood scanning the interior, I noticed that there were a few big floral displays around the place that weren't there the last time I'd been in. The air was heavy with the rich scent of lilies, a flower and smell of which I was particularly fond. I wondered what they were in aid of. None of them were wreath shaped so probably nothing to do with recent death, Sigmund or otherwise. It was possible there'd been a wedding the day before, although not too likely in the middle of winter.

Jo had already pushed off for some ferreting. I went in a different direction. I knew the church well enough from touristy visits on lazy summer bike rides but I didn't *really* know it. I had no idea where something like a briefcase could be concealed, so it was simply a matter of looking everywhere it could be.

I started in what I thought to be the places least likely to be disturbed by either casual visitors or more regular ones: those involved in the upkeep and business of the church. I found a lot of dust and the paraphernalia of a small remote house of worship clogging and cluttering up the areas tucked away from where the congregation would gather, if indeed there was still a congregation worthy of the label frequenting St Rumwold's.

I found it slipped in behind a low bookcase that was higgledy-piggledy with Bibles. It was well tucked away, not to be seen or found by anyone other than a determined searcher or a spring cleaner. The discovery gave me the biggest thrill I'd had for a long time, not least because it was my idea that it could be in the church.

I called Jo and held the case aloft much as I've seen various Chancellors of the Exchequer do with their packed lunches on Budget Day. She came trotting up the aisle and her eyes were sparkling with intrigue in what remained of the half light. She smiled at me and congratulated me on my detective work.

The briefcase was of the executive type, like a small suitcase. It was the kind of case men chained to their wrists in films because they were full of precious stones or gold bars or top secret documents. It was not particularly heavy. No gold bullion then. I shook it and didn't hear the noise of diamonds ticking against each other.

'What are you doing?' said Jo, with a maternal tolerance.

I had to admit to being terrifically excited by the find. I met Jo's stare and saw the professional exterior had softened somewhat to be replaced by something childish. We smiled at each other, like a couple of big kids on Christmas morning.

'You want to open it here?' I said.

'No. I think we should take it back to Mrs Swaine and let her do the honours,' said Jo.

'I hope you're joking.'

'Of course I am, you dunce. Come on, get on with it. Let's find out what was worth two lives and a load of deceit.'

'I hope it's not locked or wired with explosives,' I said, as I positioned my thumbs on the catches.

'Wait a second,' said Jo. She went and stood behind a solid-looking wall. 'OK. Ready when you are.'

I pretended she was joking and gently applied pressure to the catches. They weren't locked and it didn't blow up. I lifted the lid.

Jo hurried back over. She looked down at the contents and said, 'Jesus fucking Christ.' Out loud. In a church. If I hadn't been feeling the same thing I might have remonstrated with her for her blasphemy.

The case was packed with bundles of twenty-pound notes. I lifted a hand with the intention of picking one out and received a quick slap on the back of it for the idea.

'Close the lid, David. Don't touch anything in there.'

I understood but I didn't immediately shut it. With only my eyes, I quickly tallied the packets of twenties – eight wide and three across: twenty-four. I shut the lid and shared that with Jo.

'How much altogether, do you think?' she said.

'If it were only twenty-four and let's say they are bundles of a thousand pounds that's twenty-four thousand pounds. If there are two layers that's forty-eight thousand. I think there could be at least four layers. That's nearly a hundred grand in used notes.'

'That's worth killing for,' she said.

'Yeah, but not yourself.'

38

If it had been just me, I'd have shoved a fiver in the donations box, left quietly, whistled my way back to the car, driven home, locked myself in my bedroom, emptied the contents of the case on the bed, stripped off and rolled around in it all. But what we did next was, of course, entirely Jo's call. It was her case and so, as far as I was concerned, it was her briefcase.

My senses, temporarily overwhelmed with a sudden release of the mind-altering drug called adrenalin, stood down from DEFCON orange to green. I became aware again of my surroundings. The hushed, simple but dominant atmosphere descended like holy fallout to bring a calmness and gravity to proceedings. I was able to smell the flowers again; I could hear what the big open space was doing to our voices; I noticed a saintly, red-robed statue in a niche, hands clasped in front, staring down on us. Waiting to see what we would do.

'What now?' I said, and I realised I was deliberately keeping my voice down.

Jo inhaled very deeply, like someone about to plunge into freezing water. When she let it go she said, 'Silverhurst.'

Like I said, it was entirely her call, but I couldn't help myself. 'Are you sure?'

She turned her police eyes on me. 'What do you mean?'

I turned my 'take a reality check' eyes on her. 'Jo, there could be a hundred grand in here. Think about it.'

'I don't have to, David. It's not mine. The case belongs to the next of kin of Nigel Tate.'

'What about the contents?'

'And the contents.'

'Who says?'

'I says.'

I knew I was disappointing her but, like I said, I couldn't help myself. It was still a lot of money. 'If this is "dirty" money, something come by dishonestly, whose is it then?'

'What are you trying to do?'

'Just playing devil's advocate.'

'In here? Is that wise?'

'I'm encouraging you to consider all the angles.'

'There are no angles. There's just a straight line.'

'As in straight and narrow?'

'If you like, and it leads back to Silverhurst.'

I was losing. I'd probably already lost, but like a trainer with no arms I just couldn't throw the towel in. 'Shouldn't you at least see exactly how much is in there and whether there might be some important documents under the money?'

'Important documents?'

I was clutching air where there should have been straws. 'Something to help you in the investigation. This is about being a detective for you, right? Solving puzzles of the human variety?'

'As much as it's about anything.'

'So, what if you hand this over to Mrs Swaine and she decides to keep things from you?'

'That's her prerogative.'

'Because she's a woman?'

'No, because she's my client. Anyway, why would she if she wants answers?'

'Maybe she'd get them. Maybe they're in here. And then she wouldn't need you.'

'So? Job done. Move on.'

'But you wouldn't know. Could you live with that?'

'I'd have to.'

'But you don't have to. Listen, I understand the money is going to your client. Your decision. No problem. But why don't we first just check everything out? Just so we know. Just so you know.'

I was getting to her. It was in her hesitation. It was in the fact that we were still standing there talking about it. And it surprised me.

I went for the kill. 'What if there is something very illegal going on and there is something about that in here?' I tapped the lid for emphasis. 'Something that could have an effect on innocent lives? You said yourself, you wouldn't keep something like that from the authorities.'

'We can't look in it here,' she said.

'Agreed. Let's go home. Check everything out. And then you can call your client and share the find with her. It's just a delay. It's not going to hurt anyone, is it?'

I took off my jacket and concealed the case under it as we walked back to the car. It's funny how being in the wrong and knowing it can make you feel. Fifteen minutes earlier, I couldn't have cared less who saw me arrive, park and walk up to the church. Now, I kept a keen lookout for anyone who might be able to provide descriptions of us and my distinctive 'tank'.

Jo was quiet on the drive back and I didn't probe at her silence for fear of her changing her mind. She had the case on her lap and stared out of the window at nothing. My personal curiosity regarding the contents of the case was threatening to cloud my judgement if it hadn't already.

All was quiet at home on our return. Only the night lights for the shop were on. I let us in the back.

'Upstairs or down here?' I said.

'Can anyone see in down here?'

'Not with the blinds properly closed.' I went over to check that they were.

Jo slumped down into one the sofas in the same secluded area where she'd had her first meeting with Rebecca Swaine. It seemed hard to believe that was less than a week ago.

There was still coffee left and I gave two mugs thirty seconds in the microwave, carried them over and sat opposite her. The case lay on the low table between us. I thought of something, got up, disappeared into the cleaning products station and returned with two pairs of new rubber gloves. I hoped to earn a brownie point or two back with that.

'Shall we?' I said.

Jo snapped up her gaze, snapped on her Marigolds and snapped open the case. She turned it so we could both see inside. The high tide of my adrenalin was back. I was beginning to realise that lots of money had that effect on me. We carefully removed the bundles of notes and piled them up on the table. I checked one: a thousand pounds. When they were all out the case was empty. No other surprises. I was disappointed. Jo felt around for false bottoms. Nothing. Jo took out a few random notes to check them and I saw a chance to vindicate our decision to bring them home first.

'If there's counterfeit money here, we'd have to hand it in to the authorities, right?'

'Of course,' she said, holding one up to the light.

'Well then, that's another good reason for bringing it back to check.'

'These are all genuine,' she said.

'We weren't to know, were we?'

We counted the bundles. There were a hundred. We put them back neatly, shut the case and peeled off our protection. I got a whiff of sweaty rubber, which stirred a potent and inappropriate memory. I went and washed my hands.

When I came back Jo had her phone out. I sipped my coffee and I said, 'Ringing her tonight?'

'Now, actually. If she wants to see me this evening, I'll drive over.'

I hid my face behind the mug and nodded my acceptance of the way things were. I wondered if Jo would want company, especially with that kind of money in the car. Not that I could imagine much happening to her between Dymchurch and Aldington. It wasn't downtown LA. She'd be lucky to pass another vehicle the whole way there.

After several rings she gave up and said, 'Not in.'

'Or not answering. Maybe she just doesn't feel like talking. She looked pretty upset at times today.'

'She has a right to be. Can you imagine: your brother and your husband deceiving you like that? And they all lived under the same roof.'

I said, 'I haven't got a brother and I hope I never have a husband, honest or not. Where do you think the money came from?'

'That's the hundred-thousand-pound question, Watson: where indeed.'

'I think it will come as a shock to your client. Hey, what if it's not Nigel's case? Maybe it's been lying around the church for months.'

Jo smiled. 'It still wouldn't be finders keepers. We'd have to declare it to the police.'

'You should ask her to describe the case to you before you go giving all that money away.'

Jo's mobile started dancing around the table and playing a tune. She looked at the display.

'I can ask her now,' she said, and answered it, looking triumphant.

She listened and her expression went from winning to grimly serious in the time it takes a stranger to say, 'Hello, Miss Cash. We haven't met. Mrs Swaine is with me. She's asked me to give you a message. She wants you to concentrate all your efforts on finding her husband's briefcase and when you do you are to ring this number. We believe it contains something that belongs to me. If you want to see your client alive again, unharmed, I want my money back. And no police. I'll be in touch.'

39

I said, 'She said what?'

Jo repeated what the female caller had said.

I said, 'Rebecca Swaine has been kidnapped?'

Jo seemed in mild shock. She said, 'That was her number. And that's the idea I got.'

'How? Why?'

'Who? We don't even know who?'

'It was a woman? A man and a woman have been looking for Nigel Tate.'

'Perhaps they've been keeping an eye on his gallery.'

'Or paying someone else to and to let them know if any one shows up.'

'And we did this morning and gave them plenty of time to get round there.'

'How would they have known where to find Rebecca Swaine?' But even as I said it, I understood: they would only have had to follow us back from London.

'Did you notice anyone following us back from London?' said Jo.

I shook my head. 'I wasn't looking, was I?'

'It looks like we might have led them straight to Silverhurst.'

'We weren't to know, were we?'

'I'm not blaming us, David.'

I said, 'Good. How the hell would they know we had the money?'

'I don't think she does. I didn't get that impression.'

'Then what was she on about?'

'We're to find it for her.'

'Well we have, haven't we? Job done.'

'Maybe. Maybe it's not hers. Maybe it's not all of it.'

'Call the police.'

'No.'

'Why?'

'She said not to.'

'You have to.'

'And tell them what?'

'What's happened.'

'Then we lose control and we give up my client's money.'

Jo and her client's bloody money. 'Didn't you say the caller said it was hers? So pay them and get her back.'

'Shhh. I'm trying to think and it's impossible with you making all that noise.'

All that noise? That hurt. It continued to amaze me how quickly Jo and I could alter our positions in arguments. Since we'd found the money I'd been urging her to think very hard about handing it over to anyone and she'd been adamant to do 'the right thing'. Now we'd had another of our role reversals.

Jo said, 'Get me a pen and paper, will you?'

I think she was just trying to get rid of me or shut me up, but I got them anyway. She scribbled a few things down and I waited.

'It's the woman and the man with the tat and the tail, isn't it?'

'Possibly.'

I tried again: 'Jo, your client has been kidnapped. You must call the police and report it.'

'One: no one mentioned the word kidnap, and she said not to. Two: maybe my client wouldn't want me to. Three: it would take time. Four: I'd lose control. Five: if every time I encountered a crime in my work I went running to the police I wouldn't have any work left.'

I said: 'One: of course she'd say that, she's kidnapped your client. Of course she doesn't want you to involve the police. Two: why the hell wouldn't your client want the police involved if she's been kidnapped, taken by force from her home? Three: so what if it takes time? It's going to take a lot more time and be a lot worse for you if something happens to your client and you did not involve the police when you should have. Four: You wouldn't be *losing* control, you'd be handing responsibility and control over to a law enforcement organisation that is trained, experienced and equipped to deal with such a situation. Five: this is different and you know it.'

Jo said, 'Yes it is,' and then completely disregarded what I thought was my rather good reflexive analysis and argument a propos her weak position. She said, 'I should have said, what money?'

'Eh?'

'She said *I want my money*. I should have said what money.'

'Did she give you the chance to?'

'Not really.'

'Call back and ask her. Then probably she'll just think she surprised you.'

'That would make me look stupid.'

'What?'

'It'll sound dumb.'

'No it won't.' I was wasting my breath; she wasn't listening to me.

'I think I should drive out to Silverhurst. Make sure this isn't a hoax.'

Of course, she meant 'we'.

We took the 'tank' and in ten minutes we were back to a place that was becoming quite familiar. We banged on the front door and no one answered. We looked in the windows. The lights were on, the curtains were open and the place was empty.

I said, 'What now?'

Jo's phone rang. She accepted the call, listened and said, 'Let me talk to my client.' Jo crooked her finger at me and when I got in close she turned the phone so that we could both hear. Jo's breath smelled like she needed something to eat.

'Miss Cash.' It was Rebecca Swaine. 'Please, no police. Do as they say. They haven't hurt me. Find what they want.'

He Made Me

'That's all you get for now,' said the woman.

'You said money,' said Jo. 'What money?'

'My money. Your client's husband took my money. You heard her. No police. Find the money, give it back and everyone can go home safe and happy. Police, and people might get hurt. People might not come back. And don't think I won't know. Like I know you and your boyfriend are at this moment standing on her driveway.'

We both instinctively started looking around. The caller, knowing that would be our reaction, laughed in our ears. 'We're not there now, silly.'

'How much is it?' said Jo.

'Enough that when you find it you'll know it. I'll be in touch and if you have any success call this number.'

The call was terminated.

'They must still be around to know that we're here,' I said.

Jo sighed rather heavily. 'Forget it, David. They might have been parked up on the way. Just watched us drive past, heading here because they'd know that's what we'd do. They won't be around here now.'

I said, 'Shit.' Then I said, 'Good job we didn't bring the money straight here from the church, eh?'

'I hope so, David.'

'What do you mean?'

'Maybe if we had, they'd have just taken it and left her alone.'

'True. How would that have made you feel?'

'Pissed off.' And I was understanding why Jo was reluctant to call in the law: she wanted to bring a satisfactory resolution to things herself – client and money united with a full and detailed explanation for everything. It was professional pride and it was potentially dangerous. It's no secret what follows pride.

40

I was hungry so I'd knocked us up a meal in the wok. We were both on the sauce. Soy for Jo, Blankety-blank for me.

'Have a drink,' I said. 'You look like you could do with one. There won't be any driving tonight.'

Jo shook her head. 'You can't know that.'

'They've probably taken her back to London, haven't they?'

'Probably.'

'You're going to try and find them, aren't you?'

'Yes. I've found the money. So I've bought myself some time. I can spend it looking for them.'

I resisted the urge to remind Jo of whose idea it had been to look in the church for the case and who it was who found it.

'Where will you start?'

'I still have friends in the force. Tat and tail sounds distinctive. He might have form.'

'Will you ask Marion Pardew?'

Jo shook her head as she sucked up some noodles. 'I don't know her well enough and I might have to explain things.'

'When will you start?'

'I hope you're not trying to make me feel bad.'

'Just asking.'

'I'll make some calls when I've finished this.'

'How do you think they'll treat her?'

'I think they'll treat her fine. They want their money back. They don't want the complications of hurting people.'

'At least we know why the gallery was broken into.'

'Maybe.'

'Come on. It must be. They didn't take anything else.'

'We can't know that for certain. But I agree with you. It's not somewhere I would have expected Nigel to keep a hundred grand but when you're running out of options you get desperate. They had to chance a look. They took it.'

'And Natalie?'

'What about Natalie?'

'They've shown they're not averse to kidnap. I'd say it's looking more likely that they have something to do with her disappearance.'

Jo made a noise to express her disagreement. 'There could still be any number of reasons why Natalie has gone off the radar.'

'Give me three.'

'Holiday, hiding…'

Jo's phone rang. She swallowed her food and answered it. I continued eating, with my eyes on her. It was a personal call and it didn't last long.

Jo pushed her plate away. She hadn't eaten much.

I said, 'How about calling them and saying you've found fifty thousand?'

'And what if they say, find the other fifty thousand?'

'What about calling them and saying you have no idea where the money is and they can do what they like to her?'

'That's not a bad idea, actually. Call their bluff.'

'I was joking.'

'Really? I'm not. I don't think they'd hurt her.'

'You can't take that risk. She's your client, remember?'

'I want to call my mate from Ashford, but if I do that she'll have to inform her DI and you saw what her problem was.'

'No. I mean, I saw she had a problem, but I don't know what it was.'

'Me.'

'Oh. What about phoning your old mate DI Sprake from Folkestone?'

'A: we didn't part on the best of terms. B: he'd have to pass it over to Ashford because Aldington comes under Ashford police jurisdiction and I'd be back with the DI with a problem.'

'The longer you leave it to call the police, the worse it's going to look. They'll say, why didn't you report it straight away?'

'I needed to make sure it wasn't a hoax.'

'That's only going to work for a certain window of time and it's nearly shut.'

'Come on, David. Think.'

'I already did. I had some good thoughts and you ignored them and me.'

She stood and paced. Then she stopped and said, 'I'm going back to Silverhurst.'

'What? Why?'

'With Rebecca Swaine out of the way, I can have a good look around. Plus I might see something that might mean something to me now, when it didn't before. And I need to be doing something. I can't just watch TV.'

'Shitty death, Jo. Are you telling me you're going to break into your client's home when she's been kidnapped?'

'I'm only doing it to try to find something to help get her back. I'm not asking you to come.'

'What if you get caught breaking and entering?'

'By who? No one overlooks the place.'

'You know I can't let you go up there alone.'

'You don't have to come in. You can just sit in the car and keep watch.'

'Be a remote accessory after the fact, whatever that means? Tell you what: I come up for moral support and if your search turns up nothing and you have no ideas and we're none the wiser about anything, you call the cops. Your Ashford mate.'

Jo considered for a second and said, 'OK.' She had her hands behind her back. She might have had her fingers crossed.

I had to find somewhere special to hide the briefcase. I couldn't leave it in the shop safe because (a) it wouldn't have fitted and (b) I didn't want awkward questions from the ladies next time I saw them about bundles of twenty-pound notes. In the end, to save time and arguments, we took it with us.

41

Déjà vu. Rebecca Swaine's driveway on a nippy still January night. The only difference from earlier was my tummy was full and I had a glass of plonk filtering through my system. A heavy darkness clung to everything. Through the bare branches of the trees, and with our elevated position overlooking the Marsh, I could make out the twinkling streetlights of the A259, the Christmas tree effect of the nuclear power station that squatted on the shingle peninsula out at Dungeness and the glow-worm effect that characterised the shipping laid up for the night in the sheltered bay of the English Channel.

I asked Jo how she intended to gain entry and she showed me her Maglite torch. It wasn't going to be subtle. I stifled a groan. She decided we should break a window on the far side of the house where it would be more discreet. Just the idea of breaking and entering had my senses on full alert. That's the dark for you. Everything seems amplified, especially bad things. I reminded myself that our proposed actions were the offspring of concern and worry regarding Rebecca Swaine's immediate future.

'Shouldn't we be wearing gloves?' I said.

'And how would that look *if* the law should happen to turn up?'

I didn't like to think of the law turning up. And then I did like to think about the law turning up – Jo would have to explain what we were doing there and she couldn't do that without mentioning the kidnap of her client. And then the police would be involved, which is what I wanted.

As I followed Jo past the front door on the narrow path I tried the handle on an impulse. The door opened, letting out a wedge of yellow light.

I said, 'Psssst.'

Jo turned. I caught a flash of teeth. She said, 'Well done. At least no one can accuse us of breaking and entering now.'

We stepped inside. As I shut the door behind us, I said, 'What can they accuse us of?'

'Nothing that would stick. Stop worrying.'

Jo called out three loud hellos. As expected, there was no reply. We didn't exchange our outdoor shoes for guest slippers.

Jo had ideas. She locked the front door and I trailed her through to Nigel's rooms. I tried not to feel that what we were doing was wrong. I tried not to feel scared. I tried not to feel.

She had a good look around, downstairs, then she went in search of Sigmund's rooms. They were upstairs off the landing that led to his studio.

Jo poked about a little more seriously, although she didn't share with me what she was looking for. Maybe she didn't know.

I had a look along his shelves and my eye was taken by something out of place. It was scrapbook size. It was a scrapbook. I took it down and flicked through it and quickly realised that this was a scrapbook of all sorts of ephemera, newspaper articles, magazine cuttings, photographs. There was even what looked like some original correspondence from the focus of the compilation: Paul Nash. There were other letters too. From other people.

I waved it at Jo and told her what it was. She didn't seem particularly interested. Probably because she didn't find it. I held on to it and followed her through into Sigmund's studio. It wasn't as neat as it had been when I'd last been in there. It looked like someone had been searching for something.

Jo let out a long breath. It was one of her mannerisms when she was frustrated by something.

She took out her phone and said, 'Time to call the cavalry.'

I said, 'Really?' because I didn't believe her.

'Yes. Really. Come on. We can wait for them downstairs.'

In the room with the fire, which was now out, I made myself comfortable on the sofa and for something to do I flicked through the scrapbook. There were newspaper cuttings, yellowed with age, original handwritten letters, many of which had an aged quality – something about the handwriting and the paper – that was confirmed by those that were dated. And there were lots of photographs: both amateur and professional-looking.

Jo was pacing with her phone to her ear. She hadn't spoken. She huffed and hung up and said, 'No answer.'

I said, 'It is Sunday night.'

Jo was tapping her phone against her chin and still pacing when I found something interesting. I had to say her name twice before she looked at me.

'Come and look at this,' I said.

She came and sat next to me. Anyone looking through the window might have believed we were happily married and spending a quiet evening going through the family photo album. All that was missing were our slippers.

'What is it now?' she said, and there was more than a hint of impatience there.

What I had was a landscape orientation black and white photograph of three men posing for the camera in front of a building, the identity of which was not immediately apparent from the picture. I could tell it wasn't that old from the faces of Sigmund Swaine and Nigel Tate. Five years at most. I didn't know the third man but he caught my eye because he had a ponytail and there was a mark on his neck, just above the open collar of his shirt. It was either a birthmark or a tattoo.

I turned it over but there were no names helpfully scrawled on the back. Jo almost snatched it from me and looked more closely. I noticed a newspaper cutting that had been tucked in the same page. There was a photograph between a headline and a block of text. There were more people in the photograph – a decent crowd – and it was harder to identify them individually. But I could make out Sigmund and Nigel – and the third man was there, too.

'Bingo,' I said, feeling rather pleased with myself. I read: 'Alumni of Royal College of Art come from all over to attend the opening of the college's new Sackler Building for painting.'

Jo said, 'What's the date?'

'November, 2009.'

'Where is it?'

'According to this, Howie Street, Battersea.'

I took the photograph back from Jo. 'That has to be tat and tail.'

'It has to be worth a look,' she said.

'What about the police?'

'I tried. I kept my promise.'

'Will you try again?'

'David, I want to check this out for myself first.'

I wasn't going to argue with her about it any more. 'OK.' I looked at my watch. 'It's gone nine. There won't be anyone there now other than security.'

'I can't go home to bed, David.'

42

At least because of the hour and the day there wasn't much traffic to speak of on the motorways. I punched our destination into the GPS and sat back to enjoy the ride. Jo was driving. And the way she was driving it wouldn't take long.

Howie Street was short and given over mostly to buildings of the Royal College of Art. The one we were looking for was 'painting', which was directly opposite 'sculpture'. I had grave doubts regarding what could be discovered from driving all the way up there on a Sunday night but I understood why Jo needed to try.

The street was quiet. There were street lights. Jo brought the car to a stop by the kerb directly outside the 'painting' building. There were lights on inside the part of the building nearest to us. Behind the roller blind of the window that gave out onto the pavement a silhouette of a figure crossed the room.

We got out together and approached the entry phone system. Jo pushed the button. We heard a buzzer sound inside.

'Who is it?' said a distorted male voice.

Jo looked up at the CCTV camera that was trained on our position, depressed the intercom button and said, 'Can I have a word, please. Face to face.'

'Why?'

'Because I need to contact someone to do with this department and it's urgent.'

Surprisingly, we weren't told to bugger off. A man wearing the uniform of the private security sector came to stand behind the clear glass door. Maybe he was just bored and we were a bit of stimulation in his mundane routine.

We had a conversation through a few millimetres of glass. 'Go on then, what's so important?'

'Can you give me a telephone number of one of the 'senior people who runs this place?'

'Why?'

Jo held up her industry-recognised identification card and said, 'I'm a private investigator. My client is in serious trouble and I have good reason to believe that someone who could help me with my enquiries might have been a student here at one time.'

The man looked to be thinking about things. He said, 'Can't it wait until the morning?'

'My client is missing as of this evening. In very suspicious circumstances.'

I'd thought to bring the scrapbook with us. I gave it to Jo to see if she wanted to use it. She did.

'We're looking for someone who was at the opening of this building in 2009. He's an ex-student of the RCA. I just need to speak to someone who can identify him for me. That's all. Please. Just a phone number. You can call them if you like and relay my message. I'm not exaggerating when I say this could be a matter of life and death.'

The man scratched his face. He said, 'Wait there.'

He was back in a minute with a bunch of keys and another security guard. He unlocked and opened the door to admit us. I held up my finger and nipped back to the car for the briefcase. I didn't feel comfortable leaving a hundred thousand pounds that wasn't mine in a car that was a car thief's wet dream.

The man gave me a questioning look.

'Valuables,' I said and smiled.

We followed him into the little office that security called home. A small television with a bad picture was making noise in the corner of the room. He turned it off and said, 'Sit down.'

We sat. I laid the case on my lap and rested my elbows on it.

'If you're going to call someone for us,' said Jo, 'it's got to be someone who's been on the lecturing staff here for a good while. The guy we're looking for was probably here years ago.'

The man nodded his understanding, picked up the landline telephone and dialled a number from a contact sheet on a clipboard.

After a few edgy seconds, he said, 'Sorry to call you so late in the evening, madam. It's security at painting in Howie Street here.'

He listened for a moment.

'No, nothing like that, madam.' He looked up and over his glasses at Jo and said, 'I have a visitor here, a private investigator. She claims that her client is missing and it could be a matter of life and death. She's asking to speak with a senior member of staff of the college.'

He listened a little longer and said, 'Yes, madam.' He handed the phone to Jo.

Jo said hello and thanked the woman for speaking to her. She repeated what she had told the security guard and said, 'I need a name for a face in a photograph. That's all. He's standing with two other gentlemen, Sigmund Swaine and Nigel Tate.'

Jo listened and said, 'That's good. They are both dead. They died last week in separate but probably related suicides. My client is Sigmund's sister. She is missing as of tonight and there is foul play involved, which I'd rather not discuss over the phone, but would be happy to tell you about in private. I repeat: I'm just after a name for a face. It really could be a matter of life and death. Five minutes on your doorstep is all I need.'

Jo listened and said, 'Thank you very much.' She gestured for a pen and paper, which was handed over quickly. She scribbled down the address and read it back. Then she handed the phone back to the security guard.

We sat quietly while he took his instructions, said 'Yes, madam' twice more and hung up.

'Mind if I just make a note of your credentials, madam?' he said to Jo.

Jo handed over one of her business cards. He looked up at me.

I showed him the only identification I had on me: my plastic driver's licence.

He looked faintly disappointed and noted down my details. And then we were seen off the premises.

Before he shut the door on us, Jo said, 'Thanks very much for your help.'

He said, 'Good night and good luck,' and went back inside.

43

It was only the second time I'd needed the GPS since purchasing the car. If things carried on the way they were going it might even turn out to have been worth the indulgence.

The London boroughs were appropriately quiet for a late Sunday night in the middle of January.

Herbert Street in Camden was not hard to find. One of the good things about being in the metropolis and relying on satellite navigation was that there was no danger of being directed into a field. The house we were looking for was not hard to find either. It was the only one in the street in the iron grip of scaffolding and shrouded with plastic sheeting, as Jo had been told over the phone.

Mrs Jenner had the door open for us before we'd negotiated the builder's debris that cluttered the concrete handkerchief of front garden. The light spilling out helped us see what to avoid tripping over.

'Miss Cash?' she said.

Jo shook the hand that was offered and then so did I. I gave my name because it seemed the right thing to do.

'You'd better come in. Please, wipe your feet. As you can see, it's a terrible mess out there.'

We made appropriate noises of understanding and performed our ice-skating impressions on the mat. Mrs Jenner showed us through to a small parlour. It was cold in there; the heating hadn't been on. It was clear that she hadn't been using the room prior to our arrival. It was formal and tidy and made me think of a proper reception room, something part of the house but not the home.

Mrs Jenner gestured to seats and we sat. I sneaked a quick look at the artwork on the walls. It was mostly sketches. The only thing they had in common was similar mounting and framing. I wondered if they were hers, or ex-students' work, or valuable because they were done by someone famous. They looked a bit simple.

I saw her looking at the case I'd brought in with me, as though it had all been a ruse and she expected me to try to sell her insurance or something. I set it down on the floor next to my chair.

In the dim light cast by the little shaded bulb mounted in the centre of the ceiling, Mrs Jenner looked a pretty old bird, but sprightly with it, I reckoned. Her hair was completely grey, silver really, and short, and her face was heavily wrinkled, but her eyes, behind her designer specs, were sharp, intelligent and clear. She was a small woman but I could imagine her cowing others younger and bigger than her.

'Thanks for agreeing to speak with me, Mrs Jenner,' said Jo. 'I'm sorry to call on you so late on a Sunday night. It really could be a serious matter.'

'Over the phone you said foul play is involved.'

'Yes. My client has been abducted against her will.'

I sat and wondered if there was any other kind.

Jo said, 'I received a phone call about that this evening.'

'Kidnapped?'

'It seems so.'

'Then surely this should be a police matter.'

'It is. I'm ex-police and I've been trying to get in touch with an ex-colleague to alert her, but it's Sunday night and she's not answering her phone. In the meantime I'm trying to find the missing woman, too. My client,' Jo added for emphasis.

'You mentioned Sigmund Swaine and Nigel Tate.'

Jo nodded.

'And that they both committed suicide last week?'

'In separate incidents. They both shared a home with my client, Sigmund's sister. Nigel Tate was married to her.'

'How tragic.'

Mrs Jenner didn't qualify that statement, but I imagined she was referring to the two deaths and not the union of Nigel Tate and Rebecca Swaine.

Before the woman could fire off more questions, Jo held up the picture and said, 'Do you recognise anyone from this photograph?'

Something like a happy memory passed over Mrs Jenner's features. It softened her a little and I realised that she'd been a bit tense, which was perfectly understandable in the circumstances.

'Of course I do,' she said. 'Sigmund was a brilliant artist. He had such tremendous potential. He could have been very important, in my opinion. But he lacked confidence in himself as an artist. He could never seem to be happy with anything he painted. Like so many great artists, he was a troubled man.'

Jo wasn't too interested in discussing Sigmund's mental health. She pointed to Nigel Tate and said, 'And this one?'

'Nigel. He was not a bad artist. He lacked imagination, originality, a purpose. And he was lazy. He was a little too fond of the bohemian lifestyle traditionally associated with the life of an artist.'

'Do you know the third man?'

Mrs Jenner nodded and it seemed the recollection was not a happy one. 'Lewis Edwards.'

'Was he also a student of the college?'

'Yes. Average talent. Innovative but confused with it. Could never seem to find his own style.'

'Did you tutor any of them?'

'Each of them was my student. Sigmund was the only real artist among them, the only one worth any time and effort. I'm so sorry to hear of his death. And Nigel, of course. Suicides. How awful. What a terrible waste of life. Do you know why?'

'Not yet. But I'm searching for answers for my client.'

'And now she has disappeared?'

'Yes.'

'Why are you looking for Lewis? Has he got something to do with your client's disappearance?'

'What makes you ask that, Mrs Jenner?'

'He was a bad apple, a bit of a wide boy. And you seem to be interested in him, of course.'

'Honestly, I don't know. That's a tattoo on his neck, isn't it?'

'Yes. A bird, I remember.'

'A man with a bird tattoo on his neck and a ponytail has been described as looking for Nigel Tate recently. He was with a woman.'

Mrs Jenner had nothing to say about that.

Pointing at the photograph, I said, 'This was taken at the opening celebration of the painting department in two thousand and nine. Were you there?'

'Of course.'

'Did you speak to these three?'

'Yes. Each of them, I remember.'

'Did you catch what Lewis Edwards was up to at the time?'

She shook her head. 'Sorry. If he mentioned it, I've forgotten. I wouldn't have spent much time with him.'

Jo seemed disappointed. But we'd got a name and it hadn't been too difficult. I thought we were doing well.

'Would you know anyone who you could suggest might be able to help us further in locating Lewis Edwards?' said Jo.

'The best I could do for you would be to ask around at the college tomorrow.'

'Thank you,' said Jo. 'I'd really appreciate that. Could you do it without saying why?'

Mrs Jenner smiled and she lost ten years with it. 'I should think so.'

'Do you still tutor at the college?' I said.

'Oh, yes,' she said. 'It's my life.'

We shook hands again and she saw us out, urging us to be careful where we trod and offering her hopes that we managed a swift and satisfactory resolution to our quest.

We were almost at the car when I let out a loud, 'Shit!'

'What is it?' said Jo.

'I've left the bloody money in there.'

44

By the time I'd troubled Mrs Jenner for the hundred thousand pounds and stumbled back up the darkened path, Jo was leaning against the car, talking on her phone. Whoever she'd called was talking back. I gathered it was Marion Pardew. Jo was still talking as we got in. I waited and listened.

Jo hung up and said, 'She's going to look him up. See if he's got form and if anyone knows where he can be found.'

'You didn't tell her why we're looking for him?'

'No.'

'Didn't she ask?'

'There's no proof he's involved in Rebecca Swaine's abduction.'

'Shouldn't you at least have mentioned it?'

'If something comes of it, I will.'

I let my silence speak for what I thought of that.

When I'd made my point and because I thought we could be in the capital a bit longer yet, I said, 'I saw a café that's open late. Fancy a coffee?'

'Good idea.'

We were sipping our beverages in a comfortable silence, sitting on uncomfortable stools at the window and staring out at the shadowy London street when Jo's mobile next started up. It was approaching midnight. I felt like someone out of a Hopper painting.

Jo made some room for herself and some privacy. I had to hope this was because of the couple sitting behind us and nothing to do with me, her partner.

When she came back to me, she said, 'He's not known to the police.'

I was surprised and it must have shown on my face.

Jo said, 'Not even a parking ticket.'

We sipped our drinks and contemplated our options.

Jo said, 'What if I ring them and tell them we've got it?'

'The money?'

'Yes. The money.'

'And?'

'And we can do a trade tonight.'

I thought about it. It made some sense. Maybe we should have done it sooner, if not immediately the balloon went up. It was only money. And, as far as we knew, a woman was being held against her will. Also, the money could well belong to the mystery woman and so she might well have a legitimate right to it, regardless of her methods.

I communicated all this to Jo. She made a face and said, 'Let's do it in the car.'

I hid my smirk. It wasn't appropriate. I threw back the rest of my coffee and we took turns to use the facilities and guard the money, which I was beginning to have mixed feelings about bringing with us.

Back in the car, and before Jo dialled her client's abductor, we had a quick conversation about whether or not to involve the police. Jo said no. I felt we should. Jo won. Jo always won.

Our call was answered quickly. Jo had her phone on loudspeaker. In the well-sealed confines of the car the mystery woman came through loud and clear.

'Who's this?' said Jo.

The woman laughed. It seemed genuine. 'I'll give you a point for effort. You have news?'

'We have what you're looking for?'

'Really?' She sounded genuinely surprised. 'Where did you find it?'

'We can talk about that later.'

'You are sure you have it? You wouldn't be trying to pull the wool over my eyes, would you, Miss Cash?'

'Why would I do that?'

'Let's have a little test then. How much do you say you found?'

'Let me talk to my client.'

'You're on speakerphone. Talk away. We have no secrets from each other any longer.'

Jo said, 'Mrs Swaine?'

'I'm here. There is nothing for you to worry about. We have had a frank discussion and I want you to help them find what they are looking for.' She sounded as if she was reading.

'I think I've found it, Mrs Swaine. Do you really want me to give it to them?'

'Yes. I do.'

'Happy now?' said the mystery woman. 'So how much do you think you've found?'

'Forty thousand.' I gave Jo my look but she wasn't interested.

'That's not the amount I'm looking for, Miss Cash.'

'That's all I've found. It was all in one place in used twenties. How much should there be?'

'Ten more.'

Jo said, 'Maybe he spent some.'

There was a quiet pause.

Jo said, 'What do you want to do?'

'You found it quickly.' I still don't think she quite believed Jo.

'I'm a detective. It wasn't hard to find.'

The woman let a little chuckle find us. It sounded a bit forced. She made a decision. 'Let's meet.'

'Fine with me. Will you be bringing Lewis with you?'

Another, longer pause.

'You have been busy, haven't you? I can see I'm going to have to watch you, Miss Cash.'

'Where are you? We could come to you.'

'We?'

'You've got your partner, I've got mine.'

'Why don't you come to my home, then?'

'Which is where?'

'London.'

'Whereabouts?'

She provided an address. Jo asked for the postcode for the sat nav and the woman reeled it off.

'Got that,' she said. 'We can be there in twenty minutes.'

That encouraged another pause and then another chuckle.

'You're already on your way?'

'We're already here.'

'How marvellous. I'm starting to look forward to meeting you, Miss Cash. You sound quite... interesting. Now let's just get one thing straight: Ms Swaine is here of her own free will, correct, Ms Swaine?'

'Correct,' said Ms Swaine.

'Good. So there is no need for you to start involving... others. It would only be to waste their time and cause considerable embarrassment and unwanted attention for your client. Make myself clear?'

'Crystal.'

'Super. I'll get Lewis to put the kettle on.'

She hung up.

45

I looked across at Jo. She continued to stare out of the windscreen. I gave her some thinking time. Then I said, 'I'm confused. We found a hundred thousand, you tell her there's forty and she says she's after fifty.'

'It occurred to me as I was talking to her that the demand note must be from her. She was asking for fifty in it. That pretty well confirms it, don't you think?'

'So whose is the other fifty thousand?' I said.

'I have no idea, but I think she's going to go for forty.' She turned to face me. 'You heard her.'

'The kidnapper?'

'No, Rebecca Swaine.'

'What she said doesn't mean anything under the circumstances, as you well know. They could have been holding a gun to her head.'

'I know.'

'If we walk in there with the money and no support we deserve all the trouble we get. It's not sensible, Jo.'

She surprised me by grinning. 'I know. What's your idea?'

'We go in without the money. If all's well we go and get it and hand it over.'

'Leave it in the car, you mean?'

'No. Too obvious and too easy for it to be taken away from us by a determined party, who, worst case scenario, if they are particularly determined and armed, let's say, and not wanting to leave any loose ends...' I'd made my point.

Jo said, 'Bit dramatic.'

'So is abduction and holding someone against their will for tens of thousands of pounds in cash.'

'Where then?' Jo stole a glance at the dashboard clock. 'Time's getting on.'

A thought occurred to me. 'What about Mrs Jenner's? It's only down the street.'

'And how would you explain that to her?'

'She doesn't have to know. Why don't we just hide it in the mess of her front garden? It's as good a place as any and probably as safe as anywhere else. We're only going to be a couple of hours at most.'

'You hope.'

'If all goes well.'

Jo said, 'Hide a hundred thousand pounds in a front garden?'

'Got a better idea?'

Jo thought about it as one of London's street-cleaning vehicles crawled by making a racket, its twirling orange rooftop light turning the street into the cheapest of light shows.

Jo said, 'We'll need to take some of it to prove we've got it.'

'Fair point.'

I'd parked in full view in a well-lit area; I didn't want my Range Rover broken into while we were quaffing coffee. I started it up and headed back in the direction of Mrs Jenner's. I stopped under a broken street light. It was as dark a place as we were likely to find in a hurry in the light pollution capital of England. We divvied up the contents of the briefcase.

We left twenty thousand in the case. We decided to hide fifty thousand in a recess in the boot – the mystery woman wasn't after more than fifty in total anyway. Then we hid ten in the car where it could easily be found, just in case we weren't believed that we'd only recovered forty in total, and someone where we were heading decided to search the car with or without our permission. (Leaving the ten for them to find quickly would give them no reason to look harder and get a nice surprise.) That left twenty – the balance of the forty thousand we'd claimed to have found – which needed to be stashed in Mrs Jenner's garden. It went into a plastic shopping bag I had in the boot.

I drove to Mrs Jenner's. There wasn't a light on. When I was as sure as I could be that I wasn't being watched, I got out, walked quickly across to the low front wall, nipped over into the garden and hid it under a folded tarpaulin. In my haste to get out of there I barked my shin on something that brought tears to my eyes with the pain and had me limping and cursing under my breath all the way back to the car.

It had started to rain while we'd been counting out the money, a steady light pattering on the roof. This had turned into something of a heavy downpour just as we arrived in Mrs Jenner's street. By the time I'd stashed the money and hobbled back to the car I was quite wet. I was going to make my new upholstery damp and that made me unhappy. To Jo's obvious and audible irritation, I wasted a few minutes arranging the picnic blanket I kept in the boot so that it covered the driver's seat. She didn't need to actually say anything. I was used to her body language and the little noises she used to express herself when her patience was being tried.

A bit defensively, I said, 'It'll only take a minute. I'm not getting my upholstery damp if I don't have to.' I had to suffer another tut.

When I was ready, I started the engine and checked the sat nav. With the hour, the weather and the lack of traffic I didn't expect it to take us long to find our way to Mrs Swaine's captors' hideout. I thought I could easily make up any lost time, not that we had a definite time to be there.

I took a last look at Jo for any signs of a change of heart and plan – her inner voice of reason and logic having spoken out and been heard, perhaps: *take the money and run.*

She said, 'What are you waiting for now? You want to check the tyre pressures, maybe run a Hoover over the footwells? It's not like we've got to be anywhere, is it? It's not like a woman is being held against her will, maybe chained up in a rat-infested cellar, desperately waiting for the ransom to be paid so that she can be released.'

I refused to be drawn. 'I'm waiting for you to say let's go.'

She shook her head and said, 'Let's go.'

As I pulled away from the kerb, I said, 'Our prints are all over the money, you know.'

'Can't be helped. Besides, we're in deeper than that now, don't you think?'

I supposed she was right but didn't say so. 'Are you going to tell me why you've kept ten thousand of the fifty thousand back?'

'It seemed like a good idea at the time,' she said, rather disinterestedly, I thought. 'And ten thousand gives us a card.'

'And what if we don't end up needing it?'

'Blimey, don't you go on sometimes?'

'Always, when my personal safety is at stake. Did I tell you, I have something to live for these days?'

'If we don't need it, I'll give it to charity. Satisfied?'

'I'll hold you to that.' I negotiated some traffic and said, 'If this mystery woman was after Nigel Tate for money shouldn't that opportunity have died with him?'

'You'd think so, wouldn't you?'

'What do you think?'

'I think that this could be something to do with the whole family. I just don't know what. But I'm going to find out.'

I drove at a steady pace: keeping to speed limits, stopping at lights and obeying the Highway Code. The last thing I wanted was to be pulled over by some bored policeman who was jealous of my ride and looking to ruin my evening.

Twenty-five minutes later the sat nav informed us we were in the road we were looking for. I stopped the car and let the engine idle. My body was sending its signals that I was nervous. I was aware of my heart thumping, my palms were sweaty and my stomach was acting up a bit, as it always did when I thought there was a real possibility of being physically hurt.

'What's going to happen?' I said, and I realised my mouth was as dry as a ready salted crisp.

'You heard her: we're going to go and have a nice cup of tea with Mrs Swaine and her kidnappers, give them a load of money and go home with Mrs Swaine.'

'You really think so? I don't mind telling you, I'm nervous. I've got things to live for.'

'So you keep saying. No one's forcing you to come in, David. Maybe it would be best if you drove around until I need the money.'

I found the idea both appealing and appalling. I said, 'Like I could ever look you in the eye again if I let you go in there on your own. I couldn't live with myself if something bad happened to you.'

Jo turned and gave me a strange look. She wore an expression I hadn't seen on her face before: beatific. I wanted to grab a fistful of her hair and kiss her face off for it. Instead, I swallowed hard and said, 'Besides, you owe me rent.'

She smiled her knowing smile. 'Let's play it by ear, shall we. Let's give them the benefit of the doubt. Show some good faith. My copper's instinct tells me we're not dealing with violent people here. I don't think we'd have been invited round to her house for tea if they were planning on hacking us to pieces with axes.'

'Have you seen *American Psycho*?' I said.

The benefit of the doubt? I thought. Show some good faith? I put the car in gear and crawled along to the address.

Number thirty-seven wasn't hard to find. It was the only house in the street with the lights on downstairs.

We were able to park directly outside, which says something about the type of neighbourhood we'd pitched up in. Jo asked me to carry the case and she didn't say why. The front door was opened before we had climbed the half a dozen steps to the covered porch. A tall overweight man blocked our entry. He was backlit only and so his face was in shadow but as he moved his head to one side a ponytail swung loosely behind him.

'Lewis Edwards?' said Jo.

'That's right.' His accent was lazy London and there didn't seem any malice in it, but then again Sweeny Todd was noted for his affability. 'You must be Cash and Carrier.' He laughed at his little joke and I felt myself redden.

'Where's the organ grinder?' said Jo. 'Or are you going to keep us hanging around on the front step all night?'

I could see his face better now. I could see he didn't like the monkey joke. I could see he had a tattoo of a bluebird on his neck.

He pointed us in, gestured to the briefcase and said, 'You want me to take that?'

Dropping my voice a few tones and trying to sound like I wasn't bothered that he had a foot of height and two feet of girth over me, I said, 'I can manage, thanks.'

He'd found his fat man's chuckle again. It followed us down the hall.

We clomped down the hallway's varnished stripped-pine floors. The decoration, order and opulence did nothing to contradict the impression I'd got from outside that this was a highly desirable London postcode. After what seemed like a few hundred yards, we reached an open door. The room beyond was well lit, warm and occupied. We went in without hesitation or knocking. Our feet stopped making a racket as we crossed onto a very nice rug. And it was suddenly very quiet.

Rebecca Swaine was sitting to one side of an uncomfortable-looking sofa, looking uncomfortable. She wore the same clothes she'd worn on our trip to London and a troubled expression that gave her a few lines where I hadn't noticed them before. She looked tired and tense. All of these things she had a right to. She didn't look particularly pleased to see us. Her eyes quickly strayed to the briefcase I was holding.

'Welcome,' said a voice I recognised from the phone conversations. It belonged to a middle-aged woman who, even though she was sitting down, I could see was too short for her weight. She was made up to look attractive in a chubby sort of way. She had an easy smile and she used it. 'Miss Cash and Mr Booker,' she said. It wasn't a question. 'Come in and sit down. It's been a long day for all of us.'

She was sitting in a wing-backed chair to one side of an ornate marble fireplace. A living flame gas fire supplied the room with its focal point and its heat. On first impressions, neither of them struck me as the type to carry out the rather chilling threats that had been passed down the line in the initial contact. It made me think that was just some good old-fashioned bluff and bluster to get our sincere attention.

Lewis Edwards had come into the room behind us and gently shut the door. He stood in front of it but not in a threatening way. Jo and I took the empty second and matching sofa. I was right; I'd sat on more comfortable park benches.

The woman had mentioned tea on the phone but there was no sign of it. I made a note not to trust her.

'You have the briefcase, I see. That's good,' said the woman. 'I take it there's money in it?'

'Twenty thousand,' said Jo.

The easy smile tightened up a little around the edges, as if someone had pulled a thread.

'That's not what we agreed,' said the woman.

'The other twenty is safe and close,' said Jo. 'This twenty is to show we've got it. And you can get the rest when we have some answers and I'm happy that our exit is clear. Just taking precautions.'

The smile was back. 'Of course. I understand. Do you mind if I don't take your word for the contents of the case?'

'I wouldn't if I were in your shoes,' said Jo, which got an appreciative little chuckle from the organ grinder. 'Here,' said Jo, taking the case and holding it up for Lewis. 'Twenty bundles. Thousand pounds a bundle. You can count to twenty, Lewis, can't you?' This got a louder chuckle from our hostess and a hurt look from Lewis.

'I like you, Jo,' said our hostess. 'You have spirit. Women like us should get along.'

As Lewis took the case to the dining table to check the money, Jo said, 'I'm not like you. I don't kidnap people and threaten them.'

'Have you been threatened, Rebecca?' said the woman, turning to Mrs Swaine.

She uttered a terse, 'No.'

'Who are you?' said Jo.

'My name is Hayley Ruben.'

'Well, Hayley, you know that kidnap is a serious criminal offence?'

'I do,' said Hayley. 'But let's be clear – no one has been kidnapped, threatened or forced to do anything against their will. Right, Rebecca?'

'Right.'

'Rebecca is here of her own free will.'

Jo said, 'So she can leave anytime she wants to?'

'Yes. Anytime she wants to.'

Jo stood up and I felt I should too. Show some solidarity.

Jo said, 'Come on then, Mrs Swaine. Let's go home.'

Rebecca Swaine stared at the floor. She did not move. No one said anything and it was a very quiet few seconds.

'Sit down, please,' said Hayley. Her dominance and point was made.

We sat and I thought I heard Lewis snort behind us.

'Mrs Swaine doesn't want to leave until we have the money. Isn't that right, Rebecca?'

'Yes.' Mrs Swaine was being quite monosyllabic.

'How about some answers, then?' said Jo.

'What are your questions, Jo?'

'Let's start with why you were demanding fifty thousand pounds from Nigel Tate.'

'I wasn't demanding it. It's my money.'

'Why did he have fifty thousand pounds of yours?'

Hayley turned to Mrs Swaine. 'Do you want me to answer that, Rebecca?'

Rebecca Swaine gave Hayley an unkind look. 'No.'

Hayley gave an exaggerated shrug. 'Next question.'

Jo said, 'Would there be any point in any other questions?'

'Probably not. Listen, Jo: Rebecca and I have had a frank discussion. She has learned things that she would rather not have. It is her private business. You must remember, Jo, you are working for her. She is your employer. If she doesn't want to share information with you, you must accept that.' She really did sound quite patronising.

'I'm well aware of that, Hayley,' said Jo, making an effort to sound equally condescending.

'There's twenty thousand here,' said Lewis.

Hayley looked at her watch and said, 'It's getting late. Why don't we wrap this up? How soon can you get the rest of the money?'

'We can be back here in an hour.'

'Why doesn't Lewis accompany you, Mr Booker? Jo can stay here with us and we can have a nice little chat, maybe a drink while we wait for you.'

I looked at Jo and she gave me a resigned nod. I stood up. Lewis Edwards straightened himself up.

'Have fun, boys,' said Hayley. 'And no gossiping, you hear?'

With little choice, I left Jo behind and followed the bulk of Lewis Edwards out of the room, out of the house and into the dark, freezing night.

As soon as he had the front door shut he fished around in his pockets for cigarettes and lit up.

'You're not smoking in my car,' I said.

'Blimey, you too? What's wrong with everyone? She makes me go outside for a smoke.'

He'd shed that mantle of pseudo tough guy, like someone glad to get out of a coat that didn't fit him. It occurred to me that perhaps he could be encouraged to see us more alike than not.

'It's not me,' I said. 'It's her. She'll moan all the way back home. Let's have one of those, can I?'

After the briefest pause, he offered the pack. I hadn't had a cigarette for months and in that time I'd battled some keen cravings. I'd resisted and I was proud of myself. But I had to find some common ground with him and this was a first step. Besides, I didn't know that I had to be mad at him just because he was doing what he was told, like me. Maybe we weren't so unalike in our evening roles. Seconds to tough women. I knew from experience how powerful a tool that was to men who spent their lives belittled by overbearing wives, girlfriends or female bosses.

I lit my cigarette from his lighter, cupped in his hands against the breeze, and we moved out of sight of the house for a few puffs. The bond was made. The smoke hit me hard in my throat and the nicotine was a rush for my system. I managed to avoid coughing and embarrassing myself. I exhaled heavily and the air turned white with the clash of temperatures as much as the exhaled smoke.

'Thanks,' I said. 'Couple of minutes extra won't hurt.'

'You think they'll notice?' he said. 'Hayley's on such a power trip she can't get enough of it.'

I forced out a sympathetic noise. 'I know what you mean. This isn't anything to do with me. I'd rather be home in bed. Only reason I'm here is 'cos her car's not up to the journey and I don't trust her to drive mine.'

We puffed away quietly for a few seconds.

'Where is it then?' he said.

'In a plastic bag in a front garden in Camden.' I laughed hoping he'd join in. He did.

'You're kidding me? Twenty grand?'

'Her idea. I couldn't believe it, myself, but, like I said, it's nothing to do with me. I just do what I'm told. And we were in a hurry. Ready?'

We stamped out the cigarettes. I deactivated the central locking and the alarm and we got in.

'Nice,' said Lewis, getting himself comfortable. 'Wouldn't mind one of these, one day. What line of work you say you're in?'

'I run a café. This is a present to me from some inheritance money. You only live once, eh?'

'Too true,' said Lewis. 'The only time I'll ever come into money is if I have a wank in my change pot.' And with that the ice was well and truly broken. I checked in with the sat nav and off we went. I was still laughing when we got to the end of the road and it wasn't completely forced.

Lewis turned out to be quite a chatterbox.

46

We made good time back to Mrs Jenner's but that was because normal people were tucked up in bed, leaving the roads clear for the darker side of London life to play out. I'm not sure that Lewis completely believed me about the plastic bag full of money in the garden. But he had little choice when I came jogging back across the road with it.

I got in and handed it over to him. He looked inside and laughed.

'It's all there was in the case when we found it. Still, that's not my problem. You know what, if Hayley doesn't believe it and wants to "persuade" the Swaine woman to stay a bit longer, I might just push off home. I've got burgers to flip in a few hours.'

'Where did you find it?' he said. 'We had a good snoop round.'

'You know how Sigmund died?'

'Offed himself in a church, Hayley said.'

'That's where he hid it.'

'Trying to buy his way into heaven?'

After a few turns, I said, 'You knew him, right? And Nigel Tate?'

'Yeah. Long time ago. How did you find out all that?'

'Jo found a scrapbook in Sigmund's room. Photos of his past. She found out that a woman, and a man fitting your description, had been sniffing round the gallery. She's a detective. That tat makes you stand out.'

Absently, Lewis Edwards fingered his painted neck, like maybe he properly regretted it. Lots of people do when they grow older and wiser.

There were so many questions tumbling over themselves in my mind that I wanted to ask my new best friend but I didn't

want to break the spell by being crass about it. I wanted Lewis to
think I wasn't as interested as I was; I wanted him to believe that I
wasn't anything other than Jo's chauffeur. Firing questions at him
might have undermined that idea. And he'd already told me a lot
on the way across London.

When we returned, I pulled up short of the house. We'd made
good time and had a thin slice of the hour to spare. I said, 'How
about another ciggy before we face the women?' I actually wanted
one. I had to get my thoughts organised and I was bit nervous.
Lewis obliged and we stood around in the dark, puffing away,
with him clutching the plastic bag full of money.

I wanted to try my luck at cementing my relationship with
Lewis. As we stubbed out our smokes, I said, 'She paying you
well for this?'

'She's paying me fuck all, actually.'

'I'm not even getting petrol money,' I said. 'I think we're
entitled to some expenses money for tonight, don't you?'

I didn't think he was going to take the bait, but Lewis Edwards
must have been hard up. He hesitated long enough for me to
say, 'What about we split a thousand?' He hesitated some more.
Encouraged, I said, 'We go in there, you count it out and say it's
thirty-nine. What's Hayley going to do?'

'Split it how?'

'I'll take four, you take six.'

Lewis liked it. He pulled out a bundle and peeled off four
hundred for me. I shoved it in my pocket and watched him do
the same with his six hundred.

As we approached the door, I said, 'Lewis, let's not be too
friendly in there. You know what I mean? Wouldn't want any of
the women to think we'd conspired to rook them of a few quid.'

'Got it,' he said.

The three of them were all in their same seats when we pushed
in through the lounge door. I went over and stood next to Jo.
I gave her a quick wink and said with as much irritation and
tiredness as I could muster, 'Right, I've had enough of this. I've

got work in a couple of hours. If you two aren't coming now you'll have to find your own way home.' That set a tone.

Hayley said, quickly, 'Let's let Lewis count the money first. OK, Rebecca?'

'OK,' I said. 'Let him count the bloody money then.' I exaggerated a yawn.

Lewis finished counting the money. 'Nineteen thousand here,' he said. 'That makes thirty-nine thousand in total.' He might have added the last bit for Jo.

Jo looked at me. I tried my subtle wink again. It felt like a tic. 'Jesus Christ,' I said. 'You can count, can't you, Lewis?'

'Count it again, Lewis,' said Hayley. She sounded pissed off and tired.

Lewis counted it again. 'Thirty-nine.'

'I've had enough,' I said. 'I don't care how much is in there. All I know is I'm not getting paid a bloody thing for wasting my time and my petrol driving up here. I'm going home.'

'David!' said Jo. And I couldn't tell if she'd caught my drift or not. I had to hope so.

'There's eleven thousand pounds missing,' said Hayley.

'Not my problem,' I said. 'I'm leaving. You two coming or not?'

Hayley turned her gaze on Rebecca Swaine. 'Do you have the missing money?' she said.

Rebecca Swaine said, 'No.'

'And you, Jo? Have you helped yourself to any?'

I knew Jo to be an accomplished liar. She stared right back at Hayley and said, 'Why would I have taken just eleven thousand pounds when I had all that in my hands and no one any the wiser about it?'

'Is that a no, Jo?'

'It's a no, Hayley.'

I took my keys out of my pocket and said, 'It's make your mind up time. Either you ladies are coming home with me or you, Hayley, need to make up a couple of spare rooms.'

Hayley was struggling with her decision. Some of her earlier confidence and control had ebbed away. I was hoping that the quick appearance of thirty-nine thousand might encourage her to settle for her bird in the hand and a warm bed sooner rather than later.

There was something holding Rebecca Swaine there. It was something Hayley knew. Thanks to Lewis, I knew it too. I wondered if Jo had been filled in while Lewis and I were off gallivanting around London and skimming Hayley. Rebecca Swaine wouldn't be going anywhere without Hayley's assurance that her secrets were safe. And Jo probably wouldn't want to leave without her client. It was some sort of code. Like the Marines or something.

I made a show of checking my watch. I huffed and walked to the door. No one else had moved and I didn't know what else I could do other than leave. I had my hand on the doorknob when Hayley said, 'Wait.' I made my you-have-ten-seconds face. 'You ladies should go with him.' I tried to hide my relief.

'Not without your assurance,' said Rebecca Swaine. And, bizarrely, she'd managed to turn the tables on her abductor. Now she wasn't going without *her* demands being met. It could have been a first. If Hayley wasn't prepared to give it, I could see in the setting of Rebecca Swaine's jaw that she'd squat. 'I don't have the money. I don't have any money,' she said. 'I can't make up the difference of your demand. And this is nothing to do with me. It never was. You've got nearly forty thousand pounds back.' She sounded a bit desperate, pleading really, and it was a bit embarrassing to witness.

Hayley knew all that. She probably also knew that there wasn't a lot she could do that she hadn't done already to get her money back. She had to accept things – take the loss and feel fortunate that she'd got so much of her original investment back. In any case, it would be easy for her to give that assurance now and revoke it later. Now she knew who Rebecca Swaine was and where she could find her.

Lewis saw us out. He even winked at me on the doorstep. A friend for life and it had only cost Hayley six hundred quid.

47

It was coming to four o'clock. In the morning. I didn't see that very often in my new life. Being the middle of winter, it was still pitch black. And cold. The night was starting to catch up on all of us. My eyes felt gritty. It was nice to get in the car with the heating on and just drive, in the knowledge my warm bed was only a couple of hours away.

A few streets into our journey and Rebecca Swaine said, 'I want to thank you both. Neither of you had to do this tonight. You've taken some huge personal risks. I really am most grateful.'

'Like I said before, you're my client, Mrs Swaine,' said Jo, as though that covered it all.

'Even so, I want you to know that I won't forget it.'

'You know she made threats of violence towards you when she phoned us?'

'I heard.'

'Did you feel threatened?'

'No. She made a joke of it. She said it would get your attention but that she had no intention of physically harming me. As you saw, she didn't have to to get what she wanted. When and where did you find the money?'

'After we dropped you off we had the idea that maybe Sigmund had gone to the church to hide the briefcase because he knew what was in it, and that it was trouble, and he didn't want it in the house.'

'So it was in St Rumwold's?'

'Yes.'

Mrs Swaine made a noise of surprise. I was glad she didn't ask the awkward question of why we hadn't driven straight back to her home.

'You know why your husband had Hayley's money, don't you?' said Jo.

'I do now. I didn't before. I didn't know anything about anything. I have been so naive, so stupid...'

'Do you still need my services, Mrs Swaine?'

'I don't think that I do. Give me a day or two to think things through, will you?'

We all knew what that meant.

'Are you going to tell me what it was all about?'

'I understand that you want to know, Ms Cash, I really do. But I don't want to talk about it. The fewer people that know, the happier I'll be. I'm sorry. But that is my decision to make. I can only ask you to understand. If it helps, I will double your fee.'

'That isn't necessary, Mrs Swaine. Hayley was right about one thing: you're my employer. Whatever you decide I have to accept.'

And that was that, conversation wise. I would have preferred it if one or both of them had gone to sleep. But neither did. I snatched glances of them throughout the drive home. Mrs Swaine hardly moved her gaze from the side window, although I suspect her thoughts were more inward-looking. She had to work out how to deal with the recent revelations. Jo stared with a grim face at the road ahead. She didn't even look once in my direction. I just drove.

We dropped Mrs Swaine off a little after five. She offered her thanks again and asked Jo to submit her final account.

As we pulled back onto the Marsh for the last and gammy leg of our trip, I let out a long breath and said, 'Why didn't you tell her about the rest of the money?'

'I think she's had enough excitement for one night.'

'Do you think that was your decision to make?'

'OK, if you want the truth, she's pissed me off by not coming clean with me over things.'

'When will you tell her, or are you pissed off enough to consider not telling her and giving it to an animal shelter?'

'No. Certainly not. I'll call on her tomorrow. I'm too tired to bother with it all now and she doesn't deserve good news.'

I thought Jo was sounding a little bitter and twisted, and could do with cheering up. I said, 'So what bit do you want to hear first – why Nigel had the money, or the family secrets?'

Jo turned to face me. 'What are you on about now? I'm too tired to play games.'

'Lewis Edwards is my new best mate. He's all right when you get to know him. We didn't just share a journey across London and back.'

'Not body fluids?' She couldn't have been that tired if she was making comments like that.

'Cigarettes, gossip and a thousand quid.'

'So that's where it went?'

'Just sealing the deal, really. Cementing a friendship.'

'Whose idea was that?'

'Mine, actually.'

'I didn't get the impression you two were mates when you got back with the money.'

'That's just 'cos I'm a good actor. And if I convinced you, probably Hayley bought it, too.'

We agreed that as we were only minutes from home we'd wait. I wanted a comfortable seat and a mug of hot fresh coffee for my storytelling. Jo said she needed things, too. I think she meant the toilet.

As soon as we got in, I put coffee on in the shop – a rich, strong, dark aromatic blend I'd been looking forward to trying. I also stuck on some heating. We agreed to meet back in fifteen minutes. I had a quick, hot shower and changed into clean sweats. I really wanted my bed, but there was no way Jo was going to let me sleep until she'd heard it all.

48

Six o'clock and we were downstairs occupying a pair of facing two-seater Chesterfields. Mugs of coffee, plates of cake and our stockinged feet occupied the low table between us. Twelve hours previously, it had been a hundred grand in used twenties. Life is full of surprises.

'Where do you want me to start?' I said.

'Where's the sixty thousand?'

'Upstairs in my uncle's office.'

'OK. What do you know that I don't?'

'Sigmund, Nigel and Lewis were all at art college together.'

Jo made a noise and face to let me know this wasn't news.

'I'm starting at the beginning,' I said. 'According to Lewis, Sigmund was besotted by Nigel. In a gay way.' Jo continued to chew, but slower, like she could hear better that way. 'For a while they were lovers.' Some of Jo's blueberry muffin exploded out of her. 'According to Lewis, for Sigmund it was the real thing, but Nigel was swimming in both pools with equal gusto. He was putting himself about, inside and outside the campus, like the flu. Nigel broke Sigmund's heart. And Sigmund never got over it.'

'Fast forward a few years. Nigel and Sigmund bump into each other again. Nigel finds himself invited down to Silverhurst for the weekend and for reasons known only to him, he accepts.'

'Maybe he felt like rekindling an old flame.'

'Maybe. Anyway, Nigel meets Rebecca and a marriage of convenience is made.'

'Convenient for whom?'

'All of them. Sigmund because he gets his one true love back in his life and living under the same roof as him, Rebecca Swaine because Nigel can add a bit of respectability, not to mention some much-needed income, to Chez Swaine, Nigel because he thinks he's died and gone to heaven – not only does he get to live in a million-pound house, but he can avail himself of whatever gender of sexual partner he's in the mood for simply by walking into the next bedroom…'

'Rebecca Swaine knew about her brother and Nigel? I was right: Freud would have been interested in that family. That's beyond disgusting. I think even the ancient Greeks would have considered that a step-child too far.'

'I doubt it. Ever heard of Oedipus? That was one weird family. And don't forget what's in the pot here: Romney Marsh, with its rich and varied history of practices of sexual deviation, diluted blue-blooded British aristocracy with its rich and varied history of practices of sexual deviation, and a red-blooded relation of British art renown.'

'You didn't say, with its rich and varied history of sexual deviation.'

'Do I need to? Everyone knows rich and varied practices of sexual deviation are the norm from installation artists to origami enthusiasts – something about the creativity process. It's all that left-brain thinking. Plays havoc with the libido, apparently.'

'So Sigmund *was* related to Peter Nash?'

'You mean Paul Nash. Peter Nash played for West Ham United in the nineties. I don't think he is remembered for his paintings, although he did have something of a reputation in the tabloid press as a piss artist. Anyway, I'll come to that, if you'll just shut up and let me get on with it. Where was I? According to Lewis, Rebecca Swaine *didn't* know that Nigel batted for both sides when she married him.'

'But she found out?'

'I don't know. She did say they weren't sleeping together, didn't she? Ask her if you like.'

'If I like what? The idea of being turned to stone with a look? What's in this coffee?'

'Caffeine. Water. Why? Don't you like it?'

'I feel weird.'

'Could be the Rohypnol kicking in.'

'That's not funny.'

'Sigmund still paints, but only for pleasure. He's good, remember. Now, it seems that Nigel didn't just view deviance as something to influence his sex life…'

'Gay and bisexual people aren't deviants.'

'Sorry, that depends on who you talk to. The Pope doesn't have a good word to say for them and I think you'll find his opinion's quite respected around the world.'

'I know you're trying to wind me up but I don't know why?'

'I'm sorry. I'm tired and this coffee is like booze. You know I don't mean it. Nigel does not tread the straight and narrow to the front door of his professional life either. He saw a way to make some quick and easy money by utilising a bit of hush-hush industry gossip about the forthcoming fortunes of a multinational. And he got found out. Lost his job. No hope of getting another in the financial sector.'

'We know all this.'

'Almost certain prosecution and pillory.'

'So he started looking around for other ways to make some fast and big money?'

'Yes. And everyone knows that short of guessing six lucky numbers out of forty-nine on a Saturday night the chances of that are slimmer than an anorexic after Lent.'

'Unless you want to work hard at something.'

'If you say so. I've worked hard at a few jobs and I never ended up anything but workhouse-poor.'

'Spare me, will you?'

'So Nigel convinces Sigmund, who, remember, is still head-over-heels in love with Nigel and, just like people since the beginning of recorded time who are head-over-heels in love will do anything for those who are the focus of their adoration, he convinces Sigmund to do something wrong for him: paint him some fakes.'

'What sort of fakes? Oh, hang on – Paul Nash sort of fakes.'

'Well done. According to Lewis, Nigel swung it with Sigmund by playing on his ancestry.'

'So Sigmund *was* related by blood to the artist?'

'Who knows? But he was convinced he was. And that's what mattered.' I tapped the scrapbook that I had thought to bring in from the car and that had been sitting on the sofa beside me. 'And Nigel fed his belief. According to Lewis…'

'Must you keep saying "according to Lewis"?'

'I think so. Because I got all this from Lewis. So nothing's proven. It's just according to him. Hearsay.'

'Yes, I understand. I understood the first time. So now I get it, you can stop saying "according to Lewis" because I know that everything you say you got from Lewis.'

'Fine. I get a bit bored saying it anyway.'

'So Nigel just opened up an art gallery in London and started selling Paul Nash fakes. That doesn't sound very bright or legal or much of a long-term business plan.'

'No. I do wish you'd just let me tell it. According… Nigel opened the gallery with some of his ill-gotten gains while he was still at Hudson's, when he had money from his fraud burning a hole in his pocket. It was an indulgence and maybe he really felt something for Sigmund or that he owed him something. I don't know. More likely, from the picture I'm building up of Nigel…'

'Fancy yourself as a profiler now?'

'… he saw a way to risk a bit of capital that wasn't his in his own little venture. He had an art background and maintained an interest in art. He actually sold a few of Sigmund's paintings and when he and Hudson's parted company he decided to try and build on the interest. What else could he do? He certainly wouldn't have wanted to work for a living. And he actually believed in Sigmund's work.'

'How touching.'

'Convince enough people, or the right people, that something is worth believing in, or investing in, and watch the rest of the lemmings line up and fight each other off for the chance to open their wallets to, in this case, own a "masterpiece".'

'Is that how good Sigmund was?'

'Lewis said his technical ability was only outdone by his originality of style. Apparently, he was very good.'

'But?'

'But word takes time to get around. A fad or a fashion has to catch on.'

'Like loom bands?'

'Exactly. Nice analogy by the way.'

'And people weren't exactly fighting each other for the privilege of owning a "Swaine"?'

'No. I suppose one of the attractions with loom bands is that they only cost a pound a pack. People, art collectors, are a little more circumspect when they're being asked to part with a few grand for an as-yet unknown. Lewis said it only ever needs a couple of the right people to hop up on the bandwagon and the rest start parting with their cash like cowboys on a Friday night in Dodge so they don't end up kicking themselves for not getting in when prices were low, and, lo, the domino effect is born. That's art for you. It's driven by money, opinion and fashion.'

'What isn't?'

'Lots of things.'

'Such as?'

'So Lewis arrives on the scene. He calls himself an art dealer these days, by the way. Says there's more money acting as a middle man and advisor to individuals and companies with money looking to invest in future art treasures as opposed to stocks and shares than there is in applying brush to canvas. And you get out more. He says the artistic life wasn't for him. He says artistic lives are for autistic people.'

'Fascinating stuff, David, but I haven't slept for twenty-four hours.'

'Lewis walks into Tate's Modern one fine day – a new gallery he's heard about on the grapevine – and a reunion is born. He

likes Sigmund's work, he says he really does. He convinces Nigel
that he might be able to shift a few on to some of his clients and
get that snowball rolling. But he needs a favour first.'

'A fake.'

'Yes. A fake.'

'A Paul Nash fake.'

'Yep.'

'So Lewis dangles the carrot of promoting Sigmund's work
with his clients if they knock out a good fake for him?'

'Correct. This could be the saving and the making of Nigel
Tate, financially speaking.'

'Why a Nash?'

'Because that was Sigmund's style and Nash was as good an
artist to copy as any for reasons I'll get to in a minute.'

'You just said Sigmund had originality of style.'

'When he wasn't faking Nashes, he did. His fixation with
Nash and the constant influence of his paintings on Sigmund's
work was something they thought they could tap into and profit
from.'

'Are you saying they did more than one?'

'Yes.'

'How many?'

'Lewis didn't say.'

'How much did they go for each?'

'Tens of thousands, and that's an under-the-counter price.
Lewis used his contacts in the art-collecting world to pass off the
fakes as the real thing. They were a bit clever with the pricing,
I think. It is a recognised principle with fakes of all sorts that
the more expensive something is the more people are generally
inclined to believe in its authenticity.'

'Where did you get that nugget from?'

'Actually, I think it was a John Le Carré book.'

Jo rolled her eyes, even though I'm certain she's never heard of
John Le Carré. 'Wouldn't people in the art-collecting world have
noticed?'

'Apparently, there are many "missing" Nashes. Dozens of examples of his work that people know exist but no one knows where they are or who owns them. Nash had a habit of selling locally, wherever he was living at the time, to people he knew, friends and family. So they can pretty much churn out Nash-like paintings and claim that it's one that turned up.'

'So why not sell them openly?'

'Haven't you been listening? They're fakes. Anytime a Paul Nash surfaces legitimately it can expect to be scrutinised by the best in the business. I doubt very much whether a fake, no matter how good it is, would stand up to that level of interest, especially if they keep turning up. Lewis would approach a collector with a story about knowing a man who has an original Nash for sale with a dodgy provenance. The "seller" is in need of some quick cash and is prepared to let it go for a very good price.'

'And art collectors are interested in handling stolen goods?'

I laughed. 'Come on. I thought you used to be a copper. Don't sound so surprised. People are people the world over. Someone offers you a brand new plasma TV still in its box for half price so long as you pay cash and don't ask where it came from, what are you going to do?'

'Report them. It's probably stolen.'

'Well, most people would have it.'

'I don't agree.'

'Maybe I've chosen a bad example. Do you collect anything at all?'

'You mean like thimbles or fridge magnets?'

'Christ, no. OK, you know I love books? If someone came to me and offered me a first impression, first edition of *Casino Royale* for a fraction of what it would cost me on the open market, so long as I paid cash and didn't ask questions, I'd have it.'

'That's so wrong.'

'Of course it is, Jo. But if it's something that your heart really desires and you have an opportunity to acquire it for a knockdown price most people will go for it and wrestle with their consciences later if they have to. There are art collectors all over the world with private collections that have been stolen to order and that never see the light of day. They get stuffed into vaults or hung in private underground galleries where only the owner can appreciate them. You also have to factor in that with paintings, for example, there is only ever going to be one in the world of any particular example, unless it's a Monet. Those paintings of the pond in his back garden are ten a penny. If you're passionate about an artist and you get offered one and can afford the knockdown price or simply can't resist the chance to possess an example of his work, you'll have it. Do you understand?'

Jo nodded. She looked disappointed to her core.

'We'll never know how difficult it was for Nigel to persuade Sigmund to forge them. That's gone to their graves, but because he did a few, I'd bet Sigmund got a kick out of passing off his own daubs as those of his highly famous "ancestor".'

'Sounds like a nice little earner.'

'It was until they got found out.'

Jo sat up. Once again I had her full attention.

'Hayley is in an art dealer, too. Apparently she can walk a fine ethical line when she wants to. Quite by accident, she discovered that a couple of her clients had both bought "lost" Nashes. She did some sniffing around, some investigating and learned that Lewis had brokered the deals. She dug deeper and found that there were others. She had her questions and she confronted Lewis and threatened to expose him and ruin him if he didn't introduce her to the source of the paintings.'

'Why didn't you say something when you came back to Hayley's?'

'It was a minor detail. It wouldn't have made any difference. And Hayley wanted to hide behind it. Rebecca Swaine knew. Hayley wanted some Nashes for herself. Apparently, she has some very rich Japanese businessmen interested in art. Lewis said the Asian market is huge, awash with cash and greedy for Western art. Lewis reckons she could have made a lot of money. Lewis said she paid fifty grand up front for four. That's the money she wanted back, in case you hadn't twigged.'

'Thanks. I got it. So what happened?'

'Sigmund stopped painting fakes. He'd started experiencing issues of conscience regarding what he was doing. Nigel couldn't persuade him to do any more. Hayley threatened Nigel but it wasn't up to Nigel, it was up to Sigmund and he wasn't feeling the Nash vibe. Hayley was threatening to get people she knew to come round and encourage him. Nigel was beginning to panic.'

'How strange.'

'But he was strange, wasn't he? And fickle and a drama queen, apparently. He became stubborn and uncooperative. Oh, my God! I just had a thought. You remember in the church Sigmund shouted "I know what you want. I know why you're here"?' Jo nodded and her brow was creased, as though she knew what I was going to suggest. 'What if Sigmund thought we had been sent from Hayley to "persuade" him to get on with what he'd been paid for?'

'Is that possible? He'd already seen us at Silverhurst. We hadn't threatened him then.'

'But we don't know what Rebecca Swaine told him about why were there, do we? She might have said something quite untrue but ambiguous and he put two and two together and made five.'

Jo rubbed her temples, breathed out hard and said, 'I don't know. I'm getting a bit confused with all this now. I'm tired and I can't think straight. Is everyone dishonest in this country?'

'Most people, I would say, if there's enough money involved. People are greedy. Before we arrived to rescue Rebecca Swaine, Hayley had revealed all to her, including the detail that if she didn't get her original fifty thousand back she would go ahead and let the cat out of the bag.'

'But what would it matter if she spoke out about it now? Sigmund and Nigel are both dead.'

'Get ready for it: the effect on the Swaine name, her reputation. The shame of it. It's where this started, remember? Rebecca Swaine wanting to hire you to find out about her husband's secrets. It was all about her vanity. About protecting the family name.'

'But they didn't share a common surname.'

'You know what I mean. They were married. It's the way they are. It's the mentality that made Britain great. It's what the stiff upper lip is built on: pride, vanity, self-importance, their names.'

'Why did Lewis tell you all this, do you think?'

'I told you. We're mates. He's one of life's natural gossips.'

We sipped our coffees and I tucked into some cake for a quiet few moments.

Jo said, 'I can understand why they would have kept the forging business from Rebecca Swaine but why keep the harmless opening of a gallery from her when it was well intended?'

'I wondered that with Lewis. He said that in the beginning Sigmund wouldn't allow it. Just wanted it between him and Nigel. And Sigmund didn't want the fuss. Apparently, Rebecca is such a controlling and domineering woman that they didn't want her involved at all and the only way to make sure that happened was to keep it from her.'

'They probably knew her better than anyone. Did either of them actually like her?'

'Don't ask me.'

We supped and picked at our food.

Jo said, 'None of this really explains why both Nigel and Sigmund took their own lives.'

I thought about it for as long as it took me to finish my mouthful and swill it down with the last of my coffee. Then I said, 'Doesn't it?'

'No. Not to me.'

'Suicide doesn't always make sense, you know.'

'I know.'

'Remember that footballer, what was his name? Gary Speed, the Wales manager. His wife found him hanging in the family garage one morning. And no one had the first idea of why he did it. It happens.'

'I know that better than you, but given everything involved here there must be a reason. I don't get the feeling that Nigel was the sort to take his own life because he'd sullied the Swaine family name.'

'Maybe it was because he was finished. No regular job, no hope of getting one in his industry, facing investigation by the FSA, and now his little sideline had been rumbled, which had the potential to have brought a shit-storm of trouble his way. Like I said, people have topped themselves for less and we don't know what his strength of character was like. I have a question: are you going to shop them to the authorities? Laws have been broken. People have lost money, been conned out of big money.'

'Greedy people. People who thought they were buying something knocked off. I don't have any sympathy for them.'

'So you won't then?'

'I don't know. I'm going to think about it. We've still got a missing young woman to think about, remember?'

'Natalie.'

'I don't suppose Lewis had anything to say about her, did he?'

'Not a dicky bird. And now I've spent some time with the bloke, I don't think he'd hurt a fly. Believe it or not, he was all right. I liked him.'

'Wouldn't hurt a fly? So who put misery guts in the hospital?'

'Lewis said the bloke was pissed, tripped up the threshold, fell over and banged his head on the floor. That's when they cleared off. Lewis said no one touched him, they just frightened each other.'

I stifled a big yawn, which incited Jo to do her impression of a lion roaring silently. She didn't even cover her mouth. I had.

'I'm going to bed,' she said.

She disappeared off to her pit and I cleared away the crocks. Then I went to bed too.

49

I was awake again by lunchtime. And I felt OK. Sleep's much like many other things in life: it's the quality that counts, not the quantity. I'd had a solid five hours of battery charging. I was ready to go again, but I quickly remembered that there was nowhere left to go. Not with Jo's case, anyway. It was all done and dusted. Mrs Swaine had locked herself away with her new-found knowledge about the only two real people in her life and probably she'd be quite happy if she never laid eyes on Jo or me again. Ever. That meant that I was back to running a coffee shop and planning my empire building. Things could have been worse. I'd had my little bit of excitement.

And then I remembered that we still had sixty thousand pounds in cash to deal with and I got a bit excited all over again.

I wanted to ring Jo to see if she was up but I didn't want to wake her. I dressed and went downstairs to see how the ladies were surviving without me.

Jo was there, drinking and gossiping. Clearly I wasn't the only one who could recharge quickly.

I said my good mornings all round and then with a little bit of eyebrow wiggling and nodding let Jo know that we should find some privacy and discuss what to do with our windfall.

'You didn't sleep long,' I said.

'I couldn't, not with all the loose ends this case has got going on. I couldn't really switch off. Same for you?'

'No. I was out like a light and slept like a log for five hours. That was enough. It's like twenty-four hours without sleep never happened.'

Jo looked disappointed in me and I couldn't work out why. 'Lucky you,' she said.

I smiled at her. 'What are we going to do with the money?' She opened her mouth to say something but I indicated with my raised palm that I wanted to say something first. 'Before you answer that, remember this: One – no one alive knows it exists. Two – you can't give it back to any of the people who were duped because we don't know who they were. Three – you could hand it in to the authorities, I suppose, but what good would that really do? You'd just cause them problems. Four – I'm not sure Mrs Swaine would want the dirty money with the blood of her kin on it.'

'What's that noise?' said Jo. 'Oh, I know. It's the bottom of the lame reasons barrel being scraped.'

'Just trying to bring a perspective,' I said, unperturbed. 'So, what are you going to do with it?'

'Consult with my employer. Technically, it's her money.'

'I knew you'd do that.'

'What, the right thing? Come on, David. I can't keep it.'

'What about half of it? Or how about giving it to charity?'

'Haven't we been through all this once when it was all there?'

'Fine. Can't blame me for trying. So when will you cross that bridge with your employer?'

'I thought I'd give her a ring this afternoon.'

We finished our drinks and then Jo asked me if I wanted to treat her to a late breakfast down at the Martello Café. I put my ire over the money to one side and said I would.

Jo surprised me by agreeing to have a walk along the sea wall after our great British fry-ups. There was a keen easterly breeze gusting in off the Channel and into our faces but the sun was out and the overall effect was something resembling bracing. It certainly blew away the cobwebs.

We walked in the direction of Hythe as far as the converted Martello tower on the outskirts of the village, talking about this and that and inevitably aspects of the case. It was good natured and I was determined not to spoil my happiness at strolling out with my new best friend by being a broken record over the money. In fact I didn't mention it again.

We were leaning shoulder to shoulder on the railings looking out to sea when Jo's phone started up. She answered standing next to me but it wasn't until the call was finished that I learned who it was.

Jo said, 'You'll never guess who that was.'

I said, 'In that case, give me a clue.'

'Missing person reappears.'

I thought. 'Natalie?'

'The one and only.'

'Where's she been?'

'She didn't say.'

'What did she want?'

'To know why I was looking for her.'

'And?'

'She's agreed to see me.'

'Does she know about Nigel and the gallery?'

'She didn't sound like it and I didn't want to frighten her off.'

'So what did you tell her?'

'I said I'd been trying to trace her because I had some money for her.'

I laughed. 'Did she ask how much?'

'Of course.'

'What did you tell her?'

'I said I couldn't discuss that over the phone and that I'd need to check her identity before I could disclose any details.'

I was shaking my head and smiling. 'You're quite devious sometimes, aren't you?'

'I'm learning, David,' she said with some seriousness.

'When are you going?'

'I said I'd call her back.'

'Where is she?'

'London.'

'I could drive you up today. We'd be there in two hours if we walk back now.'

Jo beamed at me and I felt the radiance of her smile. 'Would you?'

'Sure. I'm as keen to tie up those loose ends as you are.'

We turned back towards the village and started walking. Jo called Natalie and said she could be with her in two hours if that fitted with her plans. Apparently, it did. Maybe Natalie was hard up. They agreed a meeting place – the café opposite the gallery – and a time. All good.

50

Even though Natalie was sitting down it was quite obvious she was a tall woman and most of her height would come from the legs that were coiled around each other in expensive-looking leather knee-length boots, like highly polished tree roots. Her passport photos didn't do her justice. And they say the camera never lies. She was a stunning creature. No wonder coffee shop Paul had seemed more than a little interested in her. He wasn't at work today, thankfully. Besides, Natalie looked out of his league to me.

The three of us were sitting around the same table four of us had occupied one day before. It felt longer ago than that. Natalie had got there before us.

As well as highly attractive, she looked a mixture of anxious, nervous, intrigued and suspicious. It couldn't have been an easy look to pull off. Although on her fine features, the overall effect to someone like me was one of vulnerability, and judging by the way one or two of the other men in the place were stealing glances at her I wasn't unusual.

We knew what she looked like from the photos Jo had stolen from her flat, so we were able to identify her and walk right up to her table with some confidence. Clearly this disturbed Natalie, who hadn't the first idea of what we looked like, or that there would be a 'we' turning up.

Jo made the introductions in a professional way. She flashed her identification and then a cheeky private smile at me when she'd asked what Natalie wanted to drink. I knew what that meant; I was to do the honours.

Jo didn't wait until I returned with the tray of drinks to start on her questioning. They were engaged in conversation and it was Jo who was the one providing answers.

'Broken into Saturday night, apparently,' said Jo, and I guessed she was talking about the gallery opposite. 'How long had you worked there?'

'How are you know I work there?' If the grammar hadn't given it away there was a strong accompanying accent – Polish, Russian, Ukrainian, somewhere east of the old Berlin wall.

'I told you, I've been looking for you. I've discovered things.' If Jo wanted this statement to carry worrying connotations for Natalie it looked like she'd scored a hit. 'Mind me asking where you've been for the last few days? You've had a lot of people worried and looking for you.'

This seemed to alarm Natalie further, even though Jo had said it in a neutral way.

'Why you want to know? What is it to do with?'

'Just interested, that's all.' Jo smiled and took a sip of her drink. She was giving Natalie a void to fill if she so wished. She didn't. 'Do you know about Nigel?' said Jo.

Natalie's face hardened and her eyes seemed to glint. 'You are from his wife?'

'In a manner of speaking,' said Jo.

Natalie treated us to a sneer. 'You lie to me then. This not about money. This about warnings. Am I right?'

'Wrong.' Jo took a thousand pounds in a bundle of used twenties from her bag and put it on the table. 'It's a thousand pounds,' said Jo. 'And it's yours.'

Natalie looked between us. 'She is paying me to leave him?' There was something almost victorious in it. 'She will need more than this.'

'No, Natalie. Nigel is dead.'

Natalie looked like she'd been slapped. 'You are liar.' She looked angry but not tearful. She also looked uncertain. Her rebuttal lacked suitable emphasis.

Jo shook her head, slowly. 'You really don't know?' When Natalie didn't answer, Jo said, 'Take the money, Natalie, and put it in your bag.' Natalie hesitated, sensing some kind of trap. I couldn't blame her. It was all a bit odd.

After a long few seconds she took it and slipped it into her handbag and I considered the fish had been hooked.

'Natalie, all I want from you is some answers. You don't have to give them to me, but let me tell you why it will be in your interests to do so. One: I'll give you another thousand pounds if I think you answer me honestly. Two: if you don't give the answers to me I'll have no choice but to pass you on to my colleagues in the police.' If I hadn't known anything of Natalie's life I might have considered this an audacious move by Jo. But I did know a few things. I knew she rented a couple of pokey little rooms in an unfashionable part of London that would still have been costing her a good few hundred a month. I knew she had worked in Nigel's gallery and so was probably on minimum wage or thereabouts. I knew she didn't have a position there any more because her boss was dead. And I knew she was Eastern European and my stereotypical thinking didn't paint a rosy picture of her future job prospects. Added to that, being a foreigner and from that part of the world, I very much doubted she would want any police attention. It would be a cultural and historical thing.

'Nigel is really dead?'

'Yes.'

'How?'

'Suicide. He hanged himself.'

Natalie looked like she didn't believe it. 'When?'

'Wednesday night.'

Natalie's eyes did fill then. And I couldn't be certain she wasn't mourning the loss of a meal ticket rather than the loss of a soulmate. Jo left her alone to recover and dab away the tears that threatened to ruin her make-up. No one said they were sorry for anything.

After a little quiet, Natalie said, 'It explains things. I thought Nigel dump me. I thought he too scared to run away with me, to leave her.' She heaved out a heavy sigh. 'Wednesday he call me. He tell me to go without him. He say he will come very soon but he was missing the plane.'

'The plane?'

'We were leaving UK to be together and start new life.'

'Where?'

'Spain.'

'Let me get this straight,' said Jo. 'Nigel was leaving his wife and his life in the UK to run away to Spain with you?'

'Yes. Wednesday. He call me and say he can't make flight but I must go and wait for him and he would be coming soon.'

'Did he say why he couldn't come?'

'Yes. His passport was missed.'

'Missing?'

'Yes.'

'Lost?'

'I don't know. He say he can't find. He say me to go to hotel he booked for us and he will get flight in next day when he find his passport.'

'When did you come back?'

'Yesterday. I run out of money and he not come. I had choice – pay hotel or buy ticket back to UK. I come back. I call and call him but he never answer me.'

'So you went back to your flat and your landlady told you I was looking for you?'

'Yes.'

'Did you know what he was doing?'

It was a highly ambiguous question for a native English speaker let alone someone who did not have a mastery of English as a foreign language.

'Doing?'

'In the gallery.'

Natalie frowned. 'Selling the pictures.'

'What did you do there?'

'I talk to customers, answer telephone. Nigel say I good for business.'

'I have to ask this, Natalie: were you and Nigel lovers?'

Natalie reddened a touch, which is a hard thing to fake. 'Yes,' she said, 'we were. He loved me.'

She didn't say whether it was reciprocated.

'Your friend Irene has been worried about you. You should let her know you're all right.'

Natalie nodded. 'Why did Nigel kill himself?'

'It's a good question, Natalie. I don't have the answer. I don't think it was about you.'

I said, 'When did you last speak with him? Can you remember exactly?'

Natalie thought. 'Our plane it leave at six. Five, I think.'

'Did you ring him, or did he ring you?'

'I ring him from boarding lounge.'

Jo took out the other promised thousand pounds and handed it over. Natalie took it more easily.

Jo said, 'Thank you, Natalie. You've been a big help. I'm sorry the way things turned out for you. If I have any further questions, is it OK if I call you?'

'Is OK. Where does money come from?'

'You mean this money?' said Jo. Natalie nodded. 'I have an expense account attached to my investigation.'

We drank up and said our goodbyes. I offered Natalie a ride to the nearest Tube station but she said she'd walk.

I was in the driving seat, again. The sat nav was issuing guidance and Jo was looking comfortable in the front passenger seat as we followed instructions that would get us out of London.

'How are you going to explain the missing two thousand to your employer when you give her her husband's ill-gotten gains back?'

'She's going to get her answers. I'm going to finish this job and then I'll give her what's left at the end of it. She'll still have a good chunk of cash that she wasn't expecting.'

'So you'll tell her about Natalie?'

'Still haven't decided. But probably.'

'Any of those loose ends tied up for you?' I said.

'Possibly. Do you think Nigel intended to leave the country, or do you think he got cold feet? If he simply bottled the runaway it was a good ruse to get Natalie out of the country and his hair.'

'Having never met the bloke I don't feel qualified to make an informed guess. You could always ask Rebecca Swaine to look for packed luggage.'

'I think he was intending to leave,' said Jo. 'That would explain why he had one hundred grand in cash in his case. We know he was expecting to be investigated for dubious business practices and we know he'd been rumbled in his sideline of art forgery. His world was falling down around his ears. Maybe he thought it was time to quit while he was ahead, while he still could and with a fair nest egg to make a start somewhere. Keep his head down. Maybe move on somewhere and start afresh with Natalie.'

'Possibly. So why didn't he go?'

'You heard her: he lost his passport.'

A thought occurred to me. 'What if it wasn't lost? What if someone knew he was planning to run out on them and decided to stop him the only way they could.'

'Assuming Nigel kept his passport at home, then, that would mean it would be one of two people.'

'My thoughts exactly.'

51

Once again we had Bookers to ourselves when we returned. Just a faint hint of floor detergent hung in the air to mix with the fading smells of the business day. Time was getting on; there'd been an accident on the M20. I couldn't be bothered to plan, shop, prepare and cook dinner for one, let alone two. I offered to fund a takeaway for us and gave Jo the choice of continent to eat from. Or, I said, we could go over the road for a pint and some pub grub.

We went with option two. Being Monday and winter, we had the dining area pretty much to ourselves. There was a good fire going and the freshly pulled beer was always a welcome addition to any evening.

'I had a call for another job while you were upstairs,' said Jo.

'Really? What doing?'

'Surveillance.'

'Exciting?'

'Not really. Local business thinks one of his employees is ripping him off and selling his stuff elsewhere.'

'Oh. Still. It'll help keep the wolf from the door, won't it?'

Jo sighed and sipped her wine. 'I suppose. My dad has a saying: he says if someone wanted his business you had to want all of his business, big or small orders.'

'You never told me what he does for a crust?'

'Builder. He's wound things down a bit in the last few years. He's getting on. But he still keeps his hand in with odd jobs.'

'Well, he was right. Is right. He must miss your mum.' Jo's mum had died of breast cancer when she was in her teens.

'Keenly. Even now. He's not the man he was and I'm sure it's because of Mum.'

'Shit. Sorry.' I felt the need to change the subject, but Jo beat me to it.

'I can't waste any more of my time on something that Rebecca Swaine doesn't want me involved in any more. I'm going to give her a call and ask to see her. I've my final account to submit.'

Our food came and we both got stuck in. Clearly, it wasn't just me who felt I hadn't eaten a square meal for a week.

'How will you leave it?' I said after a few mouthfuls.

'I'm going to tell her I have new information regarding events and if she wants to hear it I'll be happy to pass it on. Other than that, I've got the money to give her. I'll call her tomorrow.'

'What about what you've learned regarding certain laws that've been broken.'

'You mean am I going to blab to my police friends about the art forgery angle?'

I had just rammed a large forkful of dumpling into my mouth and so had to nod and grunt for reply.

Jo looked to still be wrestling with her conscience over that and for some reason it amused me. I smiled knowingly.

'What?'

'Client confidentiality and ethical business practice versus the law of the land and maintaining good connections with those who can help you out in the future.'

'Something like that. It's an inner struggle. And one I haven't settled, yet.'

That was her business. Nothing to do with me and probably not something Jo would appreciate me sticking my big oar into.

We finished up with another drink and then the recent buggering up of my sleep patterns combined with a bellyful of the daily special and a couple of pints took their toll on my system.

Jo paid the bill with used twenty pound notes. She caught me looking at her and said, 'What's wrong? I get expenses.'

'In advance?'

'In certain circumstances. Talking of which, I'll be claiming for your time and transport and reimbursing you accordingly. Just so you know.'

'You don't have to, Jo.'

'Yes, I do. She can afford it and it's not even about that. I'm a professional in business. Clients must appreciate that.'

We walked home together and said our goodbyes. I headed straight for bed. I realised I was happy with my life.

52

That night I dreamt I went to Silverhurst again. I stood by a wooden gate blocking the driveway. I could not enter. There was a padlock and chain upon the gate. I called in my dream to Mrs Swaine. No answer. Peering closer through the rotting spars of the gate I saw that the house looked uninhabited.

No smoke came from the chimney, and the windows gaped forlorn. I climbed over the gate. The drive wound away in front of me all bendy. Things had changed; it was narrow and unkempt, not the drive that I knew from previous visits. At first I was puzzled and didn't understand. It was only when I bent my head to avoid a low swinging branch that I realised what had happened. I was going the wrong way. I turned around.

The drive was choked with grass and moss. On and on wound the poor thread that once had been Mrs Swaine's drive. Sometimes I thought it lost, but it appeared again, beneath a fallen tree perhaps, or struggling on the other side of a dirty ditch. I didn't remember it being so long. I came upon Silverhurst suddenly, the approach masked by the unchecked growth of a vast shrub that had exploded in all directions. I stood, my heart hammering in my breast, the strange prick, Sigmund Swaine, was glowering down at me from a dormer window.

There was Silverhurst, their Silverhurst, secretive and silent. The whitewashed walls shone in the moonlight of my dream. The replacement windows reflected the green lawns and the terrace. Generations of developers could not ruin the perfect symmetry of those walls, nor the site itself, a landmark overlooking Romney Marsh.

And then Sigmund Swaine was almost upon me, from nowhere. His manic features contorted in his noiseless screaming as he bore down on me, bare-chested, his muscular torso glistening with the sweat of his poker-wielding exertions. I turned to escape, to run for my life. One of my flip-flops came off. Gravel got into the other, restricting my capacity for flight.

I would never get away. I knew that. I turned to face him. He was gone. In his place Rebecca Swaine stood, arms outstretched towards me, dressed in a gossamer-thin full-length nightdress. Barefoot she walked towards me. It must have hurt her. Moonlight can play odd tricks upon the fancy, even upon a dreamer's fancy. By the light of the silvery moon she exuded a radiance of blamelessness, of incorruptibility. She enveloped me and pressed her lips against mine. They were all rubbery and cold. I awoke to find I was kissing my now-cold hot water bottle, and I had an erection. I felt a bit stupid for it.

Because I'd crashed and burned by nine o'clock the previous evening, I was awake by seven next morning. My head said go for a run, ventilate those images out of my mind. The rest of me said have a lie-in in the warm with Holmes and Watson. I compromised. I read a story and then chucked on my winter running gear and jogged across to the sea wall.

The wind had switched and I had to run into it all the way to St Mary's Bay. I ended up where I always ended up – standing on the covering of one of the outfalls that helped to drain Romney Marsh of its excess rainwater, staring out at the English Channel and remembering my aunt who had been drowned there by psychopaths. The pain and anger I still felt regarding my aunt's and uncle's murders had diluted over the months. But it was still there. I accepted that as I had to. As I knew I always would have to.

After a minute catching my breath and sucking in some salty air, I hopped back onto the sea wall and started home. With a tailwind and a loose top that acted as a sail my legs could only just about keep up with the rest of me as I fairly flew home.

I needed to get up to date with Bookers-related paperwork and so after showering I went downstairs, made coffee and applied myself.

Mel and Linda, the ladies that ran the place for me when I was out playing second fiddle to and chauffeuring Jo around, duly arrived and Bookers came awake, opened its door and saw a steady trickle of customers, most of whom I knew by sight and greeted warmly. The position of owner/manager was starting to grow on me. Things had settled down, routines had been formed and I was becoming comfortably familiar with my role. I had what many would consider a life of ease. It was certainly an easy life.

I had a wander around the whole estate mid-morning – ex-builder's yard/future dream home/children's play park – which cheered me up further, despite the weather's best attempts to dampen my spirits along with everything else. When I re-entered Bookers thinking about coffee, maybe a muffin and a good warm, Jo was settled at my table and reading some documents.

We greeted each other the way we always seemed to, like siblings who got on.

Jo said, 'I've spoken to Rebecca Swaine.'

'Oh, yeah? How is she?'

'I didn't ask. I'm only interested in her as a client, I'm not her doctor. I briefed her on things and she's invited *us* out for a final conference and settling of accounts. I think she wants to bury the hatchet properly on this unsavoury chapter of her life.'

'Well, let's hope she's not looking for a head for that. Or two. As it happens I'm free today.'

'David, you're free every day.'

'I didn't say I wasn't. What time?'

'Why do you think I'm here?'

'Have I got time for a quick coffee first?'

Jo pulled a face. 'Seriously? I'd rather just close the file on this. You can sit around and drink coffee all afternoon if you like. I've got another job to get on with.'

'The snooping?'

'I prefer surveillance.'

'More respectable?'

'No. It's because that's what it is. Surveillance is something professional while snooping is something amateurish.'

'It was interesting though, don't you think?'

'The Swaine case?'

I nodded.

'It made a change. I wish I could get more "interesting" cases.'

'They'll come.'

53

Mrs Swaine might have lost a little weight. The skin on her face seemed to have a touch more slackness about it, as if she was experiencing a greater gravitational pull than the rest of us. There were dark circles under her eyes. And those unusual green eyes that had seemed lit from behind when I'd first encountered her only a week before were now dull and lifeless. I almost felt sorry for her. It was hard for me to see the domineering, controlling woman I'd been led to believe she was in the defeated, deflated-looking person on the settee opposite us.

Joan had been curt and a little surly as she had been last time we'd troubled her to get out the best china and the worst biscuits. We had the same tray and the same china and the same brand of biscuits in their packaging as last time. It was all a little predictable, a bit miserable and a tad depressing.

When Joan had bustled out, possibly to eavesdrop from just outside the door, Mrs Swaine got proceedings under way.

'Thank you both for coming again at such short notice. I really appreciate the time, attention and support you've provided me with through this very difficult phase of my life. It's hard to believe it was only last Monday that I first met you both. And now I've lost my only sibling, my husband and discovered that just about everything my life was built on these days was a lie.' She was laying it on with a trowel. She pulled herself together with a visible effort, or maybe it was just for appearances' sake, and said, 'You can be sure, Miss Cash, that should anyone I know require the services of someone professional, competent and above all discreet in the future I will be very happy to recommend you.'

I didn't know what Jo was thinking, but I thought that 'discreet' seemed to get a subtle emphasis. Maybe Mrs Swaine was sending a gentle reminder about client confidentiality.

'And you, too, Mr Booker. I want you to know that I value the time, trouble and attention you've devoted to my difficulties.'

I smiled and nodded sympathy and understanding, I hoped.

Jo said, 'I'm glad, we're glad, you feel you've had good service from us, Mrs Swaine.'

'You've brought your account with you?' said Mrs Swaine.

Jo took a sealed envelope from her handbag and slid it across the table. Mrs Swaine took it with no suggestion of doing anything as vulgar as opening it in front of us. We all knew she could afford it with the ten grand she'd made from the books. What she didn't know was she was about to get a lot richer.

'Mrs Swaine,' said Jo. 'I understand that you terminated my involvement in things when we dropped you off yesterday morning, but a previous line of enquiry has since turned up some new information. I only mention this because it explains things that, now you've had some time to reflect, you might still want explained. I'm happy to relate it to you now, another time if you prefer, or to forget all about it. It's up to you.' Mrs Swaine looked a little unsure of herself. While her mind dealt with Jo's news, Jo followed it up with, 'And we also recovered some money that we believe was the proceeds of Sigmund's and your husband's... foray into the art world.'

I so wanted to look at Jo for that but to do so would have risked me bursting out laughing. Foray? I made a mental note to ask her where she got that from.

Jo was still talking. 'Before you say anything, I want to be completely transparent with you. We both know what your brother and your husband were involved in.' Mrs Swaine's head fell forward, like it was on a hinge, with what I assumed was either shame or embarrassment. Jo was prompted to say, 'Mrs Swaine, you remember I told you about client confidentiality. Both David and I are bound by that. To labour a point, what we've learned in the course of this investigation stays between us and you – my client.'

Mrs Swaine looked up at us and tried to force a smile. It was closer to a grimace. 'Who told you about Nigel and Sigmund?' It wasn't clear whether she was talking about their sexual history, their art forgery or both. She certainly looked as if she was pondering with some justifiable anxiety that there were others who knew things she would rather keep buried than made public, thereby making her a laughing stock among the gentry, or at least that's what I imagined she was fearing.

Jo looked at me and raised an eyebrow as some sort of cuing signal. I realised I was on. I cleared my throat and said, 'When I drove Lewis Edwards to get the money, he told me.' For once my brain was slightly ahead of my mouth and so I managed to stop myself saying, *he couldn't help himself; he's such a terrible old gossip*. That would only have fuelled Mrs Swaine's concerns over word spreading to soil the family name and connections. Mrs Swaine still looked deeply concerned by the news.

Jo had brought a big handbag with her. It was more of a satchel, actually. Something the pony express might have used as a saddlebag. She hefted it up onto her lap and she had Mrs Swaine's full attention.

'When we recovered your husband's briefcase from the church there was significantly more than the forty thousand pounds in it that you insisted we handed over to Hayley to buy her silence.'

Mrs Swaine did not see Jo's version of events as something to contend. She was suddenly very interested in the money, which suggested a story. 'How much more?'

'Including the ten thousand we kept back from Hayley, sixty thousand pounds more.'

The colour drained out of Mrs Swaine's pasty chops, like artificially blue water out of a flushed toilet.

'Pardon?'

'There was one hundred thousand pounds in the case.'

'I don't understand.'

'If you want me to explain why and how I'll be happy to but I should warn you, there are things to learn that might be difficult for you to hear.'

'More than finding out that my husband and brother were lovers, you mean?' said Mrs Swaine.

Put so bluntly I had to control my inclination to wince.

'Possibly not,' said Jo, remaining consummately professional, 'but potentially painful nonetheless.'

Jo took the opportunity of the lull in the conversation to take out what remained of the money. She piled it up next to the tray of tea and biscuits. It wasn't such a big pile for such a lot of money. As a psychological tactic is was a good move; a big pile of cash can soften a lot of bad news.

'There is fifty-seven thousand, four hundred pounds here.' Jo had made me hand over my four hundred pounds from my 'bonding' with Lewis.

Mrs Swaine stared at it, like someone might stare at a leprechaun that hopped onto the coffee table and started dancing.

While Mrs Swaine ordered her thoughts, Jo said, 'Two thousand six hundred went on extraordinary expenses. There is a full account of what went to whom in the envelope.'

Mrs Swaine said, 'I don't understand. Where has this come from?'

Jo said, 'Let me explain things. I took a chance that given developments and circumstances forty thousand would satisfy that woman who abducted you. It was my decision to keep ten back. It's part of the money on the table. If Hayley had kicked up an almighty fuss I could have found a way to come up with it, but with your husband dead I was fairly sure she would settle for the bird in the hand, so to speak. In fact, if you hadn't insisted on staying there until the money was handed over I wouldn't have given her a penny.'

'That is a lot of money,' said Mrs Swaine, still staring at the pile. 'Is it all the profit from their forging?'

'I can only guess yes to that.'

'So why was there a hundred thousand in the case when you found it?'

'If I'm to tell you that, I have to tell you those unpleasant things.'

'I suppose I should hear it now, so that I'm not surprised in the future. When I think of what I've gone through in the last seven days I doubt there could be much more to hurt or surprise me.'

I doubted that but shut my gob.

'Your husband had no intention of paying Hayley's money back. He had one hundred thousand pounds in the case because he was running away to Spain with the young woman who worked in the gallery.'

Jo let that settle for a few seconds. Mrs Swaine didn't bat an eyelid. Maybe it is hard to shock someone with news of their husband's heterosexual philandering when the same husband has only recently been unveiled as that someone's brother's lover. It crossed my mind that had he been offered it, Freud might have passed on the consultation as beyond his level of expertise.

'Nigel was supposed to be meeting her on Wednesday evening at Gatwick airport,' said Jo.

'Why didn't he then?'

'Because his passport went missing. According to the woman – who returned to the UK yesterday after running out of money in Spain – Nigel called her on Wednesday night and told her to go ahead without him because he couldn't find his passport and even if he had he wouldn't be able to make the plane. He told her he'd join her as soon as he could.'

'But he killed himself that night. That doesn't make sense.'

'It makes more sense when you understand that Nigel lost his job in the city because of some corrupt business dealing. As you know, he was let go by Hudson's, but the context of his dismissal meant that he left without a hope of finding employment in the financial sector once word got around. He was to be investigated by the Financial Services Authority and I've been led to believe that could have meant jail time for him. When you couple that with threats of exposure for art fraud, which would have brought a whole new set of legal problems, and the realisation that all of a sudden the escape route to the Costa del Crime he had planned had just been cut off, then perhaps his taking of his own life seems a little more understandable. Incidentally, Mrs Swaine, you don't know anything of what happened to your husband's passport do you?'

Mrs Swaine shook her head. She seemed to me to be telling the truth, thereby whittling down the list of suspects who might have had something to do with the disappearance of Nigel's passport to one.

None of Jo's disclosures seemed like news to Mrs Swaine. She said, 'It's fantastic, isn't it? How could I have been so naive? How could I have been taken in by such an evil, scheming man? You two must think that I'm a particular kind of fool.' She was still thinking about how she was going to come out of this.

'No, Mrs Swaine, we don't. Nigel was a clever man. He was a skilled manipulator. But he wasn't all bad.'

'Really? You do surprise me.'

'He opened up Tate's Modern while he was still at Hudson's, before the irregularities in his business dealings were exposed. He opened it because he believed in Sigmund's work, apparently. They weren't forging works of art then. That came later. Nigel used some of his ill-gotten gains from Hudson's to invest in your brother.'

Despite Jo giving it some feeling, Mrs Swaine appeared unmoved by Nigel's philanthropy with money come by dishonestly. (Put like that, he could have been the art world's latter day equivalent of Robin Hood.) And we quickly found out why.

'But why didn't either of them tell me? Why was I excluded from something so important in my brother's life? I've supported him in his art forever. It's always been just the two of us. I simply don't understand why they would have conspired and connived behind my back, under my roof, in order to leave me completely in the dark.'

I remembered Mrs Swaine referring to Nigel and Sigmund as the only two 'real' people in her life. I sat opposite her willing that the memory wasn't prompted for her, too. No good could come of it. But it would probably come later with the rest of the crushing torment.

'That's not something we can answer,' said Jo, and her implication was clear.

After a long pause, Mrs Swaine said, 'Do you have anything else to share with me?'

Jo took in a deep breath and indicated that she didn't.

We watched Mrs Swaine make a decision. She picked up the envelope, slipped her finger under the gummed flap and opened it. She scanned it quickly, just looking for the bottom line.

'I might as well pay you in cash, Miss Cash,' she said. 'I must say that your transparency and honesty over the money has completely put my mind at rest regarding your confidence concerning other potentially damaging aspects of this whole horrible episode. Thank you.'

She counted out the necessary number of bundles and then put two more on top.

'Mrs Swaine...' was about as far as Jo got.

'Call it a bonus for a job well done. I don't want any arguments.'

Mrs Swaine saw us out. We all shook hands. On the doorstep I said, 'If you want me to, I can see if the chap I sold your books to still has them.'

Rebecca Swaine smiled at me and something of her old self touched her features. 'Thank you, Mr Booker. To be honest with you, I don't miss them. I never looked at them. I'm even thinking of thinning the library out a bit more. Maybe you'll be able to put me in touch with someone?'

I smiled back. 'Just let me know, Mrs Swaine.'

As we went to leave a thought occurred to me. I turned back and said, 'Mrs Swaine, do you remember what you told Sigmund regarding the reason for our visit the first time we came here?'

Jo looked interested in the answer. Mrs Swaine thought for a long moment and said, 'I think I told him that you were looking for Nigel. Something to do with his business. Why do you want to know? Is it important?'

I shook my head and smiled and said, 'I just wondered, that's all.'

54

A strong winter sun had barged its way through the clouds of earlier and when we were back in the car I made a decision for us.

'Where are you going?' said Jo, as I turned left out of Silverhurst instead of right.

'I want to show you something. It'll only take a few minutes.'

'What? I don't like surprises.'

'Tough. Talking of surprises, how do you feel about being paid with dirty money from the proceeds of criminal activity?'

'We don't know that every note in that briefcase was from the sales of fake Nashes, do we?'

'No, but it's a fair guess.'

'I like to think that the money she paid me with was money earned honestly through the sale of Sigmund's own paintings.'

We laughed.

I drove along Giggers Green Road as far as the first left, cruised the short distance to the turning I needed and took us left again down the narrow road towards St Rumwold's church. I stopped in the lay-by we'd stopped in when we came looking for Nigel Tate's briefcase.

'What are we doing back here?' said Jo, although she didn't sound terribly cross about it.

'I want to show you something.'

She didn't argue with me. Perhaps it had something to do with how well she'd just been paid.

We walked back to the church and I led her up the garden path. She followed me as I stepped onto the grass of the graveyard, ducked under the spreading sagging limbs of the yew tree and around to the south-facing side of the place. There were benches there against the church wall. I sat down and motioned for Jo to join me.

She sat and said, 'Well?' She sounded on her guard and it occurred to me that maybe she feared I was going to propose, or something, which made me laugh.

'What's funny?' she said.

'Nothing. Don't look at me, look that way,' I said.

Romney Marsh was spread out before us. The flat landscape, broken up only by the legacy of enclosure – lined with random and irregular hedgerows – and dotted with the odd clump of trees, stretched out for miles. It wasn't clear enough to see as far as one could on a clear day but the stretch of the landscape was quite impressive.

Jo said, 'Why am I looking at this? Is there something I'm missing?'

'Because she's beautiful, Jo,' I said.

'She?'

'Romney Marsh. All true Marshens refer to Romney Marsh as "she".'

'Why am I not particularly surprised?'

'… and the sun's out and we've been here twice already – one of my favourite places in the world – and not appreciated it.'

'This isn't a God thing, is it?'

'No! It's about a lovely view, that's all.'

We sat and soaked it up for a few minutes. The sun was on my face and I felt quite content as I pointed out places and landmarks I knew, thereby showing off my extensive local knowledge.

Just as I was about to remark on something that caught my eye, a fat drop of rain hit me on the knee. This was followed by several more in quick succession falling around us. Disappointingly, Jo seemed almost pleased. She stood up and said, 'It's going to piss down any moment and I haven't got a coat on.'

She could have been a mystic. Within seconds the glorious winter sunshine had been replaced by dark brooding skies and the heavens properly opened. We bolted around the side of the church in search of shelter.

'It'd better be open,' called Jo over her shoulder.

'The house of God is always open,' I said. And it was.

We burst into the little porch and the hailstones that had quickly replaced the rain hammered down on the tiled roof, as if someone had emptied a crate of ball bearings directly above us. There was no sign of abatement and with little else to do after we'd read the local notices Jo decided to push into the church proper and stir the trapped air and a memory.

The church was bloody chilly, as one would expect for the time of year in an old church with stone walls feet thick. It was quite gloomy inside, too. No candles burned now. Jo strode away down the aisle towards the back of the church and where Sigmund had pitched off. I didn't ask what she was looking for. Perhaps it was just a macabre interest.

I wandered around looking at things that took my interest until I found myself at the place where I'd found Nigel Tate's briefcase. I smiled at the memory. As my eyes naturally roamed around the spot, my attention was caught by a black bin liner that looked like it was being used as a protective covering for something. It wasn't very visible. It was stuffed behind a bookcase that held a quantity of Bibles and children's picture books with biblical themes. I can't say why, but I was moved to investigate. Maybe Jo's detecting tendencies were contagious. I leaned in, reached out and slid the bin liner out, and felt it held something rectangular, thin and not heavy. Just the feel through the plastic of what I'd closed my hand around made my heart pick up its pace. Like a little boy who prepares to unwrap a birthday present shaped like a bicycle, I would have bet money that I knew what was in it before I unveiled it.

Carefully, I slid out a medium-sized framed painting of Dymchurch sea wall. The style was instantly recognisable. The signature confirmed it. I was struck speechless.

I called for Jo, but because my breath had been taken away hardly any noise came out. I cleared my throat, inhaled and called louder. She hurried over to stand next to me.

'Is that what I think it is?'

'If you think it's a Paul Nash fake, then I think you could be right.'

'Where was it?'

'Tucked behind the bookcase. Next to where we found the briefcase.'

'How did we miss it before?'

'We weren't looking for it, were we? We were looking for a briefcase and only a briefcase.'

'Is there anything else there?'

'You look. I'm happy looking at this.'

Jo got down and peered back there. 'Dust and cobwebs.' She sneezed.

'Isn't it stunning?' I said.

'Not my cup of tea,' said Jo, like the philistine she was turning out to be. 'Have you got a tissue?'

'Well, it's mine. And you should take more of an interest because this is what it's all been about. Life and death, broken dreams and broken laws.'

'You swallow a poet?'

My whole body was tingling with pleasure. And it was only a fake.

Then something occurred. I felt the warmth wash out of me to be replaced by something icy and bitter. I said, 'Jo.' I met her eye. I felt she knew what I was going to say. I realised I was anticipating great disappointment, preparing myself for her ruling. It was her call. It was her case, her decision and I would accept it, whatever it was, with good grace, maybe. But she was so infuriatingly honest and I wanted that picture. 'Can I keep it?'

She studied my face for a long moment and said, 'Keep what?'

'The painting.'

'What painting? I don't see any painting.'

I had to make sure she wasn't winding me up.

'I think it's stopped chucking it down,' she said, turning to leave.

I didn't say thank you. I didn't say anything. I slid it back into the black bin liner. And realised there was something else nestling in the bottom of the sack. I fished it out. An envelope. It wasn't empty. I called and went after her, brandishing it above my head, like a man running for the plane desperately waving his boarding pass.

The envelope had been opened. Jo took out a British passport and a headed letter. She checked the passport, although we both knew whose it was. No surprises there, just confirmation.

Jo scanned the letter and said, 'What's today's date?'

I told her.

She said, 'The final part of the puzzle, I'd say. This is notification from Hudson's that Nigel was to be formally investigated by the authorities. It's dated seven days ago. Two days before Nigel topped himself. Allowing for two days in the post this chimes in pretty well with the time of death.'

'What's it doing in here?'

'Maybe Sigmund took it when he took his passport.'

We let the quiet of the church possess us for a few seconds.

In an uncharacteristic display of sympathy for a crook, Jo said, 'He's the one I feel some sympathy for in all this.'

'Who? Nigel?'

'No, dummy, Sigmund. He was clearly off his trolley, deluded. He thought he was related to a famous artist, it takes over his life. He has his heart broken, his life ruined by some horrible man. He becomes a recluse, living with his controlling sister, only to have the love of his life walk back into it, marry his sister, quite possibly renew his affair, then use him and his talent to profit from, and finally learns that his lover was going to desert him once again for another woman.'

'I might have studied something like that for A level English literature but it was set in Venice or Denmark.'

'I'm honestly surprised Sigmund didn't kill them. He must have been such a tormented soul.'

'They all are,' I said, rather flippantly.

'Who?'

'Artists. It comes with the calling. Will you go back and give Rebecca Swaine the answer to one of her questions?'

'Which one?'

'Who killed her husband.'

'Sigmund?'

I nodded.

'Did he though? Nigel strung himself up without any help from a third party, according to the police report.'

'If Sigmund had hidden his passport, his way out, and with all his other troubles crowding in on him maybe Sigmund should shoulder some responsibility.'

'No, I don't think I will,' said Jo. 'It's not going to make any difference to anyone now, is it?'

Before we left I stuck a twenty – one of my own – in the collection box.

As we walked back to the car, me carrying the painting in the bin liner in two hands in front of me, Jo put her arm through mine.

I said, 'He made me.'

Jo must have been off somewhere. 'Eh?'

'Remember, Sigmund said "he made me" before he swan dived to his death. It bothered you for a while. And me. It was a bit cryptic for a man's last words. Do we think we know what he meant now?'

'He made me, as in Nigel made him paint the fakes?'

'How about, he made me, as in Nigel made Sigmund act by taking his passport so that Nigel couldn't leave him?'

'Or, he made me, as in Nigel made Sigmund the person he was?'

'Maybe, he made me, as in Nigel completed Sigmund?'

'That's too sad.'

'All right, what about, he made me, as in, and here I burst into song: "He made me love him, I didn't wanna do it, I didn't wanna do it."' And despite, or because of, my horrible singing and the crass inappropriateness of my outburst we laughed all the way back to the tank.

Epilogue

Some time after I wrote up this account – in true Doctor Watson style – of Jo's and my first proper outing together in the private sector, an article appeared in one of the Sunday broadsheets that had me laughing into my coffee and cake and then scrabbling around for my phone to get hold of Jo and get her downstairs sharpish. I'd read it through twice more before she showed up looking peeved that I'd got her out of bed on a Sunday.

I sat her down with her favourite coffee-based drink in *my* special wing-backed chair, a sure indicator that this was important, and then handed her the neatly folded article I wanted her to read, while I went and chatted amiably to one or two of my Sunday morning regulars. But I watched her.

'Missing' Nashes resurface to shock art world while a talent is lost and found.

The art world has been rocked in recent weeks by revelations of forging and the meteoric rise to fame, albeit post-mortem, of a widely acknowledged modern master.

Romney Marsh, once described by RH Barham as 'the fifth quarter of the globe' (which made his maths about as good as mine) *nestles in a corner of the county of Kent in the south-east of England. Probably best known for its breed of sheep, which have been exported as livestock as far away as Oceania, it has also attracted the attentions of several important artists over the years as they have gone through the many and varied phases of their careers. Among the most notable of these who called Romney Marsh home for several years was Paul Nash (1889–1946) who is probably best known for his work as a First World War war artist.*

In the 1920s, Nash spent time in the sleepy seaside village of Dymchurch, where the conflict between sea and land was to engage and influence him significantly. Nash's interest in the sea wall – that testament to human ingenuity and endeavour which has kept the English Channel at bay for centuries and allowed thousands of acres of rich farmland to be reclaimed from Neptune's grasp – provided the basis for some of his most recognisable and iconic post-war works.

Jump forward almost a hundred years to the present day and Nash's influence in that part of the world is still going strong. Enter Sigmund Swaine who, rumour has it, was a direct blood descendant of Paul Nash – his grandfather being, perhaps, the result of an affair between married man Nash and a local woman. Whatever the truth of that, the influence of the story has reached its paint-stained grasp into the twenty-first century.

It is no secret that many of Nash's works from his time on Romney Marsh went unrecorded and into local ownership – Nash would often sell to friends and casual acquaintances. These are part of what are referred to in the art world as the 'missing' Nashes. It is believed that potentially dozens of these paintings could be hanging unnoticed, unappreciated for what they are, on the walls of a good many homes in the area.

Sigmund Swaine, a graduate of the Royal College of Art, lived for most of his adult life like a recluse with his sister, Rebecca Swaine, in a roomy period property that sits atop the hills overlooking Romney Marsh. On a clear day, one can see all the way to where the English Channel meets Romney Marsh at Dymchurch – all the way to where Paul Nash spent years of his life recording the area for posterity and our appreciation, with brush, paint, canvas and his genius.

Sigmund Swaine grew up encouraged to believe he was a blood relation of Nash. The truth of this has yet to be proven, but to Sigmund, a man who built his life on the idea, it will make no difference now. Sigmund took his own life earlier this year by leaping to his death from the rafters of St Rumwold's church, a place only a good stone's throw from Silverhurst.

What drove this newly acknowledged genius to the ultimate act of self-destruction remains, according to his sister, Rebecca – who kindly agreed to be interviewed for this article – a complete mystery. She says that Sigmund had spent his adult life a troubled man, drifting in and out of periods of depression and uncertainty. His demons had tormented him and he sought solace and distraction in his art.

Enter the villain of the piece, who, ironically, has arguably turned out to be the one responsible for catapulting Sigmund's name and work to the attention and high praise of the most respected critics in the art world today, not to mention a good and increasing number of well-heeled collectors and investors in fine art.

Nigel Tate, who shared the Swaine family home at Silverhurst, also took his own life in mysterious circumstances only a day before Sigmund ended his. (Police continue to assert that there is no suggestion of foul play in either death.) It was Tate who, with his unexplained hold over the emotionally vulnerable Sigmund, coerced, according to Sigmund's sister, the impressionable Sigmund into producing several 'missing' Nashes, which subsequently found their ways into the hands and then onto the walls of a number of private art collectors. How many were created we may never know, especially as those who paid tens of thousands of pounds for the fakes will be naturally reluctant to offer themselves up for public ridicule. Or will they be the ones having the last laugh?

How did this happen? According to Silvia Jenner, senior faculty member at the Royal College of Art and one-time tutor of Sigmund Swaine, factors such as the replication of style, essence of Nash's spirit and faux-authenticity of the painting are as extraordinary as they are exquisite. It is, we are assured, impossible to determine one of Sigmund's fakes from a genuine Nash simply with the naked eye.

But the exposure of the lucrative scam that ran for months is not the end of the story. When Sigmund Swaine was not rattling off fakes of 'missing' Nashes to satisfy the orders of his devious mentor he was painting in his own peculiar style. There is no doubt that the style of Paul Nash is a strong influence, but Sigmund's work is described by art dealer, art college student friend and now curator of the estate of Sigmund Swaine, Lewis Edwards, as having a breathtaking originality of style, which is only matched by his technical ability and vision for representing the themes of his work with a flair and uniqueness that has seen appreciation of his work inflate, both economically and critically, to the extent that a decent-sized Sigmund Swaine is now in danger of fetching as much as one of the missing Nashes he sought to create.

Sigmund's early and tragic death has ensured that there is a limited number of his works available for study and fewer for purchase. This is another factor that has seen the salerooms buzzing with anticipation and the bandying about of six-figure purchase prices. For now it is the wish of Sigmund's sole surviving relative, Rebecca, that Sigmund's work will make a tour of Europe's most important art galleries before being auctioned in London sometime next year, an event that this journalist looks forward to with eager anticipation. Lest anyone should remain in any doubt regarding the importance of this chapter of British art history and its impact on the art world, it has been confirmed by Rebecca Swaine that a household name Hollywood director has been in touch with her personally to discuss the possibility of her cooperation over the commissioning of a blockbuster movie documenting Sigmund Swaine's life and death.

As a footnote and final thought to this incredible and moving modern tragedy, it is this particular art lover's lament that once again history repeats itself. Once again a unique talent devoted to his traditional art has been lost prematurely, dying in virtual poverty and complete obscurity, without recognition in his lifetime of his talent, only to be 'discovered', celebrated and profited from after his death. This art lover appeals to those who fund and promote the arts to give less time, attention and money celebrating piles of house bricks, farm animals dunked in preservative, and the unmade beds of unimaginative and lazy 'artists'. Look both backwards and forwards to the traditional arts that give pleasure to, and can be understood by, thousands, and endure in a culture's consciousness long after the bricks are thrown into a skip, the preservative has evaporated, the sheep's carcass rotted away and the unmade bed stripped of its dirty laundry for washing.

The End

A Note from Bloodhound Books

Thanks for reading He Made Me. We hope you enjoyed it as much as we did. Please consider leaving a review on Amazon or Goodreads to help others find and enjoy this book too.

We make every effort to ensure that books are carefully edited and proofread, however occasionally mistakes do slip through. If you spot something, please do send details to info@bloodhoundbooks.com and we can amend it.

Bloodhound Books specialise in crime and thriller fiction. We regularly have special offers including free and discounted eBooks. To be the first to hear about these special offers, why not join our mailing list here? We won't send you more than two emails per month and we'll never pass your details on to anybody else.

Readers who enjoyed He Made Me will also enjoy

Bad Sons also by Oliver Tidy.

Bad To The Bone by Tony J Forder.

A Note From The Author

Hello,

First, thank you for taking a chance on downloading this book. I hope you found something in it to enjoy.

Second, I invite you to visit me at olivertidy.com where you can find out more about other books I've written. You can also find me on Facebook and Twitter.

Third, if you enjoyed the read, please leave a comment to that effect with the retailer you obtained it from. That sort of thing is really important for an indie author/publisher. Readers' comments are all we've got to go by.

Best wishes
Oliver Tidy

FREE BOOK OFFER!!

Tap this link olivertidy.com to receive a free ebook.

Also by Oliver Tidy

Ebook titles available in my Romney and Marsh Files series:

#1 Rope Enough Amazon UK Amazon US (A free download while stocks last.)

#2 Making a Killing Amazon UK Amazon US

#3 Joint Enterprise Amazon UK Amazon US

#4 A Dog's Life Amazon UK Amazon US

#5 Particular Stupidities Amazon UK Amazon US

#6 Unhappy Families Amazon UK Amazon US

#7 A White-Knuckle Christmas Amazon UK Amazon US

Ebook titles available in my Acer Sansom series:

#1 Dirty Business Amazon UK Amazon US (A free download while stocks last.)

#2 Loose Ends Amazon UK Amazon US

#3 Smoke and Mirrors Amazon UK Amazon US

#4 Deep State Amazon UK Amazon US

Ebook titles in my Booker and Cash series:

#1 Bad Sons Amazon UK Amazon US

#2 He Made Me Amazon UK Amazon US

Ebook collection of three short stories - one in each of the above series.

Three Short Blasts Amazon UK Amazon US

CPSIA information can be obtained
at www.ICGtesting.com
Printed in the USA
LVHW091350251120
672673LV00012B/165